A GAME FOR THE YOUNG

David P. Philip

First published 2015
By Rowanvale Books Ltd
2nd Floor, 220 High Street
Swansea
SA1 1NW
www.rowanvalebooks.com

A CIP catalogue record for this book is available from the
British Library.
ISBN: 978-1-909902-99-2

To my family

Caroline and Emilie

PROLOGUE

'You know this can't go on,' the detective warned, offering a lukewarm cup of tea from across the table. A gesture of kindness under the guise of friendship. But they weren't friends.

To Ellie's left, a mirror she presumed to be two-way spread over one third of the wall. To her right, a door securely bolted from the outside served as a reminder that there was little choice to her scenery. The walls around her were a dull beige.

'Your silence implies guilt, Miss Swanson,' the detective said, turning over another page from his case file. The noisy bustle from the corridors outside had reduced to a distant mumble.

'Are you charging me?' she asked.

'I'm questioning you.'

'Then when can I leave?'

'You are entitled to legal counsel if it would make you more comfortable.'

'It would make me more comfortable to leave.'

The detective remained cold, holding a long and intrusive gaze before slowly selecting four photos from his folder. He placed them evenly spaced apart in front of her.

'Please look at them,' he said, speaking softly.

Seeing their faces Ellie gave a faint smile. Her mouth contorted to a grimace as she held back the tears.

'You remember your friends, don't you?'

She took a sip of her tea to control her quivering chin, her eyes resting on the pictures before glancing to the mirror.

'We're alone,' he assured her.

In her dreams she could still feel them. Remember their touch, their smell. Her focus was drifting.

'Will you tell me what happened to them?' the detective asked, pulling her attention back into the room.

'They're not my friends,' she whispered. 'They're my family.'

* * *

Feeling young, he walked as though floating through Oxford's Botanic Gardens. The sun was warm and glowed in a way he'd never seen before. The water was cool, the fruit was ripe and the grass shone with beautiful shades of green.

Finally all scores were settled, and never before had he felt so content.

He took in the arrangements of flowering plant life; they were breathtaking this time of year. The gardens were laid out in an array of elegant flower beds linked together under a soft carpet of grass lawns and pebbled footpaths - the polished result of four centuries of lavish attention.

A small flock of hummingbirds sang whilst nesting in the branches of an old English Yew tree. They held his gaze for a moment before it passed above the tree line to take in the famed Magdalen Bell Tower, watching over the gardens as if it were keeping them safe.

Pausing next to the rose garden, he took a deep and full breath. It had been years since he last came here and he'd chosen the perfect day to enjoy the gardens in April's spring.

It was a moment to savour and yet somehow the smile on his face began to fade. His expression changed from contentment to a pensive fear; something troubling grew inside of him. Something dormant and elusive but he could feel it building in the back of his mind, an inner pain rising to the surface.

He lifted his right hand to his temple, wincing as the pain gradually grew with intensity.

With a jolt he began to shake uncontrollably, a look of uncertainty and panic washing over his face. He reached into his jacket pocket and pulled out a mobile phone, but it was too late, his hands had begun to spasm and he dropped the phone onto the gravelled footpath beneath him.

A young couple holding hands by the water fountain watched in disbelief as they saw a man suddenly cry out in pain and fall to his knees. The scream echoed through the gardens, freezing its visitors like statues.

For a brief second there was only silence, but it soon broke, followed by the shouts of concern and the crunching sound of running feet on gravel.

He lay down on his back, staring up at the clear blue sky as the heads of strangers circled above him, their voices muted under the throbbing agony.

His eyesight was beginning to blur, the feeling in his legs had left him. As he felt his body slowly turning numb he closed his eyes in acceptance of his fate. There were no regrets, for he knew now that this was how it had to be.

Everything was as he had dreamed.

CHAPTER ONE

HAWKING

TWO YEARS EARLIER

It was late January and the seasonal weather had brought with it a cold and bitter winter. By 3.00AM the soft wind had become a freezing chill and the windows of the John Radcliffe Hospital in Oxford were showing the first signs of frost.

This was one of the bases of operations for the Biomedical Research Centre, a defining partnership between the University of Oxford and its surrounding Hospitals.

Throughout the empty corridors and closed reception areas an eerie stillness hung in the air, like a school playground with all the children missing. Only the Accident and Emergency Department remained open, responding to the infrequent patients arriving throughout the night for treatment.

In the west wing of the Hospital, in a laboratory, sub-basement level to the Medical Sciences Office, a young postgraduate student sat alone in the darkness, slumped over his desk, a solitary desk lamp offering the only light in the room.

James McCarthy sat in his wheelchair, arms crossed out in front of him and head rested. He had one half of a pair of headphones plugged in to his right ear and was listening while an mp3 player slowly made its way through his eclectic music collection. His left ear was free to listen to the instruments on his desk purr and click with another kind of repetitive rhythm.

In front of him, his laptop ran a search program connected to a frequency emitter. The program was rotating through EM waves, continually modifying the emitter with new frequencies, oscillating at varying units of gigahertz and terahertz.

A digital microscope observing a small glass slate of cells sat linked up to a desktop computer running continual scans, poised to record the imagery based on movement.

A seismometer, commonly known for its use in recording earthquakes and other seismic shifts, read the activity fed back through the CPU whilst drawing a continuous and uneventful straight line down the middle of its digital display panel.

Alone in the dark, James remembered the sense of pride he had felt when this first started. When he was enlisted to be part of a project that could one day change the world, something that would triumph over every scientific accomplishment achieved in the past century.

His disability had made him accustomed to sitting and observing for great lengths of time. Composure was everything, but overnight research was taking its toll, overpowering any enjoyment he could get from the covert nature of his work.

He had been at this for weeks now, weeks of nothing. It had seemed inevitable at first, simply a matter of time. Every hour lost was an investment. But as the days and weeks rolled by his patience had begun to fade. *Someone else needs to take over, it's only fair.*

James hated this laboratory. During the first few nights of the experiment his fear of the dark that he had suppressed as a child had almost resurfaced. The silence of the laboratory at night offered a chilling atmosphere, like a morgue under a full moon. But he understood why it had to be this way; the access to the equipment, the isolation, the necessity of secrecy. It was all essential.

James slowly raised his head and rubbed his eyes, jaded and semi-conscious. He couldn't hold out much longer. He squinted, barely making out the time on the monitor; it was 3.04AM. His eyelids were heavy and his head was cloudy. This had become an all too familiar feeling. His secret second bedroom was beginning to feel comfortable again, a home away from home. He had two more hours before he needed to clean up and get out. There was time to rest.

His thoughts became more and more distant. He closed his eyes and breathed deeply to relax his upper body, letting the white noise from the equipment fade away whilst the glow from the desk lamp kept his face warm. Slowly darkening, he soon passed, accepting the eventual drift into a peaceful sleep.

Within minutes James was resting comfortably. The laptop on his desk clicked as the program switched to the next frequency. The repetitive purr and ticks soon followed.

It was faint at first. The seismometer offered a minor ripple, but another soon followed, then another and another.

With a sudden twitch the lines grew thicker, darker and wider in succession. The PC responded with an alarming ping, recording the cellular reaction being sent through the microscope.

James heard the beeps as if from a distance. He was slower to react. Gradually opening his eyes, he stared with a narrow gaze at the monitor. The alert sounded for a second time. A message was now displaying on the screen in front of him. 'Processing...'

He froze, disorientated, so used to the rhythm and ticks. Seconds passed before a third alert sounded with another message. *Frequency Registered.* James could feel himself waking up, his head beginning to focus. *Registered?*

His head rose from the desk as he rubbed his eyes, yawning, stretching. He stared again at the message. *Has it just? No... Yes, yes!* The realisation snapped him into action.

Peering through the microscope, his face lit up with excitement.

'Oh my god,' he whispered, scanning through the readings.

He took a breath and reached out to snatch his mobile from the desk, pausing for a moment before selecting a contact and dialling. His pulse raced as he lifted the phone to his ear.

'Please be awake,' he pleaded as the dialling tone began to ring out. 'Pick up, pick up!'

* * *

A mile away, in a small one-bedroom flat off St Clements Street, Ellie Swanson lay sound asleep in her bed.

A copy of *The Power of Your Subconscious Mind* by Joseph Murphy lay open face down on her bedside table.

In the darkness, her studio room was lit up only by the light blue glow that came from her alarm clock. You could barely make out the stacks of books and research material laid out over her desk and floor.

Her TV sat in the far right corner of the room, disused, collecting dust on a wooden stand that cased equally neglected DVDs and music CDs. Her laptop rested on the floor in the opposite corner, charging from an electrical point.

Her mobile was next to the book on her bedside table. The display lit up and a soft ringtone began to play out across the room.

It rang for several seconds before Ellie stirred, giving out a slight groan. She peered at the clock making out the time. It was later than usual but she knew what had woken her; this wasn't her first late night phone call. She'd stopped counting the false alarms weeks ago.

With her eyes still half closed she instinctively reached out, pressing the phone to her ear as she answered the call.

'Hello,' Ellie whispered. It was her first word of the day and her throat was dry.

'Ellie, I think we've done it. I think we've found Hawking.'

She lay motionless on her bed.

'Are you sure?' Her tone was doubtful.

'Pretty sure, this isn't like anything we've seen before. You need to see this.'

Ellie leaned forward to turn on her bed-side lamp and gather herself.

'What are the readings?'

'The program is at full alert, we've never had a probability rating this high before. Cellular response is at fifteen percent.'

'Fifteen?! Are you sure?'

'Fifteen point six.'

'Who have you rung?'

'Just you, I figured you were the most likely to answer this time of night.'

Ellie smiled, appreciating that her commitment was acknowledged.

'What's the metabolic activity?' she asked, now getting out of bed.

'Hold on.' James swung round and stared briefly at the monitor before putting the phone back to his ear, smiling uncontrollably. 'Cellular growth. There's been an increase in cytoplasmic and organelle volumes. It's taking.'

'You're sure?' Ellie reached for her clothes.

'We're at sixteen point seven.' James glanced back at the monitor. 'Seventeen percent, Ellie, she's climbing.'

'OK, OK. Call the professor, I'm on my way.' She hung up her phone and tied back her long brown hair into a pony tail. It was 3.12AM; if she hurried she could be there in twenty minutes.

CHAPTER TWO

MESSAGE IN A BOTTLE

It had been over a week since Ellie had submitted her research. More than two years of intensive study and theoretical science, packaged into a collection of documents, flow diagrams and chemical formulas that equated to one of the biggest discoveries in human history. Finally the weight had been lifted.

At first there was relief, overwhelmed by a sense of achievement. She marvelled, reflecting on what they'd accomplished and gave some thought to what it meant for her future at Oxford.

The feeling wore away quicker than she expected. Now Ellie played the waiting game, indulging in a futile attempt at returning to 'normal' everyday life.

As she expected this wasn't coming easy for her. All of the team had stepped up their commitment to the project when they realised there was realistic chance it could succeed, but Ellie had immersed herself from the start.

The world and its distractions had faded into obscurity – nothing else had mattered. Her only frustration was that this unreserved devotion to the research was known only to a select few. To everyone else, outside of the team, her consistent apathy throughout the lectures of the past year was puzzling and uncharacteristic; a balancing act she had failed to maintain. She was fortunate that her coursework had been unaffected.

It had been long over a week since the team had last assembled and nearly three weeks since she received the phone call she had so desperately been waiting for. *'Ellie, I think we've done it. I think we've found Hawking.'*

The plan was simple. Everyone packaged up their notes into the agreed format, submitted their research to the professor and waited. The professor would present their findings to the Board of Science at the University and request the funds to take the project to the next level.

Everything had seemed clear and under control. She gave her work blindly and waited patiently. But time had now passed and with hindsight playing on her mind she became mindful that nothing had really been agreed at all.

She didn't know when the professor would present their research or when they would hear the outcome. How would they find out? What kind of reaction should they expect?

During the first few days Ellie had expected to be pulled out mid-way through one of her lectures. She spent most of her time during seminars watching the entrance, expecting to see a face appear in the glass panel of the door, gesturing her to come outside.

By the end of the week Ellie began to expect a phone call from the professor or an email to the team with an update, some sort of indication on his progress. But there was still nothing, not a word. She was now becoming impatient, annoyed even.

If this had continued she would have considered approaching the professor directly herself, something the team were strictly forbidden to do, but she needed to know, she'd worked too hard to be left in the dark this way. Thankfully she wouldn't have to. Today the professor would come to her.

Like many of the courses at St Anne's the diverse subject matter was separated into modules, covered by various Professors on the basis of their expertise and experience.

Ellie was taking a Biology degree, en route to a Masters, and the modules for Molecular Genetics and Cell Membrane Structure were being run by Professor William Henry Daniels, a man Ellie had grown to know outside of the University more so than in and who the team affectionately called 'The Professor'.

Today she was set for another seminar on Molecular Genetics. One way or another, today she would find out what was happening.

Ellie started the day as a coiled spring. The time to think had given her every version of the conversation she was going to have.

She awoke early, lying in bed and watching intently as the sun rose from behind her window. The cream roller blind provided her small studio room with a soft and gentle raise in light. Soon after came the morning chirps from the birds and the occasional car setting off early to beat the traffic. She stared at her alarm clock, counting down the minutes until 8.00AM. Today everything mattered.

Ellie climbed out of her bed, tied back her hair and headed for the shower. By 9.00AM she was wide awake, fully dressed and focused, ready for the day ahead.

Her class didn't start for another hour and it took less than fifteen minutes to get to campus on foot. She paced back and forth. This would be the longest hour.

* * *

Ellie arrived at the seminar composed and with plenty of time to spare. The room was already a third full. The professor's teaching assistant, Angelo Mosso, had let the usual suspects in early to get the best seats. Given the choice she would have been among them, but that would have stuck out as strange and today needed to appear like any other day.

Ellie looked around to see that the professor was yet to arrive. This wasn't out of the ordinary.

She sat in her usual spot, greeted by Marie and Sally, two distant, *we must catch up* friends she'd come to know during the course.

'Hey you,' she said to Sally, unpacking her module book along with some notes from the previous lecture.

'Els, Marie was just saying, it's been ages since we've seen you out. Where have you been?'

'Oh I've been busy, this and that, you know.'

'What's his name?' Marie asked, leaning in for some gossip.

Ellie smiled, shaking her head. *As if!* It had been years since Ellie had even thought about getting to know someone intimately – just another sacrifice that she'd given gladly to the project.

As students drifted into class, the room volume grew until it was awash with noise - a strange collection of characters allowing for an odd mixture of conversations. Idle chat that kept them preoccupied and oblivious to the professor's absence.

Ellie tried not to clock-watch as the final minutes of the hour gave out.

She did her best not to appear relieved when the professor came through the door a handful of seconds past 10.00AM, the rest of the room remaining ignorant to his lateness.

Mid-sentence she stuttered whilst glancing over. He seemed distant, preoccupied. Unpacking his things without acknowledging the class or even thanking his teaching assistant. It was confusing. The professor's manners were usually impeccable.

After several minutes he gave a thankful nod to Angelo before turning to face everyone. Standing in front of the class and leaning back against his desk, he quietly looked out at his students.

Ellie was now facing forward, noting with intrigue the subtle differences in his composure. As always his frame carried the comfort of middle age spread and his short brown hair was seasoned with the occasional grey. But she could see that he'd not shaven. There was at least three days' worth of stubble growing on his face and his shirt, always immaculately ironed, was showing creases on the arms and shoulders.

One by one the groups began to quieten. They were accustomed to the professor telling them to settle down and take control but today seemed different and a gradual hush fell over in response to it. After a brief pause he headed for the white board.

'Good morning marines.'

'Good morning sir.' The class responded as one; it was a running joke.

'Before we get started today I wanted to touch on an important subject. Something that defines not science, but scientists; who we are and what we do.' He then picked up a red marker pen and wrote on the board a single word. He turned, for a moment studying the puzzlement on his students' faces. He had everyone's attention.

'Now, who can tell me the history of the first full-body MRI scan?' he asked. 'And lets stay away from the Nobel Peace Prize controversy if we can, please.' He began pacing back and forth in front of the class.

'An MRI is a Magnetic Resonance Imaging scan,' a student called out. 'It uses magnetic fields and radio waves to take pictures of the brain.'

'Along with the rest of the body,' the professor added. 'Yes, thank you Steven, but we hopefully all knew this.' He gestured to the room.

'Let's talk about her history.'

The professor picked out another student.

'It was invented in America,' a Spanish student offered. 'In the seventies, I think.'

'That's right, but can anyone tell me about the first full-body MRI?'

The class fell silent. A history lesson on the tools and instruments used in pathology examinations wasn't normally part of their seminars.

Ellie kept quiet. *Where is he going with this?*

The professor waited through several seconds of silence before starting.

'Cancer tissue cells have an abnormal amount of potassium and sodium. Dr Raymond Damadian knew this. Collaborating with a team of graduate students he spent years developing a device that he hoped would one day help to diagnose cancer and other serious medical conditions without cutting the body open.'

He rested against his desk.

'By 1977 they had constructed a superconducting magnet that could be used to detect the abnormal cells. It was impressive stuff for the time I can tell you.'

The professor paused, seemingly for effect.

'So it was finally ready, everything was in place. But there was just one problem... Can anyone tell me what the problem was?'

13

The room was still but for a few mumbles. He looked out at his students, appearing expectant.

'Anyone?'

It was rare for the class to be so regularly silenced. Often at least a few vocal students would have an opinion to offer, but everyone seemed caught looking to someone else for the answer.

'No one wanted to go first,' Ellie replied, her eye line fixed to the floor.

'That's right Elizabeth,' the professor said, pushing away from his desk. He still insisted on calling her Elizabeth as opposed to Ellie in front of the other students. 'No one wanted to be the first. No one wanted to be scanned. After all it wasn't safe, why be first? Why take the risk?'

The professor continued pacing.

'So who went first?' Sally asked, appearing drawn in by the story.

'Dr Damadian,' the professor answered. 'But it doesn't end there. When they tested it on him nothing happened. Damadian and his team were looking at years of research and funding wasted.'

The professor came to a stop.

'Moments of trial are often weighed by the *'what ifs'*. Perhaps Damadian was too big for the machine? Perhaps it would work for someone lighter? Someone thinner? Possibly someone younger? But who could know for sure? Not Damadian and not anyone in his team.'

The professor began pacing again.

'Someone had to believe... Someone had to see past their fear of the uncertain... It was July 3rd 1977. A graduate student volunteered. And this is known as the date the first full body MRI examination was performed on a human.'

He paused next to Ellie. Close and yet seemingly going out of his way not to give her any eye contact.

'You all want to be great scientists. I see it in your eyes. The hopes that you'll discover a cure to a disease, that you'll save lives. I was the same. And on a good day, I too will have that same glint in my eye. But what you need to remember is that with every inspiration there is always at first belief.'

He stared up at the word he'd written on the board: *Faith.*

'The very definition of an experiment is a test for the purpose of discovering something unknown. As scientists some of what we do is blind journey, an adventure even, and the amount of faith you put behind your science, the amount of belief you invest, will reflect what you get out of it. If we forget this, if we stick to what can only be proofed and formulated, we lose something. And perhaps it's not something we can put into words but it's something important, it's something that defines us.'

The class sat quietly, smiling and acknowledging his advice. Historical metaphors always seemed to pack a punch.

'You're the new breed, the next hope for the future of science. Believe in what you can offer and you'll make a difference, I promise.'

He rubbed the board clean and opened the module literature.

'OK, let's pick it up from our last session. Can you all turn to chapter seven for me please.'

* * *

Ellie sat muted and still, blankly gazing forward as the session passed her by in a two hour blur. She couldn't move on from what the professor had opened with.

She had covered the rise of the Fonar Corporation and its multiple patents in MRI technology as an essay during her A-levels. The company was founded by Dr Raymond Damadian himself.

Ellie had given it as long as she could before answering his question. She hated standing out, but she couldn't help feeling as if the question he had put to the class was for her.

Language was an incredible tool. The ability to say multiple things with a single statement. The same words sending entirely different signals depending on the tone and context.

The professor had delivered a message, in a way only he could. Subtle, delicate and allowing time for Ellie to digest it.

The clock above the white board bore down on midday as the professor began summarising the points that had been covered. The class recognised this as the round up and promptly folded up their notes.

'Your take home assignment is on my desk. I want you all to take a copy of this.' He held up an assignment sheet. The students began rising from their seats.

'Also spend some time studying up on Protein Interaction Networks and Signal Transduction ready for Tuesday's lecture. If you have any questions please take these up with Angelo.' The professor gestured to his teaching assistant.

The lecture room emptied quickly. The students bustled out of the door, their noise gradually filtering away.

Ellie sat, pretending to write, as if she were making her final notes. She said her goodbyes to Marie and Sally, and offered a series of plastic smiles and we must catch up promises she'd never keep. She packed her bag as slowly as she could, anxiously waiting for them all to leave. Poised at the edge of her seat, doing her best not to lose composure.

Professor Daniels wished the last of his students well before turning to pack up his things. 'I'll meet you in the Main Hall,' he said to Angelo, filling his leather bag with books and the remaining assignment sheets. Angelo nodded with a smile and left the room.

Ellie took a deep breath to gather herself. The professor offered a brief glance before walking over to the main door to close it. He pulled down the window blind, concealing them from the human traffic in the hallway.

She stood up, her face filled with a mixture of emotions. They stared at each other, sharing silence for a few moments before the professor began walking towards her. He didn't need to say anything. She couldn't believe it.

'They said no, didn't they?'

CHAPTER THREE

LEAP OF FAITH

'Inconclusive.'

The professor repeated what he'd told Ellie earlier that day.

It was nearing midnight and a young team of scientists had assembled on the ground floor of a Computing Laboratory – one of their agreed meeting points in the Department of Engineering Science.

They kept the room dark. Desk lamps glowed around them offering a soft light.

There were four shadows in the room: Ellie, James, another student named Sara and the professor, who was standing perched against a desk while the others sat in front of him.

'Inconclusive? What the hell does that mean?' Sara asked, rising to her feet.

Sara Morgan, a charismatic biologist studying Chemistry at Keble, was prone to speaking her mind. She was often considered fiery by the professors who taught her (or 'worked with her' as she would put it).

James was more composed. 'Are they questioning the validity of the research?'

'Not exactly,' the professor said softly. 'The Board have... concerns. Look, guys, this happens more often than you might think.' The professor tried to reassure them. 'The funding required to take this project to the next level is extensive. The Board need to ensure that all areas are covered, that the very best in their chosen fields are assembled and consulted... That the right approach is taken and that the correct equipment, support and... expertise is in place.'

'Bullshit!' Sara erupted. 'They can't do this! This is ours!'

Her face was red with fury, the vein on her neck throbbing and defined. Her fists clenched.

The professor spoke calmly.

'They can, they did and it's done. I'm sorry.' He knew what this meant to them.

'Motherfuckers!' Sara shouted at the floor, pacing up and down. The professor let it go. Sara's temper was always going to struggle when dealing with this.

'So what's the next step?' James asked, ignoring the sound of Sara kicking her chair in the background.

'There isn't a next step, not for a while. The funding is pulled. But I can assure you that all your names will be credited as key contributors to the research when it's published.'

'And when will that be?' Sara asked, barely holding back the aggression from her voice.

'Most likely in the next few years. It depends on the Muscular Dystrophy research. I hear significant progress is being made. Perhaps in a couple of years they'll...'

'Oh, come on,' James interrupted. 'It'll go private. They'll never get the funding to take this all the way. Some corporate American pharmaceutical will take this on and reap the rewards.'

The professor paused before speaking. He had to choose his words carefully.

'Perhaps... not exactly like that, but in a way... yes, that's possible.'

Sara slumped into her chair, the stages of acceptance were passing quickly and giving way to the sadness now showing in her eyes.

Whilst they had been waiting for the decision their minds had run riot. They had convinced themselves that only the very best outcome was possible.

Ellie sat waiting for her turn. Unlike the others she had been given the time to process what had happened. But it didn't make it any easier; she had watched as they arrived beaming with hope and eager to hear the news. The disappointment was unbearable.

Ellie looked around the room, deciding it was time to speak.

'Look, I don't know about the rest of you but this isn't over for me. I can't just walk away.' Everyone looked at her confused. 'Look, we've started something, and it's more than... this...' Ellie rose to her feet. 'This would be a cure to the human weakness. It would change life as we know it. How can we be expected to step back? Is it vain that I want to be part of this? I've given two years of my life... We've all given... We owe it to ourselves!'

James slouched in his wheelchair, his spirit broken.

'What are you suggesting? It's over.'

Ellie hesitated before continuing. She'd been thinking long and hard on the best way to broach this.

'Well, what did they say? 'Inconclusive', right? Fine, then we take that on board. We take it to the next level ourselves.'

'Animal testing?' James frowned.

Sara glanced at him pitifully, muttering something inaudible under her breath.

Ellie tried to sound as confident as she could.

'This isn't about the money... Screw the funding! We have nearly everything we need already. We take it to human trials.'

The room fell silent. Ellie was uncertain even as she said it, but she had done it. She had put it out there. If anything she was convinced everyone else was thinking it too.

'Who would be the test subjects?' James asked, knowing the answer.

Ellie gestured to the team, palms open.

'I can't just walk away... and I'm surprised you can?' She turned to the professor.

He had kept quiet, choosing to observe. Often a closed book, he was difficult to judge at times.

'I understand that you're angry,' he said, speaking with a tone that was more forceful than usual. 'I can't deny that I'm disappointed too, but we need the funding and this needs to be research accredited to the University. We can't go rogue. We need the support. This is too significant to act alone. The risks are...'

'I'm in,' Sara asserted, biting her nails as she spoke.

The professor recoiled. Shocked by the simplicity the team seemed to view this decision with. Considering the time they'd spent together over the past two years it was easy to forget they were so young and their immaturity at times took him off guard.

'Me too,' James said, turning to the professor for a reaction. He had begun putting on his coat.

'I'm sorry, I cannot be part of this. What you're suggesting... It isn't safe. I'd lose my job, my career.'

'You could oversee the project,' Sara offered. 'Make sure that everything was being done correctly. We'll do whatever it takes.'

'No,' the professor replied, putting a scarf around his neck and checking the time on his watch.

'But this is our chance!' Ellie tried not to sound desperate. 'You said yourself the amount of faith you put behind your science will reflect what you get out of it. This is our leap of faith. This is our moment. How can you say these things and then...'

'Do not use my words against me, Ellie!' the professor snapped. 'I wouldn't have got any of you involved in this if I thought it was dangerous.' He seemed angered by the idea that the team were doing this under his guidance.

'Let it go,' he pleaded, lowering his head with almost a whisper.

'We won't,' Sara spoke defiantly. 'We can't and you know that.'

The professor could see the determination in their eyes, the devotion. He'd seen it before.

'You don't know what you're asking,' he warned.

'All we're asking is that you trust us, Professor,' Ellie pleaded.

They knew the truth just as he did. The history of pharmaceutical publications were rife with law suits and damage claims from scientists protesting that their research had been stolen or misused in some way. This would be no different.

The professor offered each of them a glance, acknowledging the sincerity in their eyes. He knew they wouldn't let this go. *How could they? Why should they? Of course they are right.*

They were a young team and couldn't help but be ambitious, but unlike them he knew what they were asking; the risks, the danger.

The project now verged at the pinnacle of two years in extensive planning; an Everest of research had been overcome. Their opportunity was now.

He needed time. Time to think, time to assess, time to weigh everything up, but there was none. If he didn't agree tonight he may never see them again.

Was it too late to turn back? He had started this. He had put them in this situation. The responsibility bore down on him like a curse. They needed him. He couldn't risk a side project led by a team of students spinning off out of control. No, he would have to see it through. And the risks? The risks would be the ante to a reward beyond comprehension.

The professor stood, rooted to the spot, muttering under his breath and privately debating. Eventually he nodded as if in agreement with himself.

Walking to the exit, he left the group awaiting his response. He opened the door and glanced down the corridor to check it was clear.

The professor looked back at the team he'd assembled, leaving an uncertain pause before he spoke.

'Follow me. There's something I need to show you.'

CHAPTER FOUR

AN OXFORD MORNING

SEVEN MONTHS LATER

I was fifteen when I read an article in a newspaper headlined 'Student Life: An Education For The Modern Stone Age'. It was full of the sort of shit you'd expect, but the message it sent was pretty clear: If you don't know what to do with your life then go to University.
Remember when your parents told you that school was the best time of your life? Well when they said that, they meant University. They just can't remember anything else before it.
Picture a place where the onus was on you to live. To push the boundaries. To drink more than you can remember and sleep with whoever is willing. It was unlike anywhere else in the world, a home where you built the memories you would reminisce on.
If you're my age and like me then any moment from now your parents are going to suddenly corner you and ask a question you can't possibly answer: "What do you want to do with your life?"
What do I want to do? Shit I don't know. Does anyone know at my age?
What you need to remember is in that moment they don't need details. They just want to hear that you've got a plan. Trust me, when that moment happens just tell them "I want to go to University". They'll probably be proud.
Conor J. Martin

The air was fresh as Conor Martin set out for his morning run along the Oxford riverbank. The footpaths were empty at this time of day, which suited him fine. He was always one to prefer running alone.

The gravel crunched under his feet as Conor picked up the pace from the gentle jog he'd taken through the streets near Gloucester Green.

The sun was rising above the fields to the east of the City, resting low on the horizon and giving a picturesque view of the Oxford skyline.

Conor's thoughts turned to his breathing, steady and deep as he pressed on, the light breeze blowing on his back giving him a gentle push. His mp3 player thumped dance music into his ears, helping him keep a regular beat and focus.

Day five had started well. Conor was finally beginning to feel settled. His enrolment at St John's College had completed the day before, leaving him to enjoy the twilight hours of Freshers' week; three days and counting before his first lecture.

He was set to be taking a degree in the Foundations of Computer Science, three years of extensive study. Not that he found that daunting; Conor didn't really have an issue acquiring knowledge, it was knowing what to do with it that seemed to be the problem.

He had started applying for Universities six months ago, a decision pushed by the insistent questions his parents had bugged him with throughout the summer.

When it came to searching he stood by his motto. *Aim high, aim far.* It had served him well.

Oxford was the oldest University in the English-speaking world. Getting accepted had taken four applications, three interviews and more than a dozen sleepless nights in uncertainty.

Conor lifted his head to look down the bank and check the path ahead; it was clear but for the occasional dog walker. The canal to his right was peaceful and still, empty of the row boats that would soon occupy it. Beneath his feet the terrain felt rough and uneven, but the view made up for everything. He only wished there was a route like this back home.

Conor was born and raised in Leicester. He had spent his entire life living with his parents in the same mid-terrace three bedroom house off Vancouver Road. It surprised him how little he missed it. This was the first time he'd spent any real time away from home but Conor already felt the freedom that came from having his own private space.

Tennyson House was a halls of residence situated less than a mile from the University campus. It consisted of four floors and housed 160 single study bedrooms. From the outside the building gave off an almost gothic feel, with old brickwork and late eighteenth-century architecture. The windows were single-paned and bordered with Victorian design. Conor imagined it to be listed, perhaps once a Museum or Hospital, most likely protected under national heritage. It was full of history and character. The hallways throughout were carpeted with a rich cream and blue fabric and the walls were painted with magnolia, making it feel clean and fresh. Conor's room was on the third floor. It was a decent size although perhaps not as spacious as he'd hoped. It had come furnished with a single bed, a basic desk, a small wardrobe and an en suite bathroom.

Tennyson brought with it a distinguished reputation, a credited history of famous tenants and a famed view that looked out onto the Castle Mill Stream. On his first day he had found the whole experience intimidating, the scale and the prestige. But after his fourth, Conor's new home was beginning to feel comfortable. He was enjoying the simplicity of making his own decisions without his parents authorising his every move.

Conor was now an only child, and his family's history was pained by a tragic loss. He was five when his younger brother Alex died from leukaemia and ever since Conor had had his parents' complete attention; perhaps at times more than he could bear.

When it came to showing them his acceptance letter, he was greeted with a mixture of emotions. They were thrilled for him on the outside, his mother had even helped Conor pack his bags, sparing him of any tears or clichés. But he could sense the fear in their voices as they wished him luck, and felt it even more so in their over-protective hugs. Conor needed to leave the nest, he had a point to prove, and this would be good for him and it would be good for them as well.

Oxford was over a hundred and thirty miles from Leicester. It had taken close to an hour and a half to drive in his dated Vauxhall Astra, the journey blowing away rust from under the wheel arches and leaving a trail along the M1. It gave him the space he needed to grow and ensure his parents couldn't drop by unexpectedly if they missed him. This was his chance to show them that he could stand on his own two feet.

So he set out searching for a fresh start and with three commitments made. The first was that he'd keep up his running schedule and maintain a level of fitness whilst at Oxford. The second, that he'd call home at least once a week to keep his family at a safe distance. And the third... He would go into this with an open mind.

University life was an opportunity to mix with people that he would have otherwise never met. A mass of cultures, varying ages, endless variety congregated within an epicentre of activity. He would go into it with his eyes wide open, be understanding and accepting of difference and try everything at least once.

Conor's adrenaline had now pumped through his veins and warmed him under the morning sun. Time had passed and the light breeze that had once pushed him along was now cooling his face on the return journey.

By 7.00AM he was ending his run with a sprint to the finish, his heart pumping nearly in sync with the music that willed him along. Sweat streamed from his forehead as he finally slowed to an upbeat walk.

Conor panted for air as he looked out at the City, giving a moment to appreciate what he'd accomplished and wondering what memories the next three years of his life would have to offer.

CHAPTER FIVE

THE ODDS GAME

Conor and his new friend Samuel Milton took in the view as they sat comfortably in the warmth of the Eagle & Child. They watched as the rain lightly tapped against the windows, as the puddles slowly formed on the street corners. Passers-by were pulling out their umbrellas and frantically running to shelter. The tables and chairs inside quickly filled up with shivering punters shaking off the rain.

'Have you ever heard of the human regression theory?' Samuel asked, handing Conor a shot of tequila. He glanced to the new arrivals coming in from the cold. Conor shrugged.

'It's the belief that the human race will eventually peak in its ascension. Achieve all that we are capable of, and then over time, slowly regress, forgetting all that has been learned.' He picked up his tequila and gestured to the room. 'It can make you wonder, when will we know that we've peaked?'

Conor had met Samuel during his first week at University. He was staying in the opposite room at Tennyson House and had given an almost immediate impression of wealth and boyish charm. He spoke with a rich, distinctly royal English accent and projected the self-worth and confidence you would expect followed a childhood spent wanting for nothing.

'So, what are you taking?' Conor had asked him.

'Strictly class A's, often with whisky. And you?'

Samuel's dry sense of humour had taken a while to get used to. He had a cold exterior that would 'deflect questions and repel interest, a demeanour that required perseverance and patience. Instantly Conor had considered him the first test of his new mindset, an opportunity to meet someone he would have otherwise never met; and after several exhausting evenings attempting to keep up with his provocative intellect and rapid switches in conversation, an acceptance between them grew. Some would call it a friendship, but it was early days.

Conor had spent the past hour sharing memories and drinking stories from back home. Samuel listened intently in parts whilst on occasion drifting his focus, distracted by the mock Tudor character of the pub, the visible wooden beams, the lamps and roaring fire place. It offered an ambience which appeared to remind him of home.

Conor would have happily listened but depending on his mood Samuel would often be guarded when talking about where he came from and, in particular, his family.

He was also proving a strong drinker; three rounds with an accompanying shot and there was no sign of effect. Conor started to imagine that he had a silver flask of whisky tucked away in his jacket pocket at all times.

'So, how's your course going?' Conor asked, the taste of tequila still warm on his breath.

'Tiresome,' Samuel sighed.

Conor wasn't thrown by the response.

'Don't take this the wrong way, but I didn't think it was for you.' He was still confused by Samuel's choice on studying Finance Math at Pembroke.

'No offense taken, chap. To be fair it's more my attendance at University that's the driving factor here, rather than any purpose.'

'So why are you here?'

Samuel looked away, appearing to choose his words before returning his attention.

'I am here, dear boy, because I find the thought of contributing to society troublesome at best.' His tone became less playful. 'I'm here because parents like mine offer to pay the tuition fees of their children just to remove you from their sight. I'm here at the courtesy of my beloved ex girlfriend Michelle, who took my virginity and my heart and then replaced me with a pretty boy named Craig.

Turns out she's engaged now, which makes you wonder why stupid decisions aren't rewarded more often!'

He took in a mouthful of his pint and swallowed it down.

'I'm here for the stories, Conor, the experience. Something to tell my grandchildren when I have them, God forbid. I want proof that I lived... Why are you here?'

'I told you. A degree in Computer Science.'

'Oh yes, that's right. Fascinating.' Samuel rolled his eyes. 'Why are you *here*?' he asked, pointing down at the table. It was clear he meant Oxford.

Conor paused to think on his answer. No one had asked him it before. Oxford was deemed an achievement in anyone's eyes, the instinctive reaction was to congratulate him, ask what he was studying and wish him the best of luck. But Samuel didn't seem to carry the same enchantment to his new digs.

'I was jaded. No, jaded is the wrong word; frustrated would be better,' Conor admitted. 'Back home I rotated my evenings around the same bars and clubs, regurgitating a copy of a night over and over... All my life, I've just wanted to do something worth remembering. I guess I'm looking for something.'

As he spoke Conor noticed a red-head by the bar ordering drinks.

'A chance to meet people,' he said softly. She had a lean athletic body and was wearing skinny jeans and a tight pink top.

Samuel frowned, noticing Conor's sudden daze and followed his eye line to the bar.

'Remember, dear boy,' he smiled. 'Women are an odds game that's never in your favour.'

Undeterred, Conor rose from the table, wobbling slightly as he stood to his feet. Unlike Samuel the pace in which they had got through the first few rounds was not without effect.

'Just give me a minute,' he said.

Samuel watched jeeringly as Conor carefully walked towards the bar, heading straight for the girl. Weaving in and amongst the crowds and tables, he moved as quickly as he could, reaching the bar in time to see that she was being served her drinks. He casually positioned himself next to her. *Aim high, aim far.*

'Hello,' he said, trying his best to sound charming.

His greeting prompted her to glance at him for a brief second before turning back to her drinks.

'Hi Fresher.'

Conor reeled. 'Jesus, that obvious?'

'Oh, I wouldn't say that,' she said, turning her head slightly, a touch of sarcasm in her tone.

'Well, ten points in any case.'

She gave no response. Conor made every effort to keep his eye line above her neck.

'Nice place, Oxford,' he tried again. 'You live here?'

'Of course.'

'You come here often?' Quickly he regretted his choice of words.

'And why would you ask that?' she moved to face Conor, giving him her complete attention for the first time. She had dark hazel eyes.

'You don't do this very often, do you?' she asked, smiling. 'Not that I'm suggesting you're inexperienced or amateur. No, you've had some experience with girls or you wouldn't have approached at all. It's just that you've got insecurities. I'm guessing it's because this is your first time away from home. Are you studying IT?'

Conor couldn't hide his surprise.

'Computer Science. How did you know?'

'You've got a look about you.'

'I'll take that as a compliment.'

'Take whatever helps,' she said, looking away to shield a smile.

Conor caught it but played along.

'Thank you. What makes you think this is my first time away from home?'

'Well, for one thing it explains this newfound courage of yours.' She took a sip of her drink. 'You can't quite believe your luck, can you?'

He looked away before returning with a smirk.

'OK, maybe.'

The barman served the last of her drinks onto a tray and took the twenty pound note she had held out folded between her fingers.

'So, what's your name?' Conor asked, feeling a sudden need to act fast.

'Oooh, direct. I'm impressed.'

'But not enough?'

'Not today,' she took the change from the barman, giving him a wink, and turned back to Conor. 'So why Oxford? What's wrong with the University in Leicester?'

'What makes you say Leicester?'

'Well judging by your accent I'm guessing it's Leicester, but I suppose it could be Coventry or outer Nottingham even.' Conor did his best not to give her anything. She studied his face and smiled. 'But it's Leicester, definitely Leicester.'

'I have my reasons for Oxford,' Conor said enjoying her interest. 'But we don't know each other well enough and perhaps we should. Can I give you my number? You can't learn everything from a glance and I think…'

'No, not by a glance,' she interrupted. 'But by watching the way that they talk, dress, compose themselves in conversation.' Conor noticed that he was leaning against the bar and stood up straight. 'You can get enough… And after looking at you and a minute's conversation I'm guessing you were born and raised in Leicester. Perhaps a little excessively mothered from a young age, middle class of course, kept your head down in school and did well but not as well as you hoped.'

She squinted in thought. 'From there you went on to further education definitely, no doubt fuelled by binge drinking and nights out with equally testosterone driven primates. But that of course led to boredom and boredom to escapism. I'm sure Oxford felt like a logical choice.' She took another sip of her drink.

'How many points do I get?'

Conor leaned back up against the bar, wondering whether there was any point in speaking at all.

'Have you ever heard of the human regression theory?' he thought to say.

She smiled and picked up her drinks.

'Have fun, Fresher, but not too much fun. OK?'

'Don't you want to know my name?' Conor called out as she walked away.

'I don't need it,' she replied, disappearing into the crowd.

He stood at the bar, dazed by the elegance in which she had palmed him away. If the odds weren't in his favour back home, they weren't worth calculating in Oxford. He glanced back to Samuel to find him grinning ridiculously and saluting with his pint. He'd enjoyed the show.

Conor thought for a second, trying to imagine how the exchange could have played out better for him. Was it the way he was dressed? His hair? He sighed, eventually settling on a reason that his pride painfully allowed him to accept.

CHAPTER SIX

THE BEGINNING OF SOMETHING PURE

Over a month had now passed and for Conor the day-to-day life of an Oxford student was starting to take shape. The first core module of his degree was well underway and his week-by-week schedule was all but memorised.

Outside of his lectures and seminars, Samuel and Conor had already achieved several nights out that were worthy of being reminisced. The coming years held great promise, giving Conor every reason to believe that he would look back on his days at University with fond memories.

It was 10.00AM and the Computer Science class were proving noisy and boisterous as they settled in for their morning seminar. Students had been trickling in to the classroom for the past fifteen minutes, a curious mix of lonely characters with inward personalities. There were nearly thirty in total, their heads always low, eyes ever focused on their smart phones or tablets. But gathered among their own they would open up, vocal and opinionated, conversation ranging from the latest films that had hit the cinema, to up and coming video games and the pending releases of long-awaited gadgets.

Professor George A. Miller sat on his desk at the front of the room. His short height and podgy stomach fed to the IT teacher stereotype. His feet dangled as he repeatedly threw his favourite baseball lightly in the air to catch it. Generally this was how most of his sessions began; the class wasn't known to start until the professor's feet had touched the floor.

Conor was still an absent member of the classroom long after Professor Miller's soles had hit the ground. He stood at the front of the room, addressing his students.

'Memory, in the form of computational data storage, has an interesting if not cryptic parallel with the way memories are stored in our brains. Random access memory, or RAM, allows your CPU to load pieces of information out of sequence from the way they have been stored on the disk, optimising the processing of data for efficiency, no different from you reciting your childhood without having to track back through puberty...'

Conor was louder than intended as he came through the main entrance, the door slamming shut behind him to amplify his lateness. He drew the eyes of his fellow students and prompted a few mumbles. He gestured an apology to Professor Miller as he made his way to an available seat, giving friendly nods to the people he knew or those that would offer eye contact. Miller paid no attention to Conor's arrival, apart from a raised eyebrow and a brief look of disappointment.

Conor slumped into his chair and unpacked his things. It was a frustrating constant that he recently found himself running late wherever he went.

'The first examples of random access memory date back to 1947,' the professor continued. 'Back then it was called the Williams tube. This worked by storing data with electrically charged points on the face of a cathode ray tube...'

Conor was barely comfortable when he overheard two students in front of him whispering.

'I heard some guy at Merton broke it,' one student said.

'What? The code? Who?'

'I can't remember his name. Something Johnson or Jameson.'

'Bullshit.'

'No, seriously.'

'What did his code mean?'

'He wouldn't say.'

'You gullible muppet.'

'Honestly, he was like sworn to secrecy or something.'

Conor moved to the edge of his seat and leaned in closer.

'Perhaps Conor would be so kind as to take us through it?' the professor announced, the sound of his voice pulling Conor's focus back to the seminar. The class slowly turned to look at him, peering with anticipation. The professor allowed for several seconds of uncomfortable silence before he spoke.

'Would you like to voice an opinion?'

'An opinion?' Conor asked, his heart thumping in his chest. 'Of course, my opinion... Yes.' He fidgeted in his seat.

'On the advancement of Computer-Aided Verification,' Professor Miller guided.

'Yes, well... Who doesn't have an opinion?' Conor smiled.

'Indeed,' Professor Miller said, holding an expectant gaze with his arms folded.

Smiling awkwardly, Conor felt the burning stares of his classmates. He tried to speak but his mouth had turned dry. He had nothing, not even a witty retort to steal some points.

'Another time, perhaps?' Miller offered, satisfied that Conor had sunk low enough into his chair. 'Or, even better, could I have a minute of your precious time after this session, please?' he then asked.

Conor gave an affirming nod, encouraging his class to return their focus to the front. The moment passed with an embarrassment that would linger.

The hands of the main clock inched forward without urgency, it was painful. Seminars under Professor Miller had a tendency to defy the laws of time, to turn minutes into hours and the attendees from buzzing enthusiasts into lifeless drones.

Conor stayed with the session as long as he could, a concerted effort considering his usual attention span. It was well into the second hour when his eye line had drifted mischievously to his smart phone - social media was soon playing its part in distracting him.

The professor wrapped things up with a collection of playful threats on the agenda of next week's seminar. He gave some suggested research and a reminder on the pending dissertation creeping up on them. Before long the class was on its feet.

Conor kept rooted to his chair, acknowledging the students as they bundled their way to the exit, shrugging off the occasional smirk and whisper. He listened to the rumbling sound of his classmates from behind the main doors until the room had softened into silence.

Lining up the excuses in his head, he rose from his chair and made his way to the front of the classroom. Professor Miller was packing away his things when he glanced up to observe Conor's walk of shame.

'Mr Martin,' Miller said, 'There's something I need to ask you...'

He packed away his notes and closed his bag, turning to him with a curious expression on his face.

'Are you my Woody?'

'Sir?' Conor approached, looking puzzled.

'It's a question I sometimes ask myself.' Professor Miller finished shutting down his laptop and projector before walking round his desk to lean up against it.

'In 1953 a student named Allan Stewart Konigsberg enrolled in the City College of New York under the University's illustrious film program... From the outset he appeared a promising student. Young, perhaps. Presumptuous, maybe. Like so many his age, yet to appreciate the way of the world.' He offered a nod to Conor.

'It only lasted a short while before it became apparent that there was a problem. Whether it was the course or the work or the tutors, I don't know. But what was clear was that something didn't quite sit right with him. He was unsettled, the University didn't seem to match his perspective on things.' The professor held a long gaze at Conor.

'Eventually, after a succession of poor grades, he was kicked out... Not that this was to be the measure of him. He went on to write, to direct, to inspire. By then he was known by his stage name, Woody Allen.' The professor let his words sink in for a few seconds.

'So, considering that the greatest teaching failure of all is to not recognise potential, when I have a student consistently going out of their way to try and fail in my class I always ask myself the same question: is this student my Woody?'

Conor stared at the floor.

'Well? Are you?' the professor pushed.

'I don't know,' he answered softly, raising his head.

'Of course not,' the professor agreed. 'Neither of us do. This is something we need to figure out together, you and I. But we need to do it quickly, Conor, and this starts with you arriving to my seminars on time and prepared. Understand?'

'Yes, sir,' Conor nodded.

'Alright. Then I'll see you next week. Now off you go,' the professor gestured to the exit.

* * *

Thirty minutes later and Conor was opening the door to his bedroom at Tennyson House.

He threw his bag and jacket on the floor before collapsing on to his bed. His head heavy in thought, he stared at himself in the mirror across the room.

The professor's words had carried weight this time, a warning he couldn't ignore. How did he let it get to this? He needed to pull himself back, to bring himself closer to the rails. The risks he was taking were getting him in trouble. *Just one more night*, he told himself. Putting on the travel kettle, he set things up for a strong cup of coffee.

Landing on his desk chair, he ran his finger over the keyboard to his laptop, disabling the screensaver and dissolving the rotating images from the screen.

The progress bar of a decryption engine appeared in front of him.

It started as a myth, a whisper around campus. Conor first heard the rumours over a pint with Samuel and then again during a Digital Systems workshop a week later. Some were saying that it began in Cambridge, but no one truly knew. It was never first hand, always a friend of a friend or the roommate of a stranger.

There was no explanation given, nor did there appear to be any pattern or connection, but students at the University were being chosen, singled out. Those who were selected spoke little of it, only to say that they had been sent a mysterious message, an encrypted invitation that they found in their mailbox or slipped under their door.

The message would contain a code that was unique to each student; a series of numbers and letters which would appear at random, encrypted by an elusive cipher.

Quickly, gossip had speculated on its purpose, the prize of breaking the code ranging from University acknowledgement to the absurd, but from there the stories would differ. Some would attempt to break it and fail whilst others instantly discarded the code refusing to participate in whatever this was.

Even now he couldn't believe it. It had been four days since Conor had found a mysterious code in his mailbox, sandwiched between a pile of takeaway menus and college leaflets.

Everyone was talking about it, but not once did he imagine being chosen. To him this represented one thing alone: a test. An opportunity to stand out among the elite. To rise above the cream of Oxford.

For every minute since that day his thoughts had rarely strayed from the task. Everything had changed. He rubbed his eyes and felt the stubble that was growing on his face. Was this a joke? If it was he had played the role of the fool convincingly.

Conor had spent the past three nights staying up until the early hours trying every decryption technique he could think of, endlessly searching for help from the internet. Nothing had worked. There was little to go on except to analyse the code against every encryption method known and the options seemed infinite.

He held up the card to the light, reading the code with pained frustration:

125.137.PB:A-B.TXT
CICRX PRBDG BPCBZ
20/11/15, 10.30AM

The deadline had brought with it stress that was proving difficult to mask. Conor's vague lecture contributions had already got him noticed, for all the wrong reasons, but the late nights had now pushed him beyond his usual 'just in time' arrivals and into inexcusable lateness.

It was only a few minutes past 12:30PM and already Conor's eyes were showing the bloodshot story of insomnia. When he looked in the mirror all he could see was his weathered face peering back at him, desperate for rest. His occasional yawns grew closer together. As the kettle boiled he reached for the caffeine.

The only truth he could console himself with was that this was his last night. Either he broke it tonight or he didn't; either way tomorrow was the deadline and he craved the end one way or the other. Conor tried to focus, shaking off the morning and settled in for what was to be another long session in front of his computer.

CHAPTER SEVEN

A FRIEND IN NEED

Samuel Milton strolled across the shingled courtyard outside Tennyson House, kicking the odd pebble as he walked. The temperature was starting to drop during the evenings and he could see his breath appear in front of him as if he were smoking.

In his right hand he held a new top-of-the-range smart phone. It had arrived by special delivery that morning with a message that had brought both frustration and a confused sense of obligation to his afternoon.

'Thank you for the lovely gift, mother, very subtle,' he said, the mobile pressed to his ear.

He never thought his absence would cause her to behave so desperately. Starved of attention, she was suddenly taking great interest in his life.

Samuel had fallen in and out of her affections enough times to know when he was being used. He remembered the story his grandmother had once told him about how, as a baby, he knew the face of his au pair long before he recognised his own mother.

He could picture their lofty estate on the hills in Winchester, even more deserted than usual. He never did understand their infatuation with owning a property that was fit to house a small village.

She was alone and it had now dawned on her that the endless spa sessions and ladies' lunches had left a gaping hole where their relationship should have existed. Clear as day she was back-peddling in an attempt to remain part of his life.

A smile grew across Samuel's face as he sensed the call coming to an end.

'OK mother, if you need to get hold of me I'll be on this number. OK, bye mother, yes, yes, I love you too. Speak to you soon.'

He hung up and exhaled a deep breath. Having just come home following another tiresome day of lectures and study, appeasing his mother with the pretence of affection was the last thing he needed.

Finance Mathematics required the application of formulated methods to decipher relationships and patterns within strings of numerical data. During his time at the University he would learn differential and integral calculus, advanced equation theory and matrix algebra.

He remembered choosing the course while he was back at home, watching curiously as it fed his family's insatiable appetite for wealth and finance. In truth he didn't know what he'd do with the qualification if he got it. Samuel was set to enjoy his years at University as if they were his last taste of true freedom. His student visa provided the immunity he needed to shirk the reality of adulthood.

He held the phone in his hand and stared at it for a brief moment. Samuel smiled, imagining his mother in a phone store asking the shop assistant for the most expensive handset available, most likely making a point to state that money was no object.

He refused to think on it. With aggression boiling in his veins, he snapped and threw the phone into the sky. Its ultra-thin case sliced through the air as it landed with a splash into the canal. He watched as it hit the water, stroking his hands clean as the ripple faded.

'If you need to get hold of me I'll be on this number.' She wouldn't ruin this for him, no matter how hard she tried.

As he sprang up the stone steps and walked into the warmth of Tennyson his nostrils filled with the rustic smell of oak furniture and polish. To his right stood a wall of pigeon-slot mailboxes for the tenants; to his left, an empty visitor's area where two leather sofas and a glass coffee table sat disused in the corner.

The walls of the ground floor were decorated with framed black and white pictures, each taken from the oldest rooms in Tennyson House, moments of time from the nineteenth and early twentieth century. He briskly walked through the reception area and headed for the stairs, the wooden floor giving a soft echo with every step.

When Samuel got to his room he dumped his leather Ashwood satchel on the floor, threw his jacket on a tub chair in the corner and checked the time. Within forty minutes, he was dressed in an Armani shirt, putting the finishing touches to his hair and smelling of Gucci aftershave.

Samuel took one last look in the mirror before placing his comb on the glass shelf below it, nodding his head to the sound of a music channel playing at an excessive level from his television.

He checked the time. The night was all planned out in his head. After catching up with two of his new American friends on the first floor, they would set off for the Red Lion. A destination chosen with purpose. They had all watched in amusement as Samuel repeatedly tried and failed with the blonde behind the bar, but tenacity counts.

There was just one last task before his evening could begin.

Samuel hit the power button on his remote control as he headed for the door. Leaving his room, he walked across the hall and knocked with repetitive rhythm on Conor's apartment.

For the past three nights Conor's absence had been both acknowledged and intriguing, but a fourth night was becoming unsociable and Samuel wasn't having it. He'd drag him out kicking and screaming if he had to.

He pressed his ear to the door and waited impatiently, tapping his finger against the frame, giving it a few seconds before unleashing another string of heavy thuds.

Founded on honesty and fuelled by alcohol, his friendship with Conor over the past couple of months had taken him by surprise.

Thinking of home, the few friends he could speak of were the sons of politicians and bureaucrats, none of which he could consider true. Over time it had led him to harbour a distrusting nature, a state of mind that his ex-girlfriend referred to as *'impossible to accept'.*

It had made his friendship with Conor especially important to him and the sudden change in his behaviour that much more confusing.

Still there was no answer. With his patience worn he reached for the door handle, rattling it loudly in the hope he wasn't about to walk in on something that could ruin their friendship entirely. Turning the handle, Samuel applied some pressure until the door clicked and gave way. Gently he pushed it open.

The room was in murky darkness. He could make out the silhouette of a wardrobe with its doors left open, a selection of clothes scattered over the bed. He sniffed the air, taking in the smell of strong coffee and cheap deodorant.

Flicking the light switch he noted the only thing that mattered. Conor was gone.

'Lock your door next time old boy,' Samuel mumbled playfully to himself. 'You never know who may be about.'

Enjoying an opportune moment to pry, Samuel stepped into Conor's room, swiftly closing the door behind him.

Opening the drawers to a cabinet, Samuel stumbled across a family picture of a young Conor sitting with his parents at a restaurant table. He stared at it closely, unable to stop himself from feeling jealous. Seeing the affection in their eyes, the smiles on their faces, the goofy, happy body language. *How the other half live.* Gently he returned the picture to where he had found it.

Whilst turning his head to the en suite, something caught his attention; a glint from the corner of his eye. A small piece of white card.

Son of a bitch! Samuel walked over to Conor's desk to pick up the code resting out in the open. *Why didn't you tell me?* He held it up to the light, turning the card over to check it front and back before discarding it with a flick towards the desk.

Once fascinated by the mystery, Samuel was, like so many others, disillusioned. There were four pupils in his class alone working on codes, tempted by the lucrative cash rewards being offered to them. Wasting weeks, months of their lives on an unbreakable cipher.

Samuel lifted the lid to Conor's laptop and pressed down on the space bar. He glared intently at the screen as the screensaver disabled.

First appearing puzzled, he soon signed.

'Oh Conor,' he whispered. 'You should know better than to play against a child at a kid's game.'

CHAPTER EIGHT

EVERYTHING HAS MEANING

The new day had started with a focus that disconnected Conor from the caffeine headache bidding for his attention. He woke wide-eyed and alert long before his alarm clock needed to help.

He had spent most of the morning marvelling at his achievement, or at least he believed it was his to claim. Despite the excitement of the code's sudden decryption, the mystery and circumstance surrounding it had brought an anxiety that gave everything he looked forward to an uncertain sting.

It had been late afternoon the day before when, in a sulk, Conor had succumbed to the idea that perhaps the code was unbreakable. Or at least that was to say that it couldn't be broken in the time he had to work with. His decryption engine continued to run, offering cross comparisons and cipher analysis, but a reality had begun to dawn that if he could break it, he would have done it by now.

As the day drew into evening his seated composure sank from an upbeat lean forward to a lazy slouch. He watched as the sun set from his window, an accepting smile across his face.

With a sigh Conor changed into his running gear, intent on burning off the stress that had built up over the past three days and as he left Tennyson and stepped into the cold, a sense of relief lifted the weight from his shoulders. Failure was at least a conclusion, it was over.

The night carried the usual chill in the air as the road lighting lit up a course down Walton Street near the Radcliffe Observatory. The route he set out looped round and round, cooling his head and relaxing him of any thoughts, the tarmac footpaths smooth under his feet.

Nearly two hours had passed before his exhausted frame stumbled through the car park heading for home, steam rising from his forehead as his body heat met the cold. Yearning for his bed and the rest it would offer, he burst through the door to his room and took a cool bottle of water from the portable fridge under his desk.

Taking long, indulgent gulps, Conor felt his breathing begin to slow and the burning in his chest subside. He slumped on to his bed, exhaling loudly as his body fell into the mattress. His eyes closed for several seconds before they opened again, slowly letting his thoughts stray back to the code. Sitting up, he leant over to his desk and stroked his hand over the mouse pad, watching with little expectation as the screensaver dissolved.

He squinted in confusion; the progress bar was gone. The view he had grown accustomed to had changed, replaced instead with a message. Conor dropped the bottle he was drinking from. *Cipher Decode Success*.

Even as he read it, Conor couldn't believe what he was seeing. It was the Enigma cipher. *Of course! The Enigma*. He remembered reading about the Enigma when he was studying the ergonomics of World War Two during his History A-Level. It was invented by the German engineer Arthur Scherbius at the end of the First World War and although initially used commercially, it was made famous by the Nazi German Military in World War Two for communicating encrypted orders and controlling engagements.

Encrypting and decrypting a message on the Enigma machine required four key settings.

First was the wheel order, three rotors which dictated the sequence *(125)*. Second was the initial position of the rotors *(137)*. Then came the Plugboard settings, these permitted variable wiring that could reconfigure connected letters to effectively swap before and after the main rotor scrambling unit *(PB: A-B);* and finally the ring settings, the position of the alphabet rings relative to the rotor wiring *(TXT)*. Conor looked at the code:

125.137.PB:A-B.TXT
CICRX PRBDG BPCBZ
20/11/15, 10.30AM

It was obvious, staring him in the face the whole time. The code was even broken up into sets of five letter groups as used by the German Military.

Still unsure as to how the engine had managed to break it, he noticed that the code had been converted from 'CICRX PRBDG BPCBZ' to now read 'RADCL IFFEC AMERA'.

Considering the Enigma machine had no space bar, he immediately removed the spaces to reveal the message.

The main research library to the University of Oxford was the Bodleian, or 'the Bod' as many called it. It was one of the oldest libraries in Europe and, in Britain, second in size only to the British Library in London. Radcliffe Camera was a beautiful reading room that stood as part of the Old Library in Radcliffe Square.

Feeling the pure rush of accomplishment, Conor stared at the decrypted message, sighing in relief at its simplicity:

RADCLIFFE CAMERA
20/11/15, 10.30AM

It was 9.45AM and Conor was sat fully dressed at the end of his bed, staring at his reflection in the wall mirror.

The Bodleian Library was a twenty minute walk from where he was staying, but, deciding to leave early, he gave himself plenty of time.

He had considered talking to Samuel before leaving but was almost certain he would only try and talk him out of going, or worse insist that he came along. This was something Conor would do alone.

With his body still aching from the evening run, he stepped out of his room a few minutes before 10.00AM. Clicking his door shut, Conor noticed Samuel's door slightly ajar from across the hallway and gently pushed it open.

Instantly the smell of morning odour that followed a night of cigarettes and drinking filled his nose. Samuel was fully dressed, asleep, face down on his bed, his heavy breathing and occasional snort filling the silence in the room. Conor smiled sympathetically at his friend before quietly pulling the door shut.

He gave a yawn and covered his mouth as he walked downstairs. Being awake for most of the night had worn him down despite the adrenaline. He'd buy a sugary drink on the way to get sharp.

Heading for the main door he deviated off course to check his mailbox; it was empty but he was glad to know it.

Going down the steps, the fresh morning air helped bring some colour to his cheeks. At this time of day the early lectures were already under way and the roads had now settled from the bustling bumper to bumper of morning rush hour.

Conor decided to walk, leaving his car to gather rust for another day. With an upbeat pace he took the most direct route he could. Sticking to the pathways, his feet skimmed along the pavement as he looked up to the endearing dome growing in the distance.

Radcliffe Camera was one of Oxford's most famous landmarks, her presence ever prominent along the Oxford skyline. He was looking forward to seeing it up close.

Coming off Broad Street, Conor walked past the main entrance of the Bodleian Library just after 10.20AM. He made his way along the side road of Catte Street, with the vast stone brickwork of the Library to his right, and the grand entrance to Hertford College to his left.

He followed the road ahead through the steel gate towards Radcliffe Square until he passed the old library to his right. Conor's pace stuttered as Radcliffe Camera suddenly came into view. The sheer scale and beauty of the building took him by surprise.

Designed by James Gibbs, one of Britain's most influential architects and built between 1737 and 1749,

Radcliffe Camera (or Radcliffe Room) was one of the first examples of a circular library in England.

The architecture for the time was seen as inspired. From the outside it appeared built in three levels; the base made of brick materials sourced from local stone, the central compartment complimented with Corinthian columns which paired up between near fifteen foot windows and an upper level that finished with a beautifully designed lead dome. The interior was broken into two stories known as Lower and Upper Camera. Lower Camera was a grand reading room whilst Upper Camera acted as an archive to a wealth of literature.

Although it was not originally part of the library, Radcliffe Camera was introduced in 1860 to house Oxford's medical and scientific collections, but these were later transferred to the Radcliffe Science Library in 1861. In recent years Radcliffe Camera kept a collection of books on Anthropology, English, Film, History and Theology.

Conor walked up the stone steps and through the main entrance archway, taking in a wonderful smell of stone, oak and old parchment. He had already gone through the formal declaration process to be granted access to the Bodleian during his first month at the University. This was traditionally oral, but in recent years was now done by signing a declaration letter.

Instantly Conor understood why Radcliffe Camera was considered such an architectural triumph; he appreciated the textured interior and how the lighting from the surrounding windows gave the bookcases and tables a glow. The first floor could be seen from the ground floor study area, a huge encircling ledge that opened up to give way to a breathtaking inner dome. The stone work above the encircling archways offered subtle details that attributed to impeccable craftsmanship.

Conor walked out onto the ground floor known as Lower Camera. He scanned the room from left to right. There were surprisingly few people studying here considering the room's size, perhaps thirty-five, forty at most, spread out across both floors. Some sat reading on the ground floor whilst others typed on their laptops, seemingly using the tranquil environment as the perfect study area. He checked his watch - it was 10.24AM.

Conor tried to keep moving, suddenly aware of how peculiar a situation this was. What was he supposed to do? Did he need to go somewhere? Were they expecting him? There was nothing obvious or out of place. He didn't recognise anyone. Conor thought back to the message. Perhaps the Enigma settings doubled up to be the location of a book? A chapter, a page? There had to be something.

He sat at one of the available workstations in the centre of Lower Camera, taking a deep breath and trying not to lose heart.

Looking at the time on the monitor, he could see that it was now 10.27AM. *Should I just wait?* Conor clicked to open the library intranet and paused for a moment to think.

Raise the flag. Reaching inside his jacket pocket, he pulled out the white card containing the code and placed it on the desk in front of him.

As the time bore down on 10.29AM Conor grew agitated, frequently turning in his chair, glancing from reading room to Upper Camera. He tried to focus, to envisage what was expected of him.

The time on the monitor updated relentlessly, the seconds passing quickly until it finally refreshed to read 10.30AM.

Good morning, Conor, a message read, suddenly appearing on the screen in front of him. The sender was anonymous.

He couldn't hide the relief from his face. Instinctively Conor glanced around Lower Camera trying to figure out where it had come from. There were fixed terminal stations everywhere he looked.

Who is this? he wrote, glancing anxiously from left to right.

A friend. The response came back quickly.

Did you send me the code?

Yes, the user replied. Conor imagined the sender staring at him from afar, watching his every move.

What is this?

A project of discovery, Conor. An opportunity worth anything you could fear losing.

He frowned. *An opportunity to do what?*

Can you keep a secret?

Yes

A game for the young, the user replied. *Do you want to be part of something that will change the world?*

The grandeur of the message made him nervous. *Is this a joke?* he wrote, peering up to Upper Camera and catching the suspicious glance of an elderly man disappearing behind a pillar.

Why did you break the code? the user responded.

With a squint Conor leaned back into his chair, looking down at the small white card in front of him.

Codes are made to be broken, he wrote.

There was no response. Lightly tapping at the table as the seconds passed, he glanced at the time. It had been over a minute.

Conor shook his head. This wasn't an invitation; breaking the code had meant nothing, there was no reward. This was an interview.

He thought for a moment before typing a new response.

Because everything has meaning.

How interesting, the user responded.

Sensing that he needed to choose his questions carefully, Conor thought hard before asking; *Will you tell me your name?*

You can call me Rysbrack.

As the response came back, he caught a glance from the corner of his eye. A curious stranger he didn't recognise; a man on a laptop wearing a dark blue hoodie, his head low and hunched. Their glances met for seconds before quickly breaking contact.

Where are you? Conor asked.

That's for you to tell me, the user responded. *You only get one chance, Conor. Make it count.*

He scratched his forehead and exhaled, his eyes now darting around the room, scanning from terminal to terminal. An awkward stare caught by a young woman, a glance to Upper Camera in hope. Conor felt his nerves taking over, clouding his thoughts. Whatever clues had been offered, he'd missed them. He tried to factor in the layout of the room, picture where he would stand if the roles were reversed. This would be a guess, a shot to nothing.

You are... he typed, freezing to ponder for a final moment, looking up at his chosen target. *By the second column, next to the fire exit.* He hit return and held his breath.

Almost instantly the session terminated, his PC restoring to display the library intranet.

Conor leaned forward, the look on his face turning desperate. He closed his eyes. *Fail, Conor. Poor show.*

* * *

Appearing gormless and expectant, Conor waited for another five minutes, staring blankly at the monitor screen. His disappointment clearly visible, he glanced around the room in frustration.

Eventually he lowered his head, logged off and left, giving Radcliffe Camera one final look before heading for the exit.

Ellie gave it ten minutes before making the call. Leaning up against a bookcase secluded in the corner, she held the mobile phone to her ear.

'We've got another bite,' she said.

'Who is it?'

'Conor Martin. Twenty-one. Freshman at St John's. Studying Computer Science.'

'Interesting. How did it go?'

She sighed. 'Not as we wanted it to. We'll need to alter our plans if he's to progress to the next stage.'

'No good?'

'I wouldn't say that,' she whispered.

'Is he right for this?'

'Difficult to say,' she said. 'There's something about him.'

'This is your call. Should we proceed?'

Ellie paused before speaking softly. 'I think so.'
'You need to be sure.'
'I am sure... Yes, we proceed.'

CHAPTER NINE

PROBABILITY AND PURPOSE

In a warm, dark living room, lit up by tea light candles and glowing lamps, the professor sat comfortably on his black leather arm chair. His legs were crossed as he took slow indulgent sips from his French roast Cappuccino. It was late into the night, even for him. The caffeine did its work well.

In the background Beethoven's second movement from Symphony No 7 played through surround speakers on a low volume.

He stared with fascination at the set of files in his hand, wearing a look of intrigue and possibility. It was one of many documents laid out on the oak coffee table in front of him, but soon came the sigh, then a gradual acceptance. He took off his reading glasses, squeezed the bridge of his nose and rubbed his eyes as he laid the papers neatly on top of a second pile. Picking up his notepad, the professor scratched through yet another name.

He took a moment to close his eyes and put his hands together as if in prayer. Perhaps he needed the others to help again. The process was taking much longer than he could have imagined. Analysing the latest student records from the Science Office, cross referencing his own research; searching for the necessary pattern in the candidate's lifestyle, medical history and background. A subtle science.

Opening his eyes, he glanced away to the picture frames that sat on shelves above him, adjusting his vision from the hazy close range blur that had formed over the hours to a clearing sharpness. He squinted taking a second to look at the old photographs, frozen moments in time that told the story of a life he barely remembered.

William Daniels was born in Banbury, twenty-seven miles north of Oxford. As a young man he carried no real interest in science or medicine. His focus was more on sports, mainly tennis and although he would never go professional he was always impressed by the discipline of tennis players, the devotion to the angles, the upkeep of their skill and fitness.

The professor smiled at a faded Polaroid of himself holding a tennis racket in skin-tight shorts and a white T-shirt, his eighties haircut a cruel reminder of his appearance as a teenager. There were no other reminders of his time as a boy. Nor were there any photos of his family.

In the next frame along William carried an entirely different look about him. Taken just off the shore of Kuwait with the burning sun on the horizon, he stood with one foot perched on the tyre of a burnt out car. Shattered glass and bloodied sand lay beneath him, sunglasses covering his eyes. Red skin and dirty stubble.

He was nineteen when he enlisted to be in the Armed Forces as a field paramedic. In hindsight he couldn't explain why but for the expectation his father had placed on him. 'Every Daniels does a term of service,' he had said.

But there were no pictures of camaraderie to tell the story of this time in his life. He often debated taking the picture down to help himself forget about it entirely.

When William returned from the Persian Gulf everything had changed. His friends and family would often ask but he refused to discuss it, at times side stepping with responses such as, *'One must look to where they are going and not where they have been'*. What was clear was that he'd seen enough of war and when he served his notice in the mid-nineties, no one questioned it.

After an initial spell of soul searching, William became interested in pursuing a career in medicine - perhaps working for the government in medical research or for the Cancer Research centre at The Royal Marsden in

Chelsea. Months passed in thought. Eventually he opted to apply for a scholarship studying Neurology at the University of Oxford and his acceptance was treated as a sign that he was on the right path.

Close to home and settled for the first time in years, William felt a sense of belonging at the University; with the campus and the people around him. He grew more attached throughout the course of his degree. It just felt right in a way he couldn't explain.

He stared at his graduation photo, remembering the feel of the scroll in his hands. By then he was a man; you could see it on his face.

Passing with noted distinction opened doors for William, raising the eyebrows of the observing professors and paving the way to a job offer – working as a Research Scientist in Microbiology. He didn't think on it, he'd found his home.

The professor looked with affection at a framed group shot taken of the research team at the old lab. Looking back, they were some of happiest moments of his life. Finding his passion in scientific study, a purpose in life that was both fulfilling and contributory.

By now William was well into his late thirties, slowly contemplating the next stage in his career. In 2006 when the opportunity came up to teach, he needed convincing. But his colleagues and peers insisted that he was perfect for the position, often taking centre stage when presenting research achievements to the senior professors or managing the obligatory annual tour with the investors. William had composure in front of an audience – 'stage presence' a friend had called it.

The responsibility of educating was never his intention, but he took to it well. The satisfaction of teaching surprised him; the excitement of meeting new students, building their trust and parting with his knowledge.

Years on, William was now a well-respected professor. His contributions to the curriculum established him with a credible reputation. Senior in his field and with three published books to his name, he was a strong practitioner in biology and genetics.

To some of his students, Professor Daniels was endeared as a father figure. His fellow professors often spoke at how they marvelled on William's ability to gain his students' trust and complete attention. He could relate with pupils from all backgrounds and all ages and was fluent in English, French and Spanish.

The professor was in his mid-forties when he headed up his first research project: a fascinating program with the brief to study the defences against cerebral deterioration; the beginnings of a notion that changed the course of his life. But the University would only support him so far. The basis of any project was on the evidence of probability and purpose, gut instincts and belief were indulgences that didn't qualify.

The professor sat smiling, his left hand stroking the short beard he was growing. He finished off his rich Cappuccino and began filing the records back into a folder on the table.

Probability and purpose? He was now leading a project so influential, so beneficial to the human race that it would touch every living soul on the planet. He couldn't wait to see the look on their faces.

CHAPTER TEN

THE BUTTERFLY EFFECT

Conor stood in the shower with his eyes closed, the steaming hot water ricocheting from his body onto the tiles. Shampoo trickled down his face, as he rested his head against the bathroom wall.

His feet felt sore. Sticking with the rural pathways of the riverbank would leave him tender for some time, and he was keeping to an ambitious running schedule despite the ever darkening sunlight during the early mornings.

That day the fog had crept in overnight, giving an atmosphere to the roads that felt gothic. He spent over an hour burning the energy from his legs before slowing to a brisk walk, the sweat on his chest soaking through on to his T shirt.

He sighed loudly before growling under his breath, still furious with himself. First impressions, that's what Conor's parents had taught him; first impressions were everything. Whether you think you remember them or not, your brain makes an almost immediate decision when meeting someone. This decision dictates how you go on to treat that person, the time you give them, the physical interest, the tone you take, everything.

Three days had now passed since Radcliffe Camera and, though Conor had not spoken to anyone about the events of that morning, he had thought of nothing else.

It was difficult to justify, but Conor was convinced that for the briefest of moments he had become part of something; something important, something special.

He checked his mailbox twice, sometimes three times daily, but there were no messages or clues waiting for him. He was left continually looking for signs, desperate for something to go on; another chance to prove himself.

There had to be a next step. There had to be something that he could do to get their attention again. The thought had seeded that the emphasis was on him to instigate the next move and that sitting around and waiting would only stand to serve another failure, a failure that could prove final.

Conor hobbled out of his en-suite to stand in the middle of his room, a woollen towel wrapped around his waist, his short fuzzy hair drying naturally and his chest bare, the muscular ripples on his stomach on display.

He checked the time whilst reaching for his clothes. He could make out the distant hum and rumble of Samuel's music from across the hall. Spraying deodorant over his body, he threw on a red hoodie and dark blue jeans.

Conor had an afternoon lecture due to start at 2.00PM, but there was time to do something first, to get something clear in his head. He nodded to himself, accepting what he needed to do. Picking up his keys and wallet, he put them in his bag and made for the door.

* * *

Conor walked through the main entrance archway of Radcliffe Camera, staring up at the dome, as he had done days before, breathing in the rustic stone and old oak atmosphere that resonates from Museums and antique art galleries.

He was slow about it this time, scanning Lower Camera from left to right, stopping to focus on the details he'd missed the first time.

The reading room was soothing, a purring hush filled with the coughs of book worms and the turning of pages. The white noise of fingers lightly tapping on keyboards. Nothing new or out of place.

He took the stairs, slowly climbing the steps to rise above the room and walk across the first floor known as Upper Camera.

Conor peered down at where he had sat the previous time he was here, imagining he was standing where his mystery contact had stood, watching his every move, making notes and observations.

He walked around the ledge, stroking the railing as he observed Lower Camera. He noted how the noise beneath reduced to barely a whisper. The finer details of the inner dome looked stunning closer to the eye.

He covered every corner, leaving nothing for chance, analysing all the angles - searching for something to go on, anything.

Time had passed into late morning before Conor began doubling back to the stairs. He glanced up at the six foot marble statue of John Radcliffe resting above the entry way. The famous physician, the public icon of Oxford. His name lent to the titles of the local Hospital, the Infirmary, an Observatory and the very reading room Conor was standing in.

Squinting with curiosity, he studied the plaque beneath it. Peering closer to make out the small print, his eyes widened. *'Carved by John Michael Rysbrack'. Rysbrack?*

Conor turned to look over the railings. *Rysbrack!* This was it, this is where the contact had stood. It made sense: from where he was standing he could see everything. It even had the opportune blind spot to the terminal he'd sat on, the perfect vantage point.

The first test had been mathematical and historical, but this was cultural? They were challenging him, probing him for weaknesses.

How must he have looked? No doubt another test would have been waiting for him on Upper Camera. *He had failed at the first hurdle.*

Slowly descending the stairs, Conor returned to the terminal on Lower Camera, glancing up to the spot where he had just stood, willing a face to appear from the shadows.

Logging on to the PC, he thought to recreate the previous day, to entice his mystery contact out of hiding. *What would be the trigger?*

As he struggled on the answer, an alert message drew his attention to the top right corner of the screen. A message was in his inbox.

David P. Philip

A reservation had been made in his name against a novel, due for collection from the main desk. Opening the mail he read the title: *A Second Chance at Eden* by Peter F. Hamilton.

Looking up he saw a young girl seated at the enquiry desk, working her way through a small line of impatient students. Conor joined the queue, bouncing on the balls of his feet and peering over the shoulders of the people in front.

Trying not to fidget, Conor's palms grew clammy with irritation as the queue diminished at a steady pace. Finally it was his turn.

'I'm here to pick up a reservation,' he said, handing the young girl his student card. 'Conor, Conor Martin.'

'I can read,' the girl said, swiping his card and looking rattled. Others were queuing behind him.

'*A Second Chance at Eden*?' she asked, typing on her computer.

'That's it! Yes, sorry. That's it.' He tried to control his enthusiasm.

Leaving the desk she turned to open a cabinet.

'Here you go,' she said, retrieving the novel and passing it to him.

'Thank you.'

Grasping at the book, he gritted his teeth to hide the relief. *Back in the game.*

The novel was bound with leather. It felt thick and padded, but was also light and soft to touch.

Sitting at a free table in the reading room, he looked around Lower Camera as he opened the cover.

There was no message or code in the inner sleeve, but it was never going to be that obvious. Flicking through the pages, he scanned the blurring text in the hopes that something would stand out. It appeared to be a standard edition. *Is the code in the story? There has to be something.*

He looked at the cover intently, holding it up to the light. The bound felt luxuriantly textured, real leather. Opening the pages and bringing it closer to his nose, he began to notice that there was an odour. He could smell something...

As the fumes travelled up his nostrils, a vile stench registered on Conor's face, making him jolt in his seat and recoil. His breathing became short and erratic as his wind pipe filled with fire, the air turning to a taste of mould. A strange feeling swarmed on the back of his throat: the revolting vapour had reached his lungs.

He put the book down and pushed it to the other side of the table. He leaned away from his chair to cough violently, reaching for clean oxygen. It was disgusting. *The taste.*

Red-faced and almost dizzy, he took a minute to get his breath back, his coughing subsiding to a gentle wheeze.

The scene he had made in the otherwise near silent reading room had drawn everyone's attention. He looked around to see the faces of puzzlement and worry encircling him.

Picking up the book, Conor rose from the table and placed it in his bag. Feeling a rush of blood to the head disorientate him, he held onto one of chairs and focused on the floor.

Stumbling out of the entrance and down the stone steps into Radcliffe Square, Conor felt the cool on his face, the foggy breeze breaking against the surrounding buildings.

He paused to take in a series of deep, full breaths, allowing the fresh air to fill his lungs.

Taking his time, he made his way down the gravelled footpath, his feet feeling heavy and the crunching noise of his footsteps louder than usual.

Almost in a daze, he could feel himself sweating despite the cold; a dizziness overwhelmed him. He looked back at the doorway before turning, his neck giving out to let his face fall forwards.

Hunched and faint, he dropped his bag on to the grass without thought. Sitting down to rest beside it, he lifted his head to see that the brickwork to the Bodleian had become blurry and hypnotic.

He could feel himself drifting, his eyes glancing to the bag. *What have you done?* He felt his stomach churning, the energy inside him draining away.

Conor lay down on his side, instinctively forming the foetal position. The grass felt icy and wet on his cheeks.

Using what strength he had left, Conor looked back to Radcliffe Camera, making out the blurred silhouette of someone standing in the doorway.

He felt the need to cry out but it was too late, there was nothing left. His eyelids were made of lead, his breathing heavy. He was fading in and out of the light.

As his eyelids began to close for the final time he watched helplessly as the dark blur inched closer towards him.

CHAPTER ELEVEN

AWAKE WITHIN A DREAM

Conor stirred for several minutes, passing in and out of consciousness. His head was drowsy and pulsating with pain. His body felt distant and light, slowly growing heavier.

The feeling of his bed felt strange. The pillows were airy and cheap and the sheets thin and crisp to touch. As he opened his eyes he could see a bright room painted with light magnolia. A TV played in the background on a low volume.

Gently Conor got his bearings. There was a needle in his left hand, making it feel itchy, and... something else; someone was holding his right hand.

He turned his head slowly, his eyesight focusing to see the familiar face of home.

'Mum?' he whispered.

'I'm here, sweetheart,' she replied softly. Her watery eyes carried bags. They were a sore colour of red. Her make-up had long since worn away, showing the wrinkles on her face. She was leaning over from a bedside chair, dressed in white jeans and a red flowery shirt, her light brown hair tied back into a pony tail.

As he looked around Conor saw that he was in a small Hospital room. The sterile smell was unmistakable.

His father broke away from the Grand Prix highlights to stand over his mother's right shoulder.

'I'll get the Doctor,' he said, nodding and smiling to Conor. He was immaculately dressed as always, wearing a light grey suit and white shirt. It was clear to see that he was relieved on the inside, but he acted as a rock for Conor's mother, doing his best to hide his emotions.

'Where am I?' Conor asked as his father left.

'The John Radcliffe Hospital, my angel,' she replied tenderly.

'What happened?'

'They don't know. We got a call saying that you collapsed outside the library. That you'd been taken by ambulance to the Hospital.' She held back a whimper. 'They've been performing all these tests...' She stopped herself and covered her mouth.

Conor's memory was returning to him. He began to remember how he had felt. The nausea, the dizziness, the stench of mould clinging to his wind pipe.

He glanced around the room before returning his attention. He could see the pain in her eyes.

'I'm alright Mum,' he said, offering a faint smile. 'I'm OK.'

She closed her eyes to compose herself, her thumb gently stroking the silver crucifix she wore around her neck. Her hands quivered as she lifted them to cover her mouth.

Her darkest fears were reserved for Hospitals. Everything around her would have served as a reminder of Alex, his little brother.

Conor sat up, prompting her to react.

'Easy. Take it easy now, sweetheart,' she said.

'How long have I been out?'

'Two days.'

'Two days?!' Conor cringed.

The doctor gave a courteous knock on the door as he opened it. He looked to be in his mid-thirties, he had short blond hair and was wearing a long white coat. He had blue eyes and thin-framed glasses. Conor's father stood close behind him.

'Good afternoon, Conor, awake at last,' he said, entering the room. His mother squeezed Conor's hand before backing away to give the doctor room.

'My name's Doctor Riley. How do you feel?' he asked, approaching the bed.

'Fine, I guess.'

'Are you sure? How's your head?' He shone a torch into Conor's eyes.

'Fine, fine,' Conor said, wincing at the light.

'Eyesight? Hearing?'

'Yeah, good.'

'Can you touch your thumbs with your fingers for me please?' Conor did as he was told.

The doctor pressed a stethoscope to Conor's chest.

'Deep breaths.'

Conor took long exaggerated breaths and exhaled loudly.

'Can you tell me what happened?' the doctor asked, taking the stethoscope away and putting it around his neck.

'I was hoping *you* could,' Conor said, repositioning himself on the bed.

'You don't remember anything?'

Conor thought back to the book, the nausea, the dark blur approaching him.

'Not really,' he lied. 'I remember feeling sick, resting on the grass. I'm not sure what happened.' Conor ran out of words. He never was a good liar.

'Interesting.' the doctor spoke with a soft tone. 'So it remains a mystery.' His honesty prompted a shared look of concern.

The doctor glanced to Conor's parents before he explained.

'You arrived in a mild coma, seemingly induced through a reaction to a chemical compound. You were demonstrating symptoms of respiratory arrest, liver failure, but establishing the source has been a riddle. There have been numerous theories, nothing conclusive. We've performed every test we could think of over the past twenty four hours. You've been something of a pin cushion to the Pathology team I'm afraid.'

'What do you think happened?' Conor's father asked. 'The other doctors wouldn't say.'

'Well, we can't be sure. Nothing has come back conclusive,' the doctor replied honestly.

'Yes, but you said there were theories?' Conor's father pushed.

'Well my theory is a little far-fetched, but I believe Conor inhaled microscopic mould spores. Cladosporium or Aspergillus, most likely.'

'Spores?' Conor's mother frowned.

'It's very rare,' Dr Riley defended. 'And more common in types of vegetation, but some older pieces of literature have been known to gather a form of mould as they deteriorate. When the reader then turns the pages a fragmented gas is given off.'

Doctor Riley turned to Conor.

'Should you be allergic or inhale too much of it, the lungs can spasm, causing hypoxia, respiratory failure. In extreme cases the body can shut down in response, although, a reaction of this scale is baffling, unheard of as far as we know. We've been treating you for suspected pneumonia.'

'Were there any traces of spores in his system?' Conor's father asked.

'That's the frustrating part. Aspergillus in particular is a very weak compound and would be eaten up by the antibodies in Conor's system long before he got to us - possibly to the point where it would be virtually undetectable.'

Conor's parents exchanged a glance.

'It's a theory, but it hangs on what Conor was reading at the library,' the doctor said.

Conor was sat in silence looking down at his feet. Glancing up he suddenly noticed the faces of everyone in the room now staring at him.

'What were you reading, sweetheart?' his mother asked.

The question threw him. He wasn't ready for it.

Conor leaned forward. His bag was resting on a plastic chair in the corner.

'I... I can't remember. Can you pass me my bag? I think I wrote it down.'

'We've already checked it, we couldn't find anything,' the doctor said.

His father picked up the bag and brought it over, resting it gently on Conor's lap. He sat up to open it, figuring he could just pass the doctor the novel and say that he got it from the enquiry desk. He wouldn't be lying. It would take them away from asking why he was there.

Opening his bag, Conor looked inside to find a sickening feeling waiting for him. The book was gone. Whoever did this to him had taken it.

'It must be in here somewhere,' Conor said, continuing to act out his story. He confusedly searched through the rest of the compartments to check whether anything else had been taken.

'I... I can't see it.'

The doctor sighed with disappointment.

'It's OK, but try to remember if you can. If my theory is correct, that book might be sending me a few more customers.'

'Is it serious?' Conor's mother asked.

'Well, we'll keep him in for another night to be sure, check his blood pressure and run a few tests. But no, I don't think so and you should make a full recovery quickly.'

The doctor glanced back to Conor. His mother smiled, looking more and more relieved.

'We don't need to do any more intrusive tests so you're free to drink and eat as you'd like,' the doctor said. 'There'll be a care worker round in a while to take your order for dinner, but if you can't wait there's a canteen on the ground floor. Just head down the end of the hall and take the lift on your left. You can't miss it. You need lots of vitamins, I'll get some orange juice brought to you.'

The doctor picked up Conor's chart at the end of the bed and made some notes.

'If you don't have any more questions, I'll leave you to it.' He clicked off his pen and placed it in his top left corner pocket.

Opening the door, he turned back to Conor.

'If you need me or one of the nurses, just press that red button over your right shoulder, OK?' He pointed to a button on the wall. Conor nodded, smiling thankfully.

'Thank you, Doctor,' Conor's parents called as he closed the door.

Barely seconds had passed before Conor's mother was back by his side. Offering a comforting smile, she leaned forward to hold his hand.

'Do you want to come home?' she asked, her voice sounding hopeful. Conor rested his head on the pillow. If only she knew.

* * *

In the west wing of the Hospital, sub-basement level to the Medical Sciences Office, the soft tapping of a keyboard rose outside the door to one of the laboratories.

Inside, James McCarthy sat in the dark. His face was lit by a desk lamp and the glare coming from the monitor screen.

It was 2.20AM and the skeleton shift had given him all the opportunity he needed. The admin at the Pathology unit offered a thorough analysis of Conor's vital statistics - a medical and biological audit.

A handful of written notes provided the final comments from attending Doctors. James scanned through them intently, nodding his head and making side notes of his own.

He gave himself thirty minutes, no more. He couldn't risk it. If the results were found to be missing it would be difficult to put them back unseen.

Satisfied, he logged out of the PC and carefully reassembled the paperwork. Closing the folder shut, James picked up his mobile and dialled out.

'Hello,' the professor answered.

'It's me.'

'How did he do?'

'He aced it. Everything is in the green. We can proceed.'

'Excellent. Let's hope it's not all for nothing.'

CHAPTER TWELVE

EMPTY PROMISES

Conor waved, watching fondly, as his mother blew kisses through the rear window. Her eyes were tearful and full of worry as the car pulled away.

It had taken time, but Conor could feel himself slowly returning to full strength. He fuelled his body as best he could, drinking lots of water and eating healthy food. He stuck to Doctors orders, doing as he was told and resting an average of twelve hours a day. He even had an inhaler with a prescription dosage of Salbutamol for whenever he felt short of breath.

Five days of obsessive attention had passed. It would mean calling them every other night and returning home at least once a month, but he had finally shaken the hand of his father and given his mother a long, emotional hug goodbye.

Alone at last he was able to think, reflecting on the events of the past week, and yet the reality of what had happened still dazed him. Radcliffe Camera was now clear in his memory, if he closed his eyes he could almost picture the blurred figure coming towards him whilst he lay helplessly on the grass.

There had to have been purpose to the book, whether it was a punishment or a warning; perhaps something more cryptic. Yet with all the possibilities circling Conor's thoughts he could only fall back to one absolute fact: once again he was left with nothing. No answers or anything that could resemble reasoning.

For days he had kept himself awake, thinking long and hard during the late hours of the night until finally he came upon a decision. A conclusive thought that cleared his mind.

He didn't want anything more to do with this.

Whatever this was, it wasn't why he came here. He'd lost his way and needed to get back on track. If he was contacted again he'd ignore it. If they approached him, he'd ask to be left alone. He was done.

Conor had slept soundly ever since.

With his parents gone he needed to focus. The professors had been supportive, providing him with notes from the lectures he'd missed to bring him up to speed. But as Conor immersed himself in study a knock at the door soon followed and Samuel, with almost majestic timing, reappeared, spearheading a campaign to draw him out for a social drink.

By the time he agreed the afternoon was bearing into evening and daylight had all but diminished into night.

It was 7.45PM, though it could have been midnight in Conor's eyes. He covered his mouth to shield a yawn as Samuel chose their table, neatly overlooking a cast iron fireplace. The warm rustic venue of the Wheatsheaf carried the comforts of a Victorian cottage. They made themselves at home.

'Spores?' Samuel questioned, placing his pint of Guinness on the table.

'That's what he said.'

'Mould put you down for two days?'

'Apparently,' Conor offered. 'Allergies have put people in comas before now.'

'Skin and food allergies, sure, but I'd have thought spores should give you a chesty cough at best? You are a precious daisy, aren't you?!'

'I'm fine now,' Conor said, smiling.

'Are you?' Samuel didn't look convinced, glancing at Conor's inhaler on the table. He tilted his head slightly to the left before breaking his stare to gaze at the fire.

'So are you going to tell me what you were doing there?' he asked softly, offering no eye contact.

'Doing where?'

'Radcliffe Camera.' Samuel turned his head to reveal a grin. 'Sightseeing? Reading up on something? What was it?'

Conor took a sip of his drink in order to keep quiet for as long as he could. He should have seen this coming.

'Oh, come now,' Samuel pushed. 'It can't take you that long to come up with a good lie. I would have thought you'd be getting better at this after spending a few days with the seniors.'

Conor subtly looked over his left shoulder to check if anyone could eavesdrop.

'Why do you want to know?'

Samuel closed his eyes and shook his head.

'Because unlike your dearest, I suspect there's more to this. Something cryptic perhaps? Are you fond of chasing riddles?'

'How did you...?' Conor's response was instinctive.

'It's in the subtleties of your behaviour, dear boy. I implore you to never commit a crime.'

'What do you want to know?'

'The truth,' Samuel said, looking back to the fire.

Looking up Conor almost spoke, but something stopped him.

'You broke your code?' Samuel pushed.

Conor gave another look over his shoulder before leaning forward.

'Radcliffe Camera.'

Samuel frowned. 'Radcliffe Camera?'

'That's what my code meant.'

'That's it?'

'That's it.'

Conor took a deep breath, his wheezy exhale reminding him to take a dose from his inhaler.

'And then?' Samuel asked.

'And then I went there.'

'What happened?'

'There... There was a book waiting for me.' Something told Conor that the less Samuel knew the better.

'A book? What, a novel?' He looked frustrated, trying to wave the conversation on.

'It was nothing. A second chance of something or other. I opened it, flicked through the pages, checked it under the light, nothing.'

'That's it?'

'That's it,' Conor lied. *An opportunity worth anything you could fear losing.*

'How dull.' Samuel sank into his chair. 'Did you read it?'

'No, I...' Conor hesitated, anticipating the reaction. 'It must have been the one with the mould spores. I passed out soon after. I guess I dropped it. I woke up in the Hospital.'

'Are you serious?' Samuel lunged forward. 'Fuck a duck!' His voice rose above the surrounding tables, sparking the attention of the regulars and prompting confused glances from across the bar.

'You were poisoned?' Samuel whispered.

Conor shrugged. 'That's a little over the top.'

'Listen to yourself!' Samuel cringed. 'Who are you defending? Is it the people who did this to you or your own stupidity?'

'I know what I'm doing.'

'Do you? Do you *really*?' Samuel looked around to check that the punters' glances had returned to their pints of ale. He lowered his voice to help appear calm, more composed.

'I take it you're going to jump through whatever hoop they throw up for you next, no matter what I say?'

Conor stayed silent. Raising his eyebrows, he realised he didn't have an answer he could trust any more. The doubts of the previous days were already resurfacing.

'Conor, listen to me. Listen to me, please.' Samuel pressed his palms together. 'These people, they pray on the weak, the eager to please. There will inevitably come a point in all this where you will be asked to do something; a favour, a task. It will probably be illegal. Promise me that when that happens you'll stop. Just promise me.'

Samuel held his gaze to stress the point, doing what he could to show sincerity. The rumours of the code were one thing, but he knew stories of his own. Tales of seniors and post-graduates enlisting gullible freshmen to do their bidding, setting up challenges for their entertainment. He imagined his friend to be swimming with sharks; oblivious to the danger.

Conor gave him his complete attention.

'Look, trust me,' he said. 'I know what I'm doing. I promise.'

CHAPTER THIRTEEN

SENSE OF PRIVILEGE

Alone in his room, Conor busily scoured the internet, endlessly searching strings and cross-comparisons that originated from a single phrase: *'A Game For The Young.'*

Two days had passed and still nothing. His room, once tidied immaculately by his mother, had degenerated into the familiar mess he knew to be home. He rested his head in his hands, a notepad filled with scribbles to his left, the laptop to his right.

It was 8.30PM and the view was black through his window. He found himself blinking slowly, closing his eyes for several seconds at a time, fighting off the impulse to sleep.

Conor barely made out the footsteps from the corridor until they were right outside his room. There was a shadow lurking in the hallway. He could see it underneath his door. Standing, waiting. He stared in silence, watching for a moment before he spoke.

'Samuel?' There was no response.

He could hear something. A soft scratch on wood; a faint noise that drew him to his feet.

With a sudden jolt a loud and aggressive thud came from the door. A single knock that shook him to a brief recoil.

'Who is it?' Conor called out.

The shadow moved off down the hallway, whispering quiet thumps that grew distant.

Unable to let it go, Conor opened the door. Peering down the corridor, he saw the back of a young women briskly walking away towards the staircase. Wearing a long cream duffle coat and dark blue jeans. Flat soles.

'What?' Conor shouted. She slowed to a stop, keeping her back to him. Her fists clenched. Conor turned to look at his door.

In large red marker pen the stranger had written a message: 'FOLLOW.' With a sudden lunge she sprang off at pace, making for the stairs.

'What do you want?' Conor shouted, walking after her.

Reaching the top of the stairs he caught sight of her shadow vanishing, the sound of her footsteps running down the staircase. *It's them.*

He promised himself he wouldn't. Her footsteps were starting to fade. There was no time to think. This wasn't why he came to Oxford.

Think! They still had him; he couldn't convince himself otherwise. Why else was he searching the internet? Devoting his spare time to riddles? *Think!* This was his chance to get some answers.

Conor gave chase, his heart racing with every step.

He could hear his breathing wheeze under the pressure as he descended the staircase. Catching sight of her shadow growing larger on the wall against the stair rail, he tried to speed up as best he could, nearly knocking over a group of students walking up the stairs.

Bursting out of the door and into the main reception hall, Conor gasped for air, his lungs struggling as if he were breathing smoke.

Leaning up against the wall, he pulled out his inhaler for help.

He looked both ways before he saw her, by the entrance. Moving quickly through the outer door, he sprung after her.

Stepping into the night Conor felt the sudden cold hit his face, the chill on his arms making him wish he'd remembered his jacket. To his far right he caught a glimpse of her. Walking down the canal bank, fading into black, vanishing from view. Everything felt heavy: his lungs were struggling and his body was exhausted in a way that surprised him.

Conor focused on his breathing, slow and steady. Just like the Doctor had told him.

His run had now slowed to a brisk walk but he maintained the chase along the canal path, determination alone willing his limbs into a second lease of life. He could barely see her from the distance she'd built, too far away to make out any details.

With every step they moved away from the light of Tennyson, from the comfort of noise, disappearing further into the dark.

He looked up ahead, trying to second guess where she was taking him. Less than half a mile downstream there was an industrial office block overlooking the river. The lights from the office windows shone out, reflecting off the water and giving Conor just enough to make out his surroundings.

She came to the canal bridge and quickly crossed it, head turned away so that her face couldn't be seen. Conor was gaining now, the upbeat jogs he had introduced with every few steps had brought her within shouting distance, but as he crossed the bridge a waiting car on the adjoining street pulled up alongside her and she got in.

'Wait! Who are you?' Conor cried out as the car pulled away, disappearing off down the road. He panted for air, watching as the lights dimmed to black, the heavy breeze cool on his cheeks.

It was them, he knew it. He could have got to her. He *should* have got to her.

Conor stood on the bridge, bent over, coughing loudly. He spat out the saliva that had built up in his mouth. Arching his back, he stretched out to bring himself upright. Overwhelmed by frustration he gripped at the metal railing, growling under his breath. His lungs burned as he looked out downstream.

He took long excessive doses from his inhaler until the sting in his chest softened. The night air started to take its toll, giving him goose bumps on his neck. He closed his eyes, sighing with a sorrowful acceptance.

And then it happened. A moment within a dream, the likes of which he'd never seen before or would see again. Conor could see that the lights in the office block windows were turning on and off, changing the reflection beamed out across the water. They were forming a pattern. And then he saw it: the lights had spelled out *'Conor'*, as if his name had been written in the stars. His mouth opened, mesmerised at the sheer scale of what he was witnessing.

He rubbed the sweat from his forehead. The lights flickered, changing shape to now read *'Begbroke.'* Conor looked down the path and around the canal but he was alone, witnessing his own private firework display.

The lights held their configuration for a few seconds before switching up again to now read *'Park.'* Conor smiled, so impressed by the effort. The grandeur of the display, the spectacle.

The lights changed for a final time to read *'Tonight 11pm.'* And then, as suddenly as they had come, the words dispersed, returning to a scattering among the office floors.

The feeling they'd given him resembled the excitement he'd felt when he first received the code. The sense of privilege, the pride and elation. In a single moment the events of the past seven days simply evaporated. His decision to walk away was a hazy memory fading into obscurity. His faith was fully restored.

Begbroke Science Park. It made sense. Begbroke was an integrated research and development facility. It partnered commercial businesses with scientific research seven miles outside of Oxford, housing an array of new developments shared out among thirty businesses and twenty-something University research groups.

This was it. This was where the project was taking place. Conor knew it, he could feel it. Tonight he'd learn the truth.

CHAPTER FOURTEEN

NINE LIVES

Conor kept one hand on the steering wheel; the other alternated between changing gear and holding up his phone. He watched as the GPS refreshed, guiding the way. Indicating right at the roundabout, he pulled his struggling Astra off the dual carriageway and onto a more rural street called Sandy Lane.

As was customary in recent months, Conor had wound down the driver's side window to allow for some fresh air to get in, or perhaps more to allow the bad air to get out. An acute smell of burning rubber was ever present after a few miles, floating in through the fans as a warning that Conor couldn't afford to acknowledge or repair.

He drove slowly, keeping to just above the speed limit. To his right, the trees and tall fences shielded the vast six-bedroom properties that rested beyond. To his left, country cottages merged in to newly built estates overlooking a local garden nursery. As the view passed, everything opened out into clear fields that appeared an empty black at night. Over the distant tree line he could make out the lights of the Park.

Conor drove on for another minute before his phone directed him to turn left onto a small country lane.

Turning in, he slowed, noticing the dark blue signs for the Park on both sides. He took his car out of gear and brought everything to a stop, staring ahead to the steel barrier stretched out across the road, blocking his way.

Conor growled at his phone, already frustrated by the poor signal he was receiving in the countryside.

He leaned forward, making out the lights in the distance. There had to be another way in.

He was checking his rear-view mirror and putting the car into reverse, when an eerie mechanical buzzing sound triggered the barrier to rise.

They were watching. He couldn't see them, but they were out there, lurking in the dark or on the other end of a hidden surveillance camera.

Placing his phone on the passenger seat, Conor changed gear and inched his car forward beyond the gate. Old English oak trees, on both sides of the road, arched overhead as he drove on.

The vast scale of the park grew larger, ever closer. The intimidating magnitude of the office blocks and side buildings sowing seeds of doubt, his sense of invitation wearing thin. What if he was spotted? There would surely be security patrols stationed in some of the offices or grounds men observing via CCTV.

If the barrier had risen then someone was watching him, someone was expecting him, but as with Radcliffe Camera, Conor had no control. No idea where he was supposed to go or what he would do when he got there. The answers were in one of those buildings.

Turning left, he circled the main development centre. His heart raced as he scanned for clues, but he saw nothing that could make him feel welcome. The offices appeared closed and sealed, the few signs of activity reserved to a scattering of lights among the office levels.

Conor pulled into one of the parking bays, taking the car to a space in the shadows, and killed the engine. It was 10.55PM.

He waited, uncomfortable and silent. The car grew colder as the minutes passed. There were a dozen cars sharing the car park with him, acting as a constant reminder that he wasn't alone. Observing the lights from the offices, he made a mental note of the rooms and floors that were showing signs of life.

An unnerving feeling grew inside of him. He was beginning to feel more and more unsettled when a sudden chirping sound sprung from the passenger seat next to him. The break in silence made him jump.

Breathing heavily he picked up his mobile, the wheezing sound in his exhale clinging on from earlier in the night. It was a text message, though the sender was anonymous.

Conor stared down at his phone. *B Block. Back Door. TRIAD. 2nd Floor.*

He glanced back to the office blocks and then returned to his phone. *Which one is B Block?* As he reached for the door handle Conor paused. Was this that moment? The moment Samuel had spoken of; *There will inevitably come a point in all this where you will be asked to do something; a favour, a task.* It wasn't too late, he told himself. He could drive off now. Forget this ever happened, never look back. Would it matter? Did he need to know? Did he have to get his answers? For a second he tried to think how tomorrow would feel if he drove off, holding the thought for what seemed like an hour.

He sighed, unable to lie to himself. If he didn't go in there now he'd think back on this moment for the rest of his life.

'Fuck it!' Conor said aloud, pushing the door open with force to get out before slamming it shut.

Walking across the car park he headed for a mounted signpost to get his bearings. B Block was clearly marked to his left, moving at a pace just short of a jog he changed direction and made for the rear entrance. It was dark but for the lamp posts offering pockets of light on the footpaths and looking up he could see the stars shining through murky clouds, growing darker.

The pieces were falling in to place. Whoever they were they knew his mobile number and if that was the case then they must have access to his files from the Student Records Office. That would mean his address (both home and at Tennyson), his contact details, the course he was taking, everything. It would explain how they knew so much.

Approaching the rear entrance to B Block, Conor pressed himself against the back wall, clinging to the shadows. He looked to the handle, noticing that the lock was controlled by a dark metallic keypad.

Taking out his phone, he stared again at the message. *TRIAD*. Pressing the code into the pad, he held his breath.

The door offered a click as the small light above the pad turned green with approval.

Conor reached for the handle, for one last time pausing in another moment of uncertainty, imagining Samuel stood next to him and warning him off going into the building.

'I'm doing this,' he whispered. Conor pulled down on the handle and opened the door.

Immediately he heard the sound of industrial fans and the soft drone that came from air conditioning vents overhead. Conor closed the door behind him. The lights were off. His vision was limited to a few steps ahead as if he were walking through black fog.

Instinctively he reached out to a light switch on the wall but yanked his hand back. He could see enough.

As his eyes adjusted, he began to see the corridor that was in front of him; the dull beige doors that were repeating on opposing sides at various points left and right. At the end of the hallway was the outline of a large door with a smudged glass panel. What light there was shone through it to give him just enough visibility. The stone floor felt rough and icy under his feet.

His heart pounded as he walked, crouching low to the ground. The air felt cold, but grew warmer as he moved towards the door.

Reaching the end he peered through the glass, making out the rough outline of a staircase on the left-hand side and a door to his right. There would surely be a lift somewhere but he wouldn't risk it, he needed to know where he was going before he got there. Conor opened the door carefully, looking in both directions: it was clear. He didn't waste any time. With a long blink for courage he sprinted up the staircase.

As he ascended the lights grew brighter.

'Second floor, second floor,' he muttered to himself.

It happened suddenly, a noise freezing him to stone, the echo sending shivers down his spine. High above, Conor heard the cracking noise of a heavy door closing shut. Someone else was there. *Of course someone else is here!*

Looking up the steps he saw the sign for the second floor and moved quickly, leaping up the stairs and opening the door to come off the stairwell.

Gingerly Conor walked through the double doors onto the second floor. It was dimly lit, helping him make out the rows of desks divided up by waist-high partitions.

The powered down PCs came into focus; silent telephones and resting printers. Everything at an eerie state of dormancy.

Walking slowly across the office floor, he made out the larger signs that split the research teams: *'Oxford Materials Electron Microscopy and Microanalysis Group'; 'Nanotechnology Research Team'; 'Molecular & Medical Sciences'.*

Conor imagined how the office would appear during the day, bustling with activity and intriguing discoveries. The shadows played tricks on him, making out faces and the silhouettes of people in the dark. He peered from wall to wall, taking in the office floor. He rested his gaze on the meeting rooms and darkest corners, mindful of his blind spots.

No one was waiting for him. Had he got this wrong somehow? He considered calling out but thought better of it, turning to his mobile he read the message again.

Conor was walking past a series of terminals to his right when one of the monitors sprang to life. A chat message appeared in front of him. The glow of the monitor showed the frown of disappointment on his face. Slowly he approached the desk.

Good evening Conor, the message read.

You can't be serious?

What am I doing here? he typed, pulling up a chair.

You are here to collect a package, the response came back.

Conor noticed that the computer was linked to an external hard drive to his right, and it had started to purr and click.

You are now downloading the summary findings of this division's research. A progress bar appeared on the screen beneath the message.

When it completes, disconnect the drive. Place it in the leather bag to your left and bring it to us. You'll find the address in the bag.

Conor recoiled in disbelief, shaking his head and staring hopelessly at the progress bar. He scanned the room to check if he was being watched.

I won't do it, he wrote.

Then leave. The chat session terminated.

I can't do this. This was stealing. *This is stealing!* He was all alone, trespassing, stealing scientific research. This was the truth, and now he understood. In their eyes he was a gopher, a delivery boy, a pawn they were using. *Christ, Samuel was right.* If he did this, if he stole for them now, from this moment onwards they would own him. He needed to get out before it was too late. This was his last chance.

The download progress was now at 31%.

As his thoughts circled a sudden thud from across the office floor broke his concentration. Conor held his breath. Slowly raising his head, he peered over the partition, watching in horror as a middle aged, heavy looking security guard made his way towards him.

He ducked his head just in time before a flash light beamed its gaze over the partitions, lighting up everything in its path.

Conor watched helplessly as the download progressed to 53%. There was no time. He turned the monitor off and hid under the desk, disappearing from view seconds before the guard shone his light at Conor's terminal.

Strolling past, the guard moved on to the surrounding workstations, whistling the theme tune to *2001: A Space Odyssey*.

'Shit, shit,' Conor whispered, huddled under the desk. He couldn't believe this was happening. *What if they find my car?*

He needed to move but fear had taken hold. He couldn't think, he couldn't focus. The sound of the hard drive purred as it continued to steal.

Damn you, he thought, sat shivering in the corner. *Damn you for putting me in this position.* As the anger stirred in his blood he broke his frozen shape, shaking himself back to life.

Conor crawled from under the desk and poked his head out from the side of the partition. The guard was now on the far side of the office floor, doubling back. If he ran now he could make it.

Returning to the monitor, he watched as the screen loaded to show its progress. 98%, 99%... 100%. He had to get out. Could he really be part of this? If he left without the drive this would have been for nothing. He closed his eyes. *Think, think!* Conor thought back to the bridge, the light display, the sense of privilege.

Even with everything that was to come he would still look back on this moment in shame.

Unplugging the hard drive, he placed it in the leather satchel, letting the weak justifications and absurd excuses cloud his mind. His selfish desires cleared his conscience of guilt.

Crouching down he peered around the partition. The guard was thorough, carefully checking the office space, lighting up the divisions as he swept the floor. He looked as if he'd done it a thousand times. His heavy footsteps rustled on the carpet.

Conor moved in short bursts, sprinting and ducking, ever mindful of where the guard was facing and the noise he made. He came to within metres of the door, agonisingly close.

Offering a final glance towards the guard he bolted for freedom.

Conor threw himself through the doors and on to the staircase. He didn't look back. Quickly he ran, holding the bag firmly in his hand. His lungs burned. He bounced off the walls, jumping three steps at a time, allowing himself the slightest of grins as he passed the first flight of stairs.

A cracking thud rose from the ground floor, the sound slowing him to a stop. The relief he had felt shredded. Then came the noise of a radio beeping, and of footsteps rising from below, growing louder. There was another guard and he was coming up the staircase.

Staring at the shadow growing on the wall ahead, Conor began to shake in fear. He was trapped.

The double doors to the first floor smashed open as Conor burst through. His mind emptied of thought. There was no plan, his composure was now verging on panic.

The floor layout was completely different to the one above; a long and straight corridor leading away to meeting rooms and conference areas, difficult to see even with his eyes more accustomed to the darkness.

The doors passed him in a blur as he ran. Sweat now ran from his forehand, his wheezy exhale amplifying the sound of his desperation. One after the other he found the doors locked, until at last he was given an option, and with a final push he leapt through the door to the men's toilets, disappearing from sight and into pitch black.

As the lavatory entrance closed behind him he heard a creaking noise from the stairs, muted as the toilet door sealed shut.

He stood silent in the dark, taking out his inhaler to calm himself and control his breath from echoing off the tiles. Pressing his ear to the door, Conor listened intently as the sound of heavy footsteps drew closer.

The guard's radio sounded muffled.

'Hey, Harry, I'm on third. You sure you heard something? There's no one on second.'

'Probably nothing,' the guard responded, his voice loud and near. 'I'm on first. I'll do a final sweep and head back.'

'OK, see you down there.'

Conor stood motionless, staring helplessly at his only exit, listening in silence until it became unbearable. He took a single step away from the door. His face registered what was soon to happen. Inches away was the sound of heavy breath, close footsteps, a light cough. The guard was standing on the other side of the door.

* * *

Harry Trussler yawned as he pushed through the door to the gents' toilets. Hitting the light switch, he stumbled in the dark to the nearest urinal, the lighting grumbling overhead for a few seconds before shining bright. He unzipped his flies and gave a loud cough, hearing the husky growl in his lungs.

His feet were aching in the new shoes his wife had bought him and climbing up and down the stairs all night wasn't helping either.

Harry looked around the room. The toilets were laid out in an oval shape with cream urinals on the left, four wooden cubicles to his right and a line of wash basins in the centre.

He rested his balding head against the cold tiles, whistling the theme tune to *Star Wars* until he was finished.

Walking over to the wash basins, he washed his hands whilst looking at himself in the mirror, his new shoes echoing off the floor. Turning for the door, he stopped just short of the exit.

'I know you're in here,' he announced, facing the doorway. 'Spare me the trouble. What do you say?'

Harry turned with a smile on his face, waiting patiently for a response, but it didn't come. He sighed, taking slow loud steps towards the cubicles.

'Do you believe in God, son?' he asked, giving a light chuckle. 'Of course not, you kids don't believe in anything.' He reached the first cubicle and pushed the door open. It was empty.

'"The son shall not suffer for the iniquity of the father, nor the father suffer for the iniquity of the son."' Harry pushed the second cubicle door open. Empty.

'"The righteousness of the righteous shall be upon himself, and the wickedness of the wicked shall be upon you!"' He pushed the third cubicle open. Empty.

He composed himself, turning to the final cubicle. *Here we go.*

'Harry, it's Lou,' his radio blurted. 'Who's on Reception?'

'Shit,' Harry whispered, holding up his radio. 'Just doing the rounds. Karl is on third, we'll both be down in a second.'

'Hurry up. There's no one on the front desk,' Lou responded.

Harry made a face at his radio as he turned for the exit. Walking a couple of steps before stopping to turn back to the last cubicle, Harry sprang his chubby frame at the door, just like he'd seen in the movies, kicking it open with a thud.

It was empty. Empty as always. He turned for the door, unable to hide the disappointment from his face.

* * *

Conor burst through the doors to the rear entrance of B Block and out into the night. His lungs were on fire, his head barely able to focus under the pain.

It had happened so suddenly, but simplicity proved the safest option. Only seconds after the guard had turned the lights on and walked over to the urinal, Conor had appeared from behind the main door to the toilets and swiftly left in silence.

He now ran, holding nothing back, adrenaline pumping in his veins, his legs heavy and clumsy. He sprinted for his car, clutching the bag tight in his hand and fighting back the urge to cough his lungs out onto the car park.

As he got to his car, Conor yanked on the driver side door to open it, forgetting that it was locked. Reaching into his pockets in frustration he pulled out his keys. There was no time; Conor got in, started the car and reversed out of the parking bay like a getaway driver.

He sped past the exit to B Block, glancing at his rear view mirror just in time to see the face of a security guard appear from the door before disappearing into the dark.

Conor thumped his steering wheel, looking at himself in the mirror.

'You stupid, stupid asshole! Is this what you want? Is it? You want to get busted? Locked up? Kicked out? Back to living with Mummy and Daddy?! Is that what you want?'

He drove on past the raised barrier, skidding loudly as he turned in to Sandy Lane.

'Shit, shit!'

* * *

Sara had enjoyed the view from the fourth floor of C block as Conor arrived. His insecurities amused her as he stopped and started.

She glanced back to her terminal, arching over the desk as she typed, never one to use her chair unless she had to. She keyed in a set of commands and turned to a second monitor showing CCTV footage throughout the park. The barrier on the east entrance lowered.

From the speed Conor was driving when he left she imagined the old boys on watch had given him a tough time, but either way the mission was a success.

Her terminal was remotely connected to the workstation on the second floor of B block. The external hard drive had disconnected from view the moment Conor unplugged it. He'd taken it.

Sara took out her mobile, chose a contact and dialled out.

'Hello,' the professor answered.

'He's on his way.'

CHAPTER FIFTEEN

FIVE MORE MINUTES

Conor was a mile into Woodstock Road, off the A44, before he finally slowed to acknowledge the speed limit. His pulse eased as he breathed deep and steady, his burning lungs soothed by the doses from his inhaler.

He gave an occasional glance to the rear view mirror, but would instantly look away. He was disgusted with himself.

It wasn't what he had just done that offended him, nor what he hadn't done. It was the rush of excitement he had felt when he drove away clean from the Science Park.

Soon after his initial outburst Conor had practically celebrated, laughing hysterically, revelling in his achievement and safety. It quickly passed on reflection, but he didn't think he was capable of something like that.

He glanced over to the leather bag resting on the seat next to him and on seeing a lay by up ahead, pulled over to bring the car to a stop.

Conor closed his eyes to think. Placing his palms together, he held himself back from punching the steering wheel.

Outside, the dark clouds above grumbled and snapped, giving way to the first drops of rain. As they fell on his windscreen Conor kept his eyes closed. The light sound of clanging taps helping him to focus. By the time he had opened his eyes the rain was in downpour.

Reaching over, he grabbed the leather satchel. It didn't take long. Conor pushed aside the hard drive and searched through the internal compartments until he found a small piece of folded up paper. The message read: *'OX1 3PD'.*

Typing the postcode into his phone, he watched as the GPS map pin pointed to an address off Parks Road less than a mile from Tennyson House.

He shook his head. Samuel had warned him, he had warned him and he was right. Conor had just refused to listen. He now sat in the palm of their hands, jumping through their hoops.

Starting the engine, he turned the windscreen wipers on full. Checking his side mirror and indicating right, Conor pulled away, heading for the lights of the city.

* * *

Driving his car along Parks Road, Conor offered a final glance to his phone before parking up on the side of the road. The scattered street lights did what they could, but everything felt dark around him. The thick rain continued to fall, making things difficult to see.

Staring through his windscreen he could make out enough to know that he was parked opposite the safety office, near Lincoln House. This was the Head Office for the Mathematical, Physical and Life Sciences Division. He'd run past it many times, remembering how the Warden's Lodgings looked like an old cottage, surrounded by a stone wall covered in light green moss.

Conor's eyes wandered to his rear view mirror. Without realising he was doing it, he began rehearsing what he would say to these people if he was given the chance.

'What could be this important?' he whispered. 'Do you understand the risks I've taken?'

His voice rose until he was shouting at himself in the mirror, making idle threats and gestures that his true self would never find the courage to say. He nearly missed the feeling of his mobile vibrating in his pocket.

Conor stared down at his phone, the calling number was coming up as anonymous. He rolled his eyes. *Enough, I'm sick of this shit!* Holding the phone to his ear he took the call. 'I'm through. Whatever this is, I'm out.'

The line went quiet for a moment.

'Give me five more minutes of your time Conor,' a deep and elderly voice spoke. 'You will have a change of heart I'm sure.'

He paused, hesitant to agree. The seniority in the man's voice was disarming.

'Fine, five minutes. But I need to know what this is. If this has been a test I think I've earned it.'

'I agree,' Professor Daniels said, pulling up alongside Conor in a black BMW. 'Let's go for a drive. Jump in the back.'

Conor stared at him through the window, mobile held up against his face. He ended the call. There was something familiar in the man's voice, a confident yet gentle friendliness, perhaps bearing a resemblance to Conor's father.

Turning up his collars, he picked up the leather bag and got out of his car, briefly stepping in to a downpour of rainfall. The professor's eyes stayed with him as he opened the rear passenger door and got in the car. On closing the door the car sped away.

At first they sat without speaking, the professor keeping both hands on the steering wheel. Conor admired the stylish interior whilst stroking the leather seats in the back, trying to be patient. The noise of the windscreen wipers filled the silence.

'Here's your hard drive,' Conor said softly patting the bag to his right.

'Thank you,' the professor said, looking at him in the rear view mirror. 'I suppose you're wondering...'

'I'm wondering why I did this,' Conor interjected, looking down at the satchel. 'But now that I've done it I need to know what it was for.'

'Fair enough.' The professor nodded. 'Before I begin can I trust that what we are about to discuss will remain strictly between us?'

'Fine,' Conor replied.

'Have you discussed anything of what you have been doing with your friends or family? The code? The messages?'

'No, no one.' Instantly Conor thought of Samuel.

The professor held a long stare in the mirror before nodding.

'My name is Professor William Daniels, I work at the University.'

They turned right onto Sherrington Road.

'Five years ago I was appointed to lead a University funded research program. Its brief was to analyse the defences against cerebral deterioration, focusing on neurobiological experimentation.'

Conor leaned forward, keeping quiet as the professor spoke.

'The research raised as many questions as it did answers, but its achievements spawned a new understanding on the limbic system. Do you follow?'

'You were studying the brain?' Conor offered.

'Precisely. Well, parts of it, at least... Three years ago, I branched off from the brief to work with a small team of students on a proof of concept theorem.'

'And this is the project?' Conor asked.

'It's not so much a project as it is a discovery,' the professor said, glancing to Conor in the mirror. He took a short breath. 'Ten months ago we established a procedure that could pass data syntax into living cells, linking synaptic pathways on delivery, synthesising the process the hippocampus attains when building long term memory.'

'I don't know what any of that means.' Conor cringed in frustration.

'We found a way to transmit data directly into the human brain; to learn something almost instantly provided that it was documented in a digital medium or recorded in a visual format.'

Conor's jaw dropped.

'We started small,' the professor continued, 'transferring short sentences of text and simple imagery. Testing that proved trivial. Over time we began to realise the true extent of the data packages that could be compiled. Entire subjects, languages, professions that would take decades to master could be compiled and transferred in a matter of hours.'

'My god...' Conor whispered, slowly resting back into his seat. 'Is this another test?'

'It's very real, believe me,' the professor assured.

'Then what's the problem? This is amazing!' Conor let his enthusiasm get the better of him. 'Who knows about this?'

'Less than a handful of people. When I attempted to raise funding we were at the early stages of our discovery. It was labelled as stem cell manipulation, high risk science, too dangerous for the University to sponsor. From an official capacity they shut us down. Since then what we have achieved has tested the known boundaries of science, but it has been done in secret, with the students themselves acting as test subjects.'

'But why the secrecy? If it works? I don't understand.'

The Professor turned onto Mansfield road.

'This is change, Conor. The world functions under tradition, a tradition established over centuries. It is so old, so rigid, that its framework feeds into every life on the planet. History tells us that these things are in place because it's the only way they could be... Imagine waking up tomorrow and being told that there was a procedure that could teach you anything, anything that you wanted to know. Subjects only available to the privileged suddenly open to the masses. Learn anything. Be anyone. The way of the world would collapse in days... Mass hysteria. Liberal revolution. This changes everything.'

Conor rested his face in the palms of hands. 'Why are you telling me this?'

'Our discovery cannot remain secret indefinitely. Like I said, we're a small team... And the time has come for us to grow, but knowing how to introduce this and who to approach is difficult and needs planning.'

The professor turned right on to Holywell Street.

'We devised a process. Steps that would test someone's suitability and commitment to the project; their curiosity, their mindset and dedication. We needed to ensure that the people we found were the right people. You are the first to pass this process.'

'But why me? Why was I approached?' Conor squinted.

'I've been reviewing candidate records for many months. At this stage the procedure has limitations, mature memory cells prove unreceptive to the transfer. But at your age the brain has only just finished growing. The synaptic mapping is ripe. The perfect conditions for this project. We nicknamed it *'A Game For The Young'*.'

'But... How?'

'These are questions that require time to explain Conor, and even more time to understand. For now, I have told you all I can.'

They turned right on to Parks Road and pulled up alongside Conor's car.

The professor had driven them full circle.

He turned to face Conor, looking him in the eyes for the first time and holding out a folded piece of white paper.

'Take this number,' he said. 'Call me at this time three days from now and tell me your answer, in or out. Don't call me before then, I need to know that you've thought this through. If you're in, you'll learn more. Perhaps more than you've ever dreamed. The risks are extreme but the rewards are beyond comprehension.'

Conor took the paper from his hand.

'Keep everything that we've discussed to yourself. We'll be watching,' the professor warned, turning to face forward and offering a final glance in the rear view mirror.

Conor struggled to move, his limbs feeling cold and shaken. It took several attempts to open the door before he got it right. He stepped out of the car and into the downpour.

He turned back to the professor.

'Thank you,' he spoke softly.

On closing the door the professor drove off, leaving Conor standing in the rain by the side of the road. The sound of thunder came from above. He stood for minutes, unable to move or think, perhaps in shock. He looked up to the sky with his mouth open, drinking the rain as it fell.

CHAPTER SIXTEEN

AIM HIGH, AIM FAR

Conor stood poised on the canal bridge, leaning up against the railings and counting down the minutes leading up to 11.30PM.

Every night since meeting the professor, he had offered a moment to this bridge. Perhaps to rekindle memories of the light show he'd seen from across the water; or maybe it was to dedicate a space and time to contemplate the professor's offer. In truth he didn't need it; his decision was inevitable. Conor's thoughts now pondered grandeur the likes of which he'd never known.

His apathy towards the IT Linguistics lecture earlier in the day was difficult to hide. He drew away from his coursework, from the University, from the education system in its entirety. Often thinking back to Radcliffe Camera: *'Do you want to be part of something that will change the world?'* Finally everything made sense.

Professor Miller had stood at the front of his class, energetically taking his students through the basics in software distribution models, his sweaty scalp and patchy arm pits giving away the fatigue clearly taking hold as the session wore on.

Conor had arrived on time, doing more than enough in recent days to drop off Professor Miller's radar. But the balancing act of being present and yet barely listening to a word was hard to maintain.

Glancing across the room, he couldn't help sizing up his fellow classmates. He observed their variations in character, the differences in learning technique. It was fascinating.

He could see how the room had organically sorted itself. How the students absorbing the lesson gravitated to the front of the class, engaged and digesting everything.

How those who didn't understand wore pained expressions on their faces, furiously copying every spoken word to compensate.

How the ones who were equally oblivious but didn't seem to care as much lingered near the back, as close to the exit as possible.

Conor tried to imagine the effect it would have if everyone in the room suddenly assimilated the information in exactly the same way, instantly understanding the course. How would that change their lives? Their future?

His decision to join the project had been made almost instantly, but the past three days had given Conor a chance to think about things properly, to contemplate in detail what he wanted. He was thankful to the professor for that. The three days were a gift, a chance to prepare himself as best he could.

Conor used the time well, studying the basics of their research. Traditional studies of memory began in the fields of philosophy and included techniques of artificial memory enhancement. Scientists have since defined the study of memory as a field within cognitive psychology, with it becoming one of the principal pillars of a branch of science called Cognitive Neuroscience.

The brain is a learning machine, designed to acquire information and then selectively retain that which is deemed unique, useful or repeated continuously, but the key attribute is emotion.

Within the core of the brain is the limbic system; the centre of higher-order thinking, learning, and memory. But memory is essentially stored in a network of cells and synaptic pathways linked together through emotional experience.

Within the limbic system is the hippocampus, a folded layer of cells and fibres that manages learning and short-term memory. Study has proven that when a memory achieves a level of significance it is passed through to the cortex to be stored as long term memory in a process referred to as 'consolidation'.

Brain Computer Interfaces (BCIs) have enabled scientists to take huge steps towards understanding and monitoring brain activity, but the concept of delivering waves of information directly to the brain was riddled with complication. It was fascinating to even think of it as possible.

Alone on the bridge, Conor watched wearily as a young couple walked passed him, happily speaking amongst themselves. He stared suspiciously as they strolled down the canal bank before glancing to his watch. It was time. Holding out the paper the professor had given to him, Conor pressed the number into his phone and dialled out, looking up to the industrial offices downstream.

'Right on time,' the professor answered.

'I'm in,' Conor said, assertive and sure of his words.

'Be at Wellington Square in thirty minutes.'

'Fine,' Conor said confidently. The professor hung up.

No more trials, no more tests. It was time to meet the truth behind the riddles, to see the project with his own eyes.

Conor needed to get moving; at this time of night there would be nowhere to park. He'd need to walk.

* * *

Coming to the end of St John's Street, Conor arrived at Wellington Square.

Deciding for the first time to leave his inhaler at home, his lungs growing stronger by the day, he was slow and composed as he walked around the Square. The fine rain had turned to sleet throughout the afternoon, leaving the damp roads to turn icy under his feet. The dropping temperature had convinced him to wear his heavy winter jacket and scarf.

Conor shivered as he rested up against the east entrance, hunched with his hands in his pockets. The park was empty and the roads were quiet. It was dark but for the street lamps which drew around the square in an outer layer of soft light.

He was overlooked on all angles by residential properties and services centres. From where he stood he could make out the Oxford Nightline to his left; a support and information service run for students throughout the night.

He tried to be patient. His eyes drifted around the park. He was unable to stop himself from feeling nervous, remembering the journey that had brought him to where he now stood, the build up and suspense. His heart thumped in his chest, the sight of a car or the noise of an engine triggering a hopeful jolt of sudden interest. *Breathe.*

He tried to stay calm, gazing with admiration at the beautiful C-class Mercedes Benz parked a few feet in front of him. A two door Coupé from the Elegance range. The perfect representation of unobtainable wealth.

It was all around him. Properties he couldn't own, cars he couldn't afford. Trophies to the professions that offered rewarding salaries and inherited wealth. *The way of the world would collapse in days.*

Conor caught himself preaching.

'How much would all this be worth if knowledge was free?' he whispered.

Feeling a soft vibration from his right back pocket, Conor pulled out his phone to see Samuel's face on the view screen. He pressed the red button to ignore the call. *Not now.*

Behind him the soft grumble of a black Honda Civic turned into the square, the engine purring as it made its way around. The tyres crackled along the road surface.

Turning the final corner the driver set the car headlights on full, beaming a blinding light in Conor's direction. He held up his right hand to shield his eyes, squinting as he tried to make out the driver.

The side window wound down a few inches.

'Hi, Fresher,' a woman's voice spoke. Conor walked closer, lowering his hand to cover the lights. *She seems familiar...*

'You?!'

'Yes, me. Get in, will you, it's freezing,' she said, closing up her window.

Conor hadn't seen her for a long time, but the impression she left was enduring. Walking around the car, he opened the passenger side door and got in, turning to see the face of the red head from the the the Eagle & Child.

'Where are we headed?' he asked as they pulled away at speed, turning left and then right onto Beaumont Street, past the Oxford Playhouse.

'Ask me when we get there,' she answered. Short and abrupt.

'Well, have I at least earned your name?' he asked.

Breaking character she gave him a smirk before answering.

'Sara. My name's Sara Morgan.'

She drove on, taking Conor through the streets at pace. They passed St Cross College and soon after St Giles Church, and then the Keble College Chapel; all a short-lived blur in his window. He offered an occasional glance, but Sara faced forwards at all times, uninterested in small talk.

They pulled off the main road, just short of Norham Gardens and began parking up on a gravel lay-by next to University Parks. Feeling the car slow, Conor looked around to second guess where they were going.

'Jump out, we're walking from here,' Sara said, killing the engine.

He did as he was told, sensing her disapproval of him that was perhaps fuelled by their first encounter.

Sara was dressed in dark blue skinny jeans, a stylish black Runway jacket, and was wearing thin leather gloves which matched her boots.

'This way,' she said, walking down a short pebbled footpath before turning right.

Following a few steps behind, they cut through onto a large black field and stepped into the dark. Conor could make out her shape in front. The white smoke from her breath. The feeling of cold wet grass on his shoes.

As they moved across the field, the outline of buildings began to form. They appeared to be headed for one of the

Lecture Theatres but were veering left from the main campus, slowly moving in on the rear entrance to one of the office buildings, the Pavilion far away to his left.

They were bearing down on Clarendon Laboratory. Conor nearly tripped as they approached a gathering of trees and overgrown greenery. The terrain changed, with the sound of broken twigs underfoot.

'Where are we?' he whispered.

Sara responded by shining a small pen light on a large steel door, secluded behind some brambles. She turned to answer, but appeared to change her mind.

'You'll see,' she replied, producing a key to unlock it.

Pulling the heavy door open, she held it ajar so that Conor could follow. He peered into the darkness, looking on as Sara descended a short flight of stairs before walking on ahead down a long and dark corridor. Her heels clicked along the concrete floor.

Hesitant for a split second, he stepped inside, closing the door behind him.

The dim light grew brighter as they approached the end of the corridor, closing in on the jeering noise of machinery and the metallic grind from the turning of cogs. Conor could smell an acrid combination of oil and rust.

Yanking open the steel shutter to the lift door, Sara stepped inside, Conor now close beside her. She clicked on 'Sub Basement Level One', prompting the lift to jump and jolt as it lowered them down, the air turning stale and growing colder. It stopped with a sudden thud as it reached the floor.

With a stiff snap, she pulled the gate open to reveal the level.

Guiding him past an Oxford University emblem, the sub basement started out as a long corridor. Darkened and uninviting, there were signs of grime growing up the walls and across the dull stone flooring. The odd fluorescent light flickered above, the buzzing hum of electricity. Their breath echoed against the ripple of their footsteps.

'What is this place?' Conor whispered.

'The dirt swept under the rug,' Sara replied.

Taking a series of turns, passing door after door, Conor began to feel that he was in a maze, a subterranean labyrinth of steel and cement. The layout was vast and unwelcoming. It felt abandoned, though retained a purpose. Oxford's forgotten warehouse for the unwanted.

Sara slowed as they approached a door marked 'SEVEN.B'.

'Do you think you could remember your way back here?' she asked, turning to Conor, a hint of sarcasm in her tone. 'If you were alone?'

He glanced over his shoulder, thinking back to the turns. *Damn.* He hadn't been paying attention. Lowering his chin, he shook his head with honesty.

'Good,' Sara smiled, facing forward before giving the door a stern thump.

Conor knew that thud, the solitary knock, the aggression and attitude. It sounded just like the knock he had heard at his door back at Tennyson. He took a step back to notice the familiarity, remembering her walk. It was her. She was the one he'd followed to the bridge.

A grinding noise came from behind the door. Conor watched with bated breath as it opened, revealing the professor standing in the doorway.

Sara walked in, offering a nod as she passed him.

'Come in Conor,' the professor said, smiling. His words made Conor feel welcome and at ease for the first time. He stepped forward, allowing the professor to close the door behind him.

The lights in the storage room purred overhead as Conor walked in, marvelling at his surroundings. Nearly fifty square metres in size, he was standing in a room unlike anywhere he'd seen before. A large storage area converted into private quarters. An odd combination of library, laboratory and a stylish living space.

The library consisted of five long mahogany book cases, positioned parallel to each other in front of a small reading table. The books contained some of the richest scientific texts published, ranging from volumes of the History of the Scientific Method to copies of published Journals from the American Chemical Society.

The professor watched with an endearing smile as Conor took it all in.

The laboratory offered a state of the art Merivaara operating table, a glass cabinet filled with medicine, a stainless steel store cupboard stocked with apparatus, a defibrillator, a drip and a heart rate monitor.

A large surgical lamp stood close to an office desk overlooking the table. On the desk sat a high specification HP ProLiant Server with three flat screen monitors.

The sitting area looked as though it belonged in the front room of a luxurious studio apartment. Surrounded by soft glowing lamps, there were two leather sofas positioned either side of an oak coffee table, an arm chair resting in front a pile of records, a laptop and a shelf showcasing a collection of framed photographs. The professor appeared to be half way through reading a copy of the *History of Julius Caesar* by Jacob Abbott.

He could appreciate the lengths they had gone to make it their own. The spit and sawdust odour of industrial metal and open concrete had been masked by the smell of polish from the bookcases, and a clinical, sterile feel resonated from the operating table.

By the sofas, a small ceramic bowl of potpourri and scented candles offered some home comforts whilst a coffee machine added to the rich aroma in the air.

'What happened to the secret knock?' James asked Sara, sat in his wheelchair by the coffee table.

'What about it, Rolo?' Sara dismissed.

James wheeled himself over to Conor, extending his hand.

'Well done, chap. I had every faith.' He gave a wink.

'Thanks,' Conor replied, accepting the handshake whilst glancing to the operating table.

'I didn't,' Sara said softly, taking off her jacket and throwing it on one of the sofas.

Conor continued to pace around the room, taking in its obscurity, when he realised there was someone else he was yet to meet.

Ellie looked up from her laptop, sat working in the corner. She had enjoyed Conor's reaction to their secret home, remembering how it had felt when they first saw this place. *'Follow me. There's something I need to show you'*.

Conor squinted as he walked towards her, puzzled by her face. He knew her? It was the same girl that worked behind the enquiry desk at Radcliffe Camera.

'Hi,' Conor mouthed. The recognition visible on his face.

Ellie smiled in return. 'Hi,' she replied quietly.

'Conor, welcome to the *Hive*,' the professor spoke loudly, buying back Conor's attention. 'From here we do our work. The research, the experiments. This is ground zero. Take a seat.' He spoke with a calming authority.

'In this room you will learn more than you dreamed a lifetime could offer, but there are rules. Disciplines we have set in place to maintain control. Understand?'

Conor nodded as he took a seat.

'Good. Rule number one is secrecy. What we do here cannot be known by anyone outside of this room.' The professor amplified the word *'secrecy'* as he said it.

'No one can know about this, not until we're ready, and I do mean no one.' He paced back and forth, his hands in his pockets.

'Rule number two: everyone partaking in the experiment submits to regular medical examinations so that we monitor their physical and mental state. This is not negotiable. Number three is the exclusion of alcohol or any recreational drugs.'

Conor gave a playful smile. It was to be expected.

'And the final rule. What is learnt by the procedure is never used for personal gain.' The professor amplified the word 'never'. 'It undermines everything we're trying to achieve.'

Leaning against the table, the professor folded his arms.

'Any questions?'

Conor raised his head before shaking it in silence.

'Alright,' the professor nodded. 'It's time we take you through what you're now part of. I suggest you take a breath. It's a brave new world.'

Staring at his laptop with blurred eyes and a head drained of thought, Conor sat alone in his bedroom. The professor's words were still ringing in his ears. The sheer scale of the previous night had blown his mind, a bleary dream he knew to be real.

It was long past midnight, soon after Conor's arrival at the *Hive*, when the team had assembled in the library study area. The variances of their characters merged into a single unit, familiar and comfortable. The professor took centre stage.

'We broke the project into three stages,' the professor had explained. 'Three stages that unlocked the power of memory.'

Gesturing to a large green chalkboard on the wall, he went through a mass of flow charts and formulas that drove from three encircling milestones: Method, Drug and Frequency. They had marked these stages with the call signs *Einstein, Galileo* and *Hawking.* They gathered their research in front of him.

'First came the method,' the professor said, pointing to the metallic headpiece positioned at the head of the operating table. It was unlike anything Conor had seen before.

Technology that receives information from the brain is well versed in neurology. For many years, non-invasive acquisition devices have enabled scientists with the ability to scan the human brain in real time, recording the residual responses to stimuli such as viewing an image or experiencing a feeling.

Extended further, this has been tailored to control external devices; interpreting signals from the brain into motor controls, allowing for machines to be built that can be literally controlled by the mind.

Focusing an artificial brainwave to a particular part of the brain required grid mapping technology to localise and coordinate the subject's limbic system. Combined with a skeletal framed head piece made from a titanium alloy, the recipient's forebrain was loaded and configured, directing the transmission as a signal through the frontal bone.

Utilising the titanium, the *take* repeatedly echoed into the forebrain, stimulating the hippocampus to implant the memory.

The team named the headpiece 'Einstein'.

'A *take*?' Conor had asked.

'That's the name we've given to a transfer of data to the brain,' Ellie explained.

'It took months of careful planning,' the professor said, the achievement warm on their faces. 'But that was only the beginning...'

From there the night had turned hazy. Conor had been hit by a tidal wave of information that left him confused; with words he'd never heard before on a subject he could barely understand.

The team would assemble four nights a week, working from 11.00PM to 3.00AM. With a steady stream of coffee flowing throughout the night, each of them would take it in turns to receive transfers of data that would strengthen their knowledge and test the boundaries of the procedure.

'Don't worry,' the professor offered, seeing the confusion on Conor's face. 'Everything will start to make sense after your first.'

That night he had barely slept.

Sitting in his room, Conor glanced to his watch. It was nearly time. But the right words continued to elude him. *How should this start?* he wondered. *How should it end?* He had attempted four versions of this letter, but the words felt empty. Even as he wrote it he knew his mother would never understand. He pictured her reading it in tears, his father comforting her with watery eyes and a stiff upper lip.

Was this real? He still felt as if he were dreaming; dwelling on an undercurrent of doubt, wrestling with an unexplainable feeling of guilt. A belief that he was unworthy. That he'd somehow stolen a place on this elite team. That they thought he was someone he wasn't.

The justification simply eluded him. The professor could have approached anyone; Conor could think of a dozen more suited candidates in his class alone.

He stared at his laptop. If this worked out for him would they even be proud? *Aim high, aim far.* That was always the plan. He rolled up his sleeves.

Mum, Dad,

I'm sorry. This will hurt.

If I were there now I'd try to explain. I'd try to tell you not to be angry or upset.

Just for a second, try to imagine having the chance to learn anything. To instantly know everything you wanted. Does it sound too good to be true?

If it wasn't, would you believe me? Would you understand that it was an opportunity worth anything? I can barely find the words to describe it.

You can argue the danger, I'm sure many will, but in the long run the change this will bring will surely make the world a better place. If it can't do that, then perhaps it will at least make it fairer.

I love you and I have done what I've done knowing in my heart that if you knew what I know now, you would do the same in my place.

If you're reading this letter then I have died. But I died being a part of something truly special, doing something I believed in. I have no regrets.

If Professor Daniels is sat in front of you now, offering you sympathy, trying to give some purpose to the pain you feel, believe him, Mum. Trust him as I did. No one is to blame. This was my choice.

All my love, always and forever.

Conor

He glanced to his alarm clock, wiping the single tear that had trickled down his cheek as he finished typing his name.

It felt different from how he expected. The anxiety and nerves were gone, replaced with an acceptance. His new life was ready to begin.

Finishing up, he removed his leather wrist watch and the small gold band he wore on his middle finger before placing them gently on the bedside table.

Lifting the letter off the printer, he positioned the paper in the centre of the bed, making sure it would be clearly visible to anyone entering his room.

Putting on his coat, he took one last look around before turning off the main light and closing the door behind him.

The sky was clear. It had rained for most of the day, leaving the air fresh and cool, the light breeze rustling the fallen leaves across the surface of the fields.

Conor cut off down a dark footpath that weaved behind a string of terraced houses, purposefully secluded so that no one could follow him. He took one last look over his left shoulder before stepping into the shadows.

* * *

Conor arrived outside the *Hive* entrance, proud to have found his way through the maze of stone and steel behind him.

He looked down to the map Ellie had sketched, raising his head to make sure of the room number before knocking with two hammering thuds. Like Sara, Conor refused to humour James's secret knock.

Each student had been given a key to the old rear basement hatch, but access to the *Hive* was reserved for the professor alone.

A few seconds passed before the grinding noise of the bolt lock could be heard. The door opened slightly ajar before Sara's head appeared, peeking through the space. She offered a nod, opening the door further to allow Conor to step inside.

He unbuttoned his jacket, looking up to take in the calm ambience of the room - the warmth that rose from portable corner heaters; the smell of coffee in the air; the sound of Johann Pachelbel's 'Canon in D major' playing through surround sound speakers.

The professor and Ellie were sat working together at the terminal opposite the operating table. Sara dealt with the door before brushing past him to return to the sofas, seemingly half way through a game of cards with James.

'Welcome back,' the professor said warmly, looking up from the monitor. 'Long walk?'

Conor glanced to his watch; he was ten minutes late.

'Slow walk,' he acknowledged, an apologetic tone to his voice.

The professor smiled, sensing Conor's anxiety.

'Please take a seat,' he said, gesturing to the chair next to them. 'We'll keep this brief. Sleep deprivation takes a while to get used to.'

'Sure, let's do this,' Conor said, sitting down whilst trying to hide his nerves.

'Let's show you what you'll be learning tonight.'

Ellie leaned back in her chair.

'I hope you're hungry,' she said with a grin, gesturing towards the computer screen. She moved out of the way to reveal an endless string of code scrolling across the computer screen, patterns of syntax highlighted in divisions of blue, white and black.

Conor stared at it in wonder.

'This looks... Great,' he said, treading carefully.

'It's the reason you're here,' the professor said.

Conor glanced to him. 'I don't follow?'

Ellie began reeling off the data index.

'Core one. Functional Programming Grade A, Design and Analysis of Imperative Programming, Digital System Architecture, Linear Algebra.'

Conor winced.

'Core two,' Ellie continued. 'Computer Graphics and Design, Object-Oriented Programming and the Models of Computation Grade A.'

'Jesus,' he whispered.

'Core three, Continuous Mathematics, Networks Modular...'

'Stop,' Conor interrupted. 'This is everything?! This is my entire degree?'

'Sandwiched amongst it we've included details on the procedure and the team to bring you up to speed,' Ellie added.

He lightly shook his head, thrown by a state of bemusement.

'Doesn't this undermine one of your rules?'

'It's a contradiction, I know,' the professor acknowledged. 'But we've learnt from past experience that this is essential, considering the pressures you will be under. We need to ensure your full attention to this project... Perhaps it's easier to consider it as a gift?'

A gift? This is freedom! This is everything. The weight of expectation was being lifted from his shoulders.

James wheeled himself over, revelling in his victory, the sound of Sara swearing under her breath behind him.

'Are we ready?' he asked, looking to Ellie.

Conor broke his stare from the code to notice everyone looking to him for an answer. He glanced to the professor.

'This is your decision, Conor. Only you can decide what happens now.'

As Conor turned his head he noticed a framed poem that the team had hung on the wall, clearly chosen to define their dedication to a greater cause.

> *What of a selfless life lived, if not for hope?*
> *To strive, to build and be remembered,*
> *In tides of fate, for the betterment of all.*
> *With eyes closed and hearts open,*
> *Our deeds shall not be forsaken.*

There was nothing else to consider. Conor rose from his chair, for the first time meaning every word. 'I'm ready.'

CHAPTER EIGHTEEN

THE GIFT

It took less than ten minutes for the team to prepare for the procedure. Swiftly dispersing to their allocated work-stations, Sara worked on a dosage of the drug they called *Galileo* whilst James wired up *Einstein* to Conor's scalp.

The professor attached sensor pads to Conor's arms and temple so that Ellie could monitor his vitals from the main server terminal.

Lying fully clothed on the operating table, Conor tried to control his breathing. The atmosphere in the *Hive* had shifted. Everyone had stepped up a gear, conducting themselves more professionally, each going about their duties with clinical precision.

The professor leaned over.

'We're going to start with a few pre-procedural checks. Is that alright?' Conor nodded, nervously consenting.

'Good, can you start by closing your left eye and following my finger please?' The professor moved his finger above Conor's eye line left and then right.

'Good, and now the right eye?'

'*Hawking* collaborated,' James announced, sat above the head of the operating table.

'*Hawking?* What's that?' Conor asked, rising on to his elbows. The professor gently placed his hands on Conor's shoulders to lay him down flat.

'We went over this. It's a frequency,' James explained. 'The frequency... It synchronises the *take* with the electromagnetic pulses in your cerebrum, allowing the hippocampus to accept the data as memory.'

'Glad I asked,' Conor sighed, staring up at the ceiling.

James smiled, remembering the excitement he had felt when it finally happened; when he had found the combination that had eluded him for months. *'Ellie, I think we've done it, I think we've found Hawking.'*

Sara finished with the doses, extracting the drugs into two syringes and placing them on a metal tray ready for the procedure. Typing a series of commands, Ellie brought up Conor's vitals, spread out across three monitors side by side.

The professor continued.

'OK Conor, if you're ready we're going to inject you with ten millilitres of the sedative Estazolam. This will put you to sleep for the duration of the procedure. We'll follow this up with eight millilitres of *Galileo* and allow a minute for it to work through your system. We then begin the transfer. Start to finish, we should be done in no longer than two hours. Any questions?'

Conor closed his eyes before lightly shaking his head. He was trembling, the apprehension clear to see on his face. The professor softly rested his left hand on Conor's shoulder.

'It'll be alright,' he whispered, offering a smile.

Lying on the table surrounded by mysterious equipment had reminded Conor of how he felt waking up in the Hospital; his mother holding his hand, the sterile smell in the air. He had then remembered that he was surrounded by the people that put him there and was trying desperately to push it out of his mind.

'I'm OK,' Conor said. *Breathe.*

The professor held his gaze with Conor for a few seconds before breaking eye contact to check his watch.

'Are we set?' he asked, looking to his team.

Conor glanced down to the base of the table to find Sara setting up a video camera on a tripod. Ellie was making one last adjustment.

'Ready,' she confirmed. James followed suit with an assertive thumbs up.

'OK guys, game faces on. Sara?' She clicked the record button on the camcorder, leaning back to check the feed before nodding to the professor.

'December 6th, time is 11.20PM. Subject: Martin, Conor J, male, aged 21. Members present are junior scientists

Elizabeth Swanson, James McCarthy and Sara Morgan. My name is Professor William Daniels, Project Lead. This is procedure one six seven of the Betterment project.' The professor began rubbing ethanol onto Conor's left arm to sterilise his skin.

Sara appeared next to him, holding up the first syringe and offering Conor a subtle wink.

'Administering the subject with ten millilitres of Estazolam.'

The students watched in silence as the professor held out Conor's arm and pushed the needle into him. In a swift motion he pressed down on the plunger.

'Conor, if you could begin counting to ten for me please.'

Instantly Conor could feel the effects of the dose, his body already drifting, his head fuzzy and weakening.

'One, t-two, three, four, f-five, siiiix, sev...' Unable to stay with them any longer, he closed his eyes. His head fell slightly to the left as he passed peacefully into a deep sleep.

'Subject under as of 11.21PM,' the professor declared, checking his wrist watch. The team quietly paused as they watched over Conor, staring at his unconscious body lying helpless on the table.

'Sara?' The professor turned to find her frozen, eyes focused on Conor. 'Sara?!' he repeated, his tone gently raised. She quickly shook herself loose.

'Sorry,' she whispered, handing him the second syringe.

He glanced briefly to Ellie, her attention drifting from the monitors for a split second to give an approving nod.

'Administering subject with eight millilitres of Galileo.' The professor pushed the second syringe into Conor and pressed down on the plunger. 'Allowing one minute for the solution to take effect.'

Ellie kept her eyes focused on the monitors.

'How's he doing?' the professor asked. 'Stable,' she responded confidently.

He appeared over her shoulder, peering down at the readings.

'Good,' he whispered.

Sara would occasionally glance to the video feed, observing Conor through the display panel.

'It feels different somehow,' James said. Ellie agreed.

'It should.' The professor looked to each of them. 'We were only accountable to ourselves before; Conor we plucked from the street. If you're feeling a sense of responsibility, get used to it.'

He took his place by Conor's side.

'OK, that's forty seconds.'

'Stable,' Ellie responded before he asked.

'If anyone has anything they want to say speak now, you won't get another chance.' The professor offered a glance to each of the team. Everyone replied with a gesture that made it clear they were on board.

James began typing the commands to begin the transfer on his laptop. He hovered his index finger over the 'Enter' key on the keyboard, looking up to the professor for approval.

'It needs to be me,' the professor said, walking over and resting his palm on James's shoulder. Leaning over he pressed down on the 'Enter' key.

'Initiating transfer at 11.22PM.'

The small light on the central head unit flickered. Almost instantly, Conor's eyelids began twitching.

'Transfer in progress,' James confirmed, the head piece beginning to purr.

Ellie remained glued to the monitors.

'Brain activity has risen eight percent... Nine percent... Twelve percent... Brain activity holding at thirteen percent.'

The professor moved closer to watch over the readings.

'Regulatory system?' he asked.

'Stable,' Ellie returned.

'Keep an eye on everything.'

'I will.'

'Progress calculating...' James announced. 'Two point four... Two point six... Two point seven. We've got a steady incline.'

David P. Philip

'Excellent.' The professor walked over to the coffee table and picked up a remote to his MP3 player. Around the *Hive* the speakers began to play Mozart's Piano Concerto No.23 in 'A' Major, bringing with it a soothing calm that allowed everyone to feel slightly more at ease.

'And now we wait,' the professor said, pinching the bridge of his nose and squinting. 'Who wants coffee?'

* * *

Time passed slowly as they waited, the team feeling every minute. Ellie stood up on occasion to walk around and stretch her legs, but would never stray far from the monitors.

The transfer had completed fifteen minutes earlier and they were steadily introducing Ritalin to Conor's blood stream to slowly wake him from sedation.

James had detached *Einstein* from Conor's head and was running diagnostic checks. Everything had gone to plan as far as they could tell, but like the others he knew the truth. No one was ever truly sure until the user woke up.

This was the first time they had attempted a transfer of this size as the subject's first. He wondered if Conor would have agreed to it if he knew.

The professor was writing in his journal when they heard the first of the mumbles from across the room, immediately everyone stopped what they were doing and encircled the table. Conor groaned as he raised his hand to his forehead.

'OK, OK, everyone stand back please,' the professor insisted. Ellie and Sara offered a few half-hearted steps in response.

'How are you feeling?' the professor asked. Conor was drifting in and out.

'Can you tell me your name?'

'C-Conor,' he mumbled. 'How long was I out?' He looked vacant and confused.

The professor looked at his watch, struggling to hide his relief.

114

'Just over an hour and half. Can you tell me your age?'

'Twenty one.' Conor went to sit up.

'Easy, easy now.' The professor put his hands on Conor's shoulders. 'Just lie still and rest for a second. Can you tell me where you were born?'

'Leicester.' Conor responded more confidently, starting to look and sound more awake.

'OK, one last question. Can you tell me what you had for breakfast this morning?'

Conor seemed unsure, squinting as the memory resurfaced.

'Cold pizza?!' he winced.

The professor gave a sigh. *Students.*

Everyone slowly inched closer to the table.

'OK, can you try and sit up for me?'

'Sure, let me just... Ah!' Conor lowered his head and cringed, suddenly appearing in pain.

'What? What is it?' Ellie jumped.

'My head is pounding.' Conor rested his forehead on the palm of his hands.

'It's perfectly normal to have a headache. Give him some Hydrocodone,' the professor said, turning to Sara. 'That should cover it.'

She walked over to the medical cabinet, sifting through the miniature containers before returning with two pills and a bottle of water. Conor flinched. *Perfectly normal?!* He swallowed them down without hesitation.

Giving what assurances he could, it took several minutes before everyone dispersed, allowing him time to think about the *take*.

'I don't feel any different?' he whispered to Ellie. She smiled, lightly tilting her head to one side.

'We'll see.'

CHAPTER NINETEEN

THE MORNING AFTER TOMORROW

Conor's alarm sounded with an uncompromising drone as the clock struck 8.00AM. Quickly silenced with a dismissive thud, he lay in his bed, wide awake, staring up at the ceiling. An impatient intensity resided on his face as he searched his mind, counting the minutes that passed him by. The night blurred into morning.

It had been just after 2.00AM when the team had disbanded, leaving Conor feeling bemused and frustrated, unable to mask his disappointment. The professor offered confusing words of assurance.

'The transfer took,' he had said. 'You just need time. Be patient and it will come to you.'

Conor had frowned, annoyed by yet more ambiguity, more delay. The professor went on to explain that when a *take* was first delivered to the brain it is initially weak, like the memory of an old dream, long forgotten. It takes time for the synaptic pathways to build. For the *take* to be accessed as memory. They called it *The Burst*.

James tried to describe the feeling as an explosion in the brain.

'It will happen at some point over the next twelve hours,' he said. 'Slow at first, but with a bit of stimulation the knowledge will burst in your mind, filling your head. The feeling is euphoric.'

The words had stayed with Conor. From that moment onwards he was essentially a time bomb, walking along a ledge with his eyes closed, waiting for the drop.

How was he going to make it through today? It could happen at any moment. With no sleep Conor had until early afternoon at best before the long night broke him. His eyes would glaze over and his thoughts would blur together. Trying to focus on anything today was going to be an exercise in futility.

Sitting up, he let one leg hang off his bed as he glanced to the mirror across the room. Wiping the sleep from his eyes, seeing only tiredness, he climbed out of bed, stretching and yawning. The thought of going for a run seemed increasingly unlikely.

Less than a minute had passed when his phone began to ring, as if reacting to his movement. He picked it up, staring at the unknown number before answering.

'Hello?'

'Are you OK?' the caller asked. It was Ellie.

'Fine,' Conor replied. It was anything but the truth.

'Did you sleep?'

'Not for a minute.' Conor pulled back the curtains, blinking as the sunlight shone through the window.

'It's probably just the Ritalin in your system keeping you up.'

'Yeah, maybe.'

'Getting anything yet?'

'I don't think so.' Conor stared at the letter he'd written for his parents, now resting on his desk. 'I'm still not sure what to expect.'

Ellie sat cross legged on her bed, looking out of her window, trying to remember the words she'd decided on before making the call. She was now regretting the timing and her decision to call at exactly 8.00AM. It took a while before she realised that the line had gone quiet.

'Ellie?' Conor spoke.

'I was just calling to... Well, I wanted to say...'

'What?'

'It's not too late... You know... You could stop... If you wanted to.'

'What do you mean?'

'If you're worried. If you feel like you've got into something and feel pressured. I just want you to know. They'd understand.'

'Are you serious?' Conor cringed at the idea. 'Ellie, I don't know how anyone could walk away from this?'

'I know,' she said softly. 'It's just that no one will think to offer you the chance now.'

'Good!'

'What are you doing today?' She ran her hand through her hair.

'I've got a lecture at eleven.' Conor scratched the small puncture wound on his arm. 'The afternoon's clear, I think.' *He hoped.*

'Trust me, just take the day off,' Ellie said. 'It's hard enough wishing you were somewhere else, but you won't be anywhere today.'

Conor smiled, relieved at how in tune Ellie was with how he felt. The sudden apathy that filled his head was intoxicating, an obnoxious sense of self-importance; but he couldn't help it. Nothing seemed to matter.

Was it the same for scientists around the world, he wondered? Trying to reintegrate into everyday life after making startling breakthroughs, curing diseases? Being part of something so profound? *Anything you could fear losing.*

'I was thinking,' Ellie said. 'I'd like to be there when it happens, one of us should be.'

'What? *The Burst?* Sure, OK. But I'm not sure it's worked.'

'Trust me,' Ellie smiled. 'You'll remember this day for the rest of your life.'

* * *

The view from Ellie's car window changed from an urban brown to a blurring green as the route became more rural. Conor sat staring through the glass in a daze, Ellie glancing left on occasion to check on him as she drove. Just over two hours had passed since they had spoken that morning, the call ending with Ellie insisting she knew the perfect spot for them to be.

Conor did what he could to clear his mind; to think of nothing in the hope that it would help bring the *take* to the forefront of his brain.

A GAME FOR THE YOUNG

It was just after 10.15AM when Ellie pulled into a gravelled car park, encircled by trees and fading bushes. Fallen leaves lay golden brown on the pebbled surface.

'Where are we?' he asked.

'Bury Knowle Park,' Ellie replied. 'I come here to think.'

'You mean to study?'

'No, I mean to think. Believe me, it's easy to stop. You need to put time aside for it.'

Stepping out of the car, Conor breathed in the fresh air and noted the absence of noise from the city. The bustle had dulled to almost silence.

They left the car behind to walk down a short public footpath, Ellie leading the way as they crossed into the park.

Raising his head, Conor took in the view. Sighing with a smile, he looked out at a vista of open green fields, divided under trodden paths and scatterings of woodland. To his left a playground played its part in keeping a small group of children entertained as their mothers rested on benches. To the far north he could make out a Mini Golf course and some tennis courts. To his right, a Tai Chi class practised barefoot on the grass.

Ellie guided Conor to a bench positioned on a small mound to the east of the park. They turned to take in the view. Ellie was right - if there was anywhere to relax, this was it.

The sun glowed in the sky, but the seasonal weather kept the air cool. A pack of runners jogged down the path, drifting near where they were sat. There were dog walkers in the distance, an elderly man feeding the birds, the occasional couple sat reading books and all peacefully resting under the backdrop of Oxford.

Ellie sat cross-legged on the grass facing towards Conor, her back to the view. He made himself comfortable on the bench.

'When will it happen?' he asked.

'*The Burst*? It varies. James takes the longest, around ten hours. Sara's the quickest, she starts getting them after about seven hours. Six and half is the record. But the first is special, it always takes the longest.'

119

'Why?'

'We don't know.' She shrugged.

'You don't know?!' Conor flashed a look of concern.

'Right,' she smiled. 'Early days remember?'

'Right,' Conor nodded, looking out across the park. 'What does it feel like?'

'Just wait and see,' Ellie said softly. 'It's worth it, I promise.'

'What do you mean?'

'It's... Difficult to describe.'

'Try,' Conor pushed.

Ellie sighed, lowering her head, struggling to find the words.

'Have you ever been travelling on a train or in a car and seen a view so beautiful, so mesmerising, that you're inspired to take a picture? You pull out your camera and take the shot, but when you look at the image it hasn't captured what you're seeing. The colours, the light. It's just not the same. You could try to describe it but you know you'll never do it justice. It's almost as if that moment was just for you. You can't take it with you.' Ellie looked to Conor. 'That's the only way I can describe it.'

They sat for at least an hour, often speaking of their homes, their past, on occasion sharing peaceful silence.

'So where are you from?' Conor had asked.

'Brighton. You been there?'

He shook his head.

'You should,' Ellie closed her eyes. 'I miss the sea.'

The thought brought back reminiscent visions of home that she had long since buried in her memory. It took her a while to picture her bedroom, the layout of the house, the colour of the front door.

Ellie was born in Hastings, along the coastline of East Sussex, although she couldn't claim to remember it well. She was barely beyond her toddler years when her father died of throat cancer, the funeral nothing more than faint images. Her mother dealt with it in the only way she could – taking them on a run of short stints in two bedroom flats and apartments along the south coast. Travelling from town to town in short succession. It was a lonely time for both of them.

She was eight when her mother remarried, leaving her old enough to disapprove and yet too young to do anything about it. She watched helplessly as her mother fell pregnant.

It didn't take long before Ellie felt as if she were a lingering reminder to a previous life.

By eighteen, her local schooling was completed. There was nothing to keep her in Brighton. Ellie was uncomfortable at home and her friends were disappearing across the country.

Considering her future, she followed suit, applying for a grant at the University of Bristol with the hope of joining their School of Biochemistry.

It took months to hear back, but by the time the rejection letter finally came Ellie had already succumbed to the concept of a local life. The possibilities that had seemed endless were slipping through her fingers, leaving her with nothing to hold onto except harsh reality.

Her last hope came in the form of an ambitious St Anne's scholarship with the University of Oxford. An unlikely dream, others would only dare to reach for.

The initial shock of her acceptance took months to fade, often coupled by the fear that it was a mistake, a prize they would snatch from her as the enrolment drew closer. Perhaps it was why she tried so hard, constantly looking to justify herself.

For the first year, Ellie kept things distant, leaving her roommates to busy themselves with parties and alcohol. Often the loner, always into her books or on her laptop. It paid off as her grades slowly elevated her to the top of the class.

She smiled, reciting the moment when it happened; when during her Molecular Genetics lecture, her Biology teacher quietly asked her to stay behind. Then came the pitch, the opportunity. She was on board before the professor was half way through presenting the project.

The team had since grown to be a family. Sara, the older protective sister Ellie could confide in; James, the younger, gentle brother she would nurture; and the Professor, the father figure she never had.

Conor watched her closely as she affectionately described them. They were a unit. The risks they had shared had brought them close, woven them together with ambition. He began to understand the scale of their sacrifice.

Ellie appeared deep in thought, but she soon broke her stare from the ground.

'How do you feel?' she asked. 'How are the headaches?' She wanted to change the subject.

'I'm OK, enjoying the view,' he said, looking out across the fields. 'I like it here.'

'Have you ever been to the Botanic Gardens?'

'No, not yet,' Conor said, his breath starting to feel short. An ache grew in the back of his head.

'Maybe next time,' Ellie said. 'If you like it here, it's worth a visit.'

He smiled. 'What's *Galileo?*' Conor suddenly thought to ask. 'Last night, I heard Sara mention *Galileo.*'

'It's a number of things,' Ellie explained. 'Your brain needs help to store memory without emotion.'

'Emotion?'

'All memories tie into emotion. We think intense stress and fear go the deepest... and love.'

'So the drug makes you afraid?'

'No.' She leaned back onto her elbows. 'It enhances the biochemical supply of neurotransmitters, enzymes, hormones and increases the oxygen in your brain, stimulating neuron growth.'

Conor exhaled a deep breath.

'It really isn't that complicated,' Ellie smiled. 'We called it *Galileo*, the father of science.'

As she said it Conor suddenly leaned forward, breathing heavy and erratic. Ellie could see his expression change, noting it with a smile.

'Let it grow in your mind. Believe you know.'

He gripped the bench and flinched, briefly closing his eyes only to open them wide. Staring intensely at the ground, he gasped for air.

'Don't hold your breath,' Ellie said, leaning forward.

Like a childhood memory, at first it had felt distant. A feeling he couldn't explain. A burning muse of fulfilment and yet it was building to pure elation. Something was rising to the surface, a recollection. And then it happened.

An explosion of memories broke through the wall in his mind, pouring through into his conscious, a rush of hormones. Conor's eyes began to water as he felt his senses increase ten levels, a desire overcoming him to cry out, whether it was to laugh or scream he couldn't understand. He was suddenly everywhere and anything. The world was limitless.

Ellie could see it in his eyes.

'The first time is always special.'

CHAPTER TWENTY

RITE OF PASSAGE

On a darkened route to the A&E Unit, Nurse Whitely made her way through the abandoned areas of the John Radcliffe Hospital at speed. Her heels clicked along the vinyl floor, her pager beeped repeatedly, prompting her pace to quicken.

She passed by the blue doors to the Heart Centre without turning back. The black and empty hallways were eerie enough at night without a stereotypical horror setting giving her the excuse to be fearful.

As she passed through the double doors they sprang back and forth, slowly resting to a close behind her.

Silently the professor appeared from within a shadow, staring intensely down the corridor until she was gone, glancing left and then right, studying every detail until he was satisfied. He turned to Ellie, who was waiting pressed against the wall in the dark, and gently nodded.

They moved briskly through the halls, hugging the walls as they passed by the Children's Hospital on the west wing, climbing the steps to the first floor near the OCMR centre, Oxford's Centre for Clinical Magnetic Resonance Research.

Reaching the white doors to the MRI unit, the professor peered through one of the glass panels. The lights were on in the waiting area, suggesting the presence of nurses and patients, but the room was empty. Dormant; resonating a similar state to many departments throughout the Hospital, appearing calm, but ready. Timing was short, if a patient from A&E required an MRI, the Doctors would burst through these doors without care.

The professor glanced down to the keypad securing the door before reaching into his pocket to pull out his mobile phone. He opened the message he'd received thirty minutes earlier and entered a code into the keypad. The lock glowed green with approval as his gloved hand gently turned the handle to push the door open.

The bland grey corridor to the right of the reception area led through to a series of evaluation rooms, each guarded by a key card lock, each with green and red light bulbs above the door frames.

A ceiling camera at the end of the hall watched over them as Ellie walked over to one of the suites. She pressed her ear against the door marked 'Gamma Three' before lightly knocking three evenly-timed taps against the wooden frame. The professor stood by the exit, watching the halls as they waited.

Sara opened the door from inside, looking calm and calculated, leaving it ajar before disappearing back into the room. Ellie followed with a quiet gesture to the professor. They both stepped inside and closed the door.

'You sorted the camera?' the professor asked, knowing the answer but wanting to be sure.

To his left, the door was open to the console room.

'It'll be feeding last night's footage for the next three hours,' James replied, sat behind one of the observation desks.

The office was dimly lit. The PC and software application was standing by, having been hacked twenty minutes earlier.

'How's the schedule looking?'

'There's nothing planned for the next six hours,' Sara assured him.

Entering the console room, the professor raised his head to peer through the glass panel into the MRI suite. In the centre of the room stood Conor, staring with wonder at the MRI machine. Ellie appeared next to him having come through the door to his right.

Looking to the patient table in front of the MRI, Conor nervously listened to the swishing sound of liquid helium cool the superconducting magnets.

Conor was initially surprised that the machine was designed by Siemens and branded a 'MAGNETOM

Avanto'. It stood over eight feet tall; Sara had told him earlier how it weighed over five tonnes. A giant doughnut of gradient coils encased by a huge magnet, it was covered with a white outer shell casing and fronted with a friendly sky blue panel. With the price tag reaching close to five hundred thousand pounds, it was quite simply one of the most expensive, beautiful and complicated pieces of stationery he had ever seen.

The team had arrived in phases, Sara's Honda pulling up nearly an hour earlier and parking opposite the Trauma Unit. The professor chose to park at the Carillion staff car park, taking advantage of the employee badge he had acquired back in October.

James handed the professor the pass codes as he took off his jacket. They were swift and slick. Conor could see them through the window, noticing the way that they moved. They had done this many times.

'Put these in,' Ellie said, handing Conor some ear plugs.

'Why?' he asked. 'What are we checking exactly?'

The professor took James's place by the PC and began typing.

'Cerebral swelling,' Ellie offered. 'Abnormal grey cells, limbic dysfunction. Think of it as a check up.'

'Details,' Conor dismissed, taking off his hoodie and passing it to her. Back in the waiting room, Sara had already relieved him of his wallet, belt and phone. He jumped up on to the table to lie down flat.

'That's right, details,' Ellie smiled. 'The fine line between knowing your shit.'

'And knowing you're shit,' Sara said, finishing her sentence from the observation room, her voice coming through the speakers.

'Enough, there's no time,' the professor hissed. 'James, watch over the camera feed, Sara, monitor the radio chatter. Ellie, come in here and pull up a seat.'

'We'll be on the main desk,' Sara said, opening the door for James as they left.

Ellie turned to Conor and gently squeezed his arm before leaving through the side door. Moments later she appeared in the glass panel of the console room.

'Lie still, Conor,' the professor said, keying in the commands to start the procedure. 'Slow and steady breaths, this will take around thirty minutes.'

'Time for a nap,' Conor said, staring up at the ceiling and putting the plugs in his ears.

'I doubt it,' Ellie whispered.

With his ear plugs in, the steady hum reduced to almost nothing; then came the feeling of the table moving backward, the MRI overhead and closing around him. The cylinder swallowed him to the point where only his legs were free from the knees down. Conor squirmed in discomfort. *Thirty minutes?!*

'OK, here we go,' the professor said.

Outside in the corridor, the green light above the door switched to red.

Quickly Conor realised that a nap was out of the question. The noise of an MRI is disturbing at first. Loud pulsating waves reverberated within the cylinder as the electricity passed through the coils.

With striking volume and intensity, the first noise resembled the sound of a loud booming drum, relentlessly pulsating for several minutes until mercifully it stopped only to switch to the sound of a police siren in close proximity, then a blender grinding metal and a high pitched squeal. It softened for moments only to repeat the process over and over. It was an assault on the senses. Conor closed his eyes, trying not to flinch as the plugs protected his ear drums.

Anxious and nearing claustrophobia, an uneasy twenty something minutes slowly passed. The surrounding encasement now felt like a prison, a sealed coffin which held him against his will. Buried alive. Visibly sweating, his breathing short and erratic, he glanced down to his feet.

'Lie still Conor, we're almost there,' the professor said, glaring at the readings as they came in, magnifying areas of Conor's brain at varying levels.

'Fascinating.'

'What?' Ellie leaned over.

'Take a look at his hippocampus. We've not seen this level of neurogenesis before.'

Ellie peered at the grey-scaled image of Conor's brain forming on the monitor screen.

'He's not like the others?'

'No. He's like you. Cut from the same cloth it would appear.' The professor leaned back into his chair. 'As if you needed an excuse.'

'Shut up,' she smiled, lightly kicking his chair. 'We'll need to compare these results with the tests from the Pathology MRI.'

'Agreed.'

Suddenly the main door burst open and Sara appeared.

'We've got company!' she shouted. 'Pile up on the A420, multiple causalities. Head injuries, suspected fractures.'

'We're done here,' the professor said, typing in a series of keystrokes and gesturing to Ellie. 'There's plenty of time.'

'That's the problem,' Sara cried. 'The accident was over an hour ago. I missed it, I can't explain... They're here. They're coming!'

In reception, James glared at the camera feed. Through the lens, a group of hectic nurses were pushing two bedded patients at pace along the west wing corridor. A doctor followed close behind, reading notes from a clipboard.

'We have to move!' he shouted over his shoulder.

Entering the side door to the MRI suite, Ellie held down a button to retract the patient table. Conor squinted at the ceiling spot lights as he emerged.

'All done?' he asked, sounding hopeful.

'Welcome to the Betterment Project,' she smiled.

'You know what to do,' the professor said from the console room, unpacking a white coat from his leather holdall.

'What's going on?' Conor asked, jumping down from the table to grab his hoodie.

'We've got doctors en route... And there's too many of us,' Ellie said, opening the side door. Leaving the room, he turned to notice the professor putting on his white coat and positioning a name badge above his outer left pocket.

'You're staying?'

'No one suspects the old man pushing the cripple,' Sara said, moving past him through to the waiting area.

'Less of the old,' the professor jested.

'Less of the cripple!' James placed a blanket over his legs and began messing up his hair.

'So where are we going?'

Following Ellie out of the door, Conor turned in to the corridor to find Sara mounted on a chair pushing aside a ceiling tile with her fingers.

'Tell me you're joking.'

* * *

Nurse Whitely thrust aside the doors to the MRI unit, her arms stretched as far as she could manage, the bed wheels squeaking as a groaning patient glided past her.

Quickly the other nurses swarmed through.

'Set us up in Gammas two and five,' the doctor instructed, walking alongside the second bed.

Dazed, the patient stared up at the ceiling, squinting with confusion at the brief sight of someone's face looking back at him before disappearing behind a ceiling tile.

Nurse Whitely swiped her key card to open the door for the first patient.

'It's OK, here we go,' she said, talking over his mumbles, drugged and stuttering, as he pointed up to the tiles above him.

'Excuse me, make way,' another doctor spoke, pushing a young man in a wheelchair past the commotion.

The nurses divided.

'OK, Judy, get started with Mr Jenkins. I'll be with you in a moment.'

As the doors closed, the bustle of organised chaos diluted to a soft rumble. The bulbs above the door frames changed from green to red. The waiting area settled once again to a peaceful calm.

CHAPTER TWENTY ONE

FIGURES IN THE DARK

NINE MONTHS LATER

The dark clouds shielded the stars in the sky. Rain was coming. The night gave a soft wind, blowing the amber leaves on the trees beneath the shade of the Chemistry Research Laboratory, a seven-storey building positioned on the outskirts of the University campus.

In the shadows, security cameras rotated with precision and sequence, the small red light under their lens giving away carefully considered positioning. The fans purred as steam rose from the ventilation system on the roof. The streets below rested quiet and still.

Inside, on the sixth floor, the darkness was diluted to a soft light by the glow of white work surfaces and chrome finishing. The tiled floor gave a subtle reflection to the windows which were otherwise a lifeless and empty black.

A light tapping came from the glass, repeating faster and louder. Outside it was starting to pour thick, heavy raindrops; the clouds had begun to snap and ripple.

Within the office, on the ceiling, a lone slab wobbled before slowly rising, gradually disappearing from view. A hand quietly emerged holding a small mirror. Manoeuvring with tiny adjustments until it had taken in the entire floor, it retracted back into the ceiling.

Without noise, the light on the motion sensor in the top right corner of the office faded from red to black.

A few seconds passed before a pair of legs dangled from the ceiling. With a calm swiftness a body eased through the space, landing softly on the desk beneath. The dark figure stepped down, now crouching low on the floor.

'I'm in,' Sara whispered.

Wearing a black balaclava with dark leather gloves, black trousers and a long sleeve shirt, she crawled along the floor before rising next to a computer terminal.

The whites of her eyes glanced back and forth. She presented a small black USB device from her pocket and slotted it into the terminal.

There was a purr as the light on the USB started flickering.

'Now,' Sara whispered. The terminal awoke with a humming noise and grumbled as the CPU began processing.

Outside the sound of rain reduced through the windows to almost nothing and yet a familiar noise grew; a realisation increasing, apparent in her eyes. The sound became louder. The noise of a siren, now prompting a move to the window. With a sudden blast, an ambulance flew past along the adjacent street, quickly reducing to near silence.

The heavy exhale could be heard from across the office floor. She returned to the terminal, low to the floor.

'Done?'

'Almost there.' James's voice responded through her ear piece.

Sara looked rattled, composure starting to fade. She glanced to the left entrance for a moment and then returned to the right.

The sound of heavy rain muffled the noises within, taking away the edge, leaving her unsure. *What is that?* A grinding noise, a buzz and then a sudden ping. *The sound of the lift doors.* She heard the noise as if were a gun shot.

'Time to go.'

'Not yet,' James protested.

'No time.'

'Wait!'

Sara stood exposed on the office floor staring intensely at the entrance. From the hallway, footsteps made their way towards the office.

'Done.'

In a single motion Sara pulled the USB device from the computer, leapt up on to the desk and jumped, pulling up and away into the ceiling. She disappeared from view seconds before the entrance quietly opened.

The silhouette of a security guard stood in the doorway. The main light flickered as it turned on, blinding the guard for a moment as his eyes adjusted.

He walked through the office slowly, scanning each of the terminals. Above him a ceiling tile gently reappeared into place.

The guard paused, looking up to the motion sensor and appearing confused. Walking over, he pulled up a chair and got ready to mount it to take a closer look. Glancing back, he noticed that the red light had returned. The guard took out his radio.

'Jimmy, are we reading sixth?'

'Just came back on, it's been triggered. Is that you?'

'Yeah, it's me,' he said, frustration in his tone. 'It must have dropped off again, glitchy fucking thing. OK, give me twenty seconds and then reset it.'

'Will do.'

The guard returned the chair to where he found it and walked to the exit, taking one last look around the office before turning off the light and closing the door. Ten seconds later and the red light flickered, making a beeping noise.

'Sensor reset.'

On the roof, Sara reappeared from the fire escape. The rain was falling thick and rattling loudly against the steel roofing. With a sudden crack from above, a bolt of lightning struck far away to the south.

Now soaking in the downpour, she moved to the far end of the right wing and peered over the edge, staring briefly before pulling away to pick up a small harness. It was worn like a rucksack, with a fastening at the chest. Quickly Sara attached the harness to a small elastic rope that was tied to the roof. Timing was key; this needed to be judged perfectly.

As another lightning strike lit up the sky, Sara stepped off the building feet first. She descended in seconds, gliding through the air at a frightening pace. The elasticated rope suddenly snapped tight, slowing the descent until the fall halted just short of metres from the concrete floor. At that moment, she pressed down on the chest harness, releasing the rope to spring back up the building, away into the night sky.

Sara landed on the ground with athletic composure. Swiftly standing upright and running off down the street, she disappeared into an adjacent alleyway.

* * *

Two hours later and the team had assembled in the *Hive*. James was lying sedated on the operating table, Ritalin being fed intravenously through a cannula in his right arm.

He'd received a *take* on the known scales and formulas of Quantum Mechanics less than an hour earlier.

The professor was sitting at his desk writing in his journal. Ellie casually watched over James's vitals, her eyes often straying. She had become less vigilant in recent months.

Conor was studying at the reading table, working his way through a list of articles Ellie had recommended on his Netbook whilst Sara read a book on Binding Proteins and DNA Sequencing.

Though transfers were frequent, the professor still insisted that the team read from books and laptops. Whether it was to keep their brain patterns conforming to regulatory methods of learning or simply to keep them preoccupied, they couldn't be sure. Ellie suspected both.

Conor, now twenty-two years old, sat noticeably differently. Over the past nine months he had received over thirty *takes* of data and with each transfer he had emerged slightly altered. Subtle at first, but stretched out over time the difference in him was now immeasurable.

The way he carried himself, his outlook, even the clothes he wore and the way he moved. He often wondered whether his parents would recognise him, although perhaps not enough to find out. It was long over four months since he had last returned home, despite the increasingly desperate voicemails his mother was leaving him.

To Professor Miller, Conor was something of a mystery. Never before had he witnessed such a turnaround in one of his students. Now a shining example on how focus can drive a student to excel, Conor had become one of his 'reliables', the precious few who he could turn to when one of his questions hung in the air without response; always aware of the answer, often sitting smug and confident as they watched their classmates struggle. The transformation would have been treated as suspicious had Conor not frequently demonstrated his talent spontaneously.

Finishing up on an article, Conor sighed before falling back into his chair.

'Controversial stuff?' Ellie asked.

'Not really, as with most things there's something for everyone.'

'What are you reading?' Sara glanced up from her book.

'An article on Yogic Science. It's about the existence of a soul. How our wisdom and self awareness can be attributed to a form of energy which conducts thought, consciously or otherwise. Interesting.'

'I thought you'd like it,' Ellie said, leaning forward. 'It got me thinking.'

'Here we go,' Sara mumbled. 'What about?'

'The definition of intelligence.'

Conor grimaced.

'The definition of intelligence is the ability to acquire and apply knowledge and skills? I looked it up.'

'Right, but how do you measure intelligence if it is given without effort?'

'I suppose that depends on your point of view,' Conor offered.

Ellie squinted.

'Maybe, but if you're knowledgeable surely that makes you aware. Doesn't that then make you intelligent? I've been sitting here thinking...'

'Oh god,' Sara groaned, taking off her reading glasses.

Ellie held up her hand.

'No, wait. Think about this for a second. Are those that would be deemed the 'intelligence' of our time truly intelligent? Or have they simply memorised the achievements of a previous generation?'

'No, I wouldn't agree with that,' the professor said, his head still low as he wrote. 'There's more genius among you now than there has ever been. We just don't stand out like we used to.' He smiled, raising his head.

'Your generation has just lost interest in acquiring knowledge, that's all.'

'Don't you mean respect? How much stock do we place on intelligence now, anyway?'

'Wouldn't you agree that intelligence brings enlightenment?' the professor asked.

'Not necessarily.' Ellie shrugged. 'Take Bobby Fischer for example.'

'The chess world champion?' Conor frowned. 'Wasn't he supposed to have an IQ of what, a hundred and eighty five?'

'A hundred and eighty seven,' Ellie corrected. 'Yet he was renowned for an unreserved hatred of Jews, a complete anti-Semite. He repeatedly demonstrated symptoms of paranoid schizophrenia.'

'What's your point, Ellie?' the professor asked.

'I'm starting to think that this technology won't solve human ignorance.'

'Interesting, and what of evolution?' he offered.

'Oh, please, don't start talking about how humans only use ten percent of the brain, that's a disproven myth and you know it.'

'No, I'm talking about the human condition.'

'Now you've lost me,' Conor said, wincing.

'The search for purpose,' the professor said. 'Our curiosity and quest to obtain new information. Wouldn't you agree that this project serves to that end?'

Ellie nodded, conceding the point.

'So what's the next step in our evolution?' Sara asked. 'Allowing computers to do the thinking for us? Humans simply processing the output?' She gestured to James, asleep on the operating table. 'Our species is already hopelessly dependent on technology.'

'Wouldn't you agree that our quality of life has improved?' Ellie asked.

'Superficially, I suppose.'

The professor frowned.

'That's a little insulting on your generation, wouldn't you say? What's your point?'

Sara sighed.

'I'm not sure. Fuck it, why does everything need to have a point?'

'It helps,' Conor groaned, turning to a new article.

Sara went to speak, but lost the will. She picked up her book.

'Who's Richard Myers?' she asked the professor.

'Pardon?'

'This book? It says that it's the property of Richard Myers.' She held up the inner sleeve.

'These are old books taken from the library. It doesn't matter.'

Sara stared inquisitively at the book before looking back at the professor.

James began to mumble as he came round, yawning and stretching, using his elbows to rest up on the table as he leaned forward.

'What did I miss?' he asked.

'Nothing, absolutely nothing.' Conor responded without raising his head.

James pressed the palm of his hand against his forehead, groaning under his breath. The Professor was soon stood over him, going through the usual checks.

'OK, follow my finger, please,' he said, moving his finger above James's eye line, left and then right. Everything seemed as it should.

'Can you tell me your name?' the professor asked.

James went to speak but as he did his face turned blank, a sudden picture of doubt and fear. His breathing grew heavy.

'I, I don't know,' he said, an agonising tone to his voice. Everyone suddenly looked up.

'What do you mean you don't know?' Sara shouted.

The team encircled the table.

'Everyone stand back, stand back!' the professor pleaded. 'Come on. Think, think. You know your name, tell me your name!'

Ellie covered her mouth, her eyes watering. The nightmares she had long forgotten were resurfacing. There was little anyone could do. It had finally happened; they had pushed the boundaries to breaking point.

She glanced to Conor for strength, her eyes focusing on his, but in doing so her expression suddenly shifted, drifting from a state of fear to nervous intrigue. She just caught something. The slightest glimpse of a smirk from the corner of her eye.

Ellie erupted, slamming the table.

'Asshole! That's your name!'

The atmosphere cut in half as James's laughter filled the room.

'Oh, come on, that was funny,' he chuckled, quickly looking to the others for support.

The room grew cold with anger and sighs of relief. No one had seen the funny side.

CHAPTER TWENTY TWO

LOST IN MISDIRECTION

The *Hive* entrance was plain and unassuming, no different from the door across from it or the countless others that came before and after. That was its brilliance. It wouldn't be stumbled upon or treated as suspicious. In the corridors of the storage floor, the icy maze of metal and concrete would rest under an unsettling silence, breaking only to the grind coming from the cargo lifts. The giant steel doors of each bay offered a dull exterior, giving nothing away as to the nature of their contents.

Across from the *Hive*, the sound proof mesh did its work well, protecting and isolating the room. Everything was designed to keep the sound, warmth and light within from escaping.

'No, this doesn't touch them!' Conor shouted from inside, rising to his feet, clearly frustrated as he paced back and forth by the coffee table.

James shook his head.

'So you don't think that with immediate access to historical fact that there wouldn't be a mass crisis in faith?' He gestured with open palms. 'What if you could learn all there was to know on evolution at infancy? You think pupils of religion, who were born and raised, would remain true to their faith?'

'That's an opinion.'

'It's historical fact.'

'Which is your opinion!' Conor stopped pacing as he folded his arms. 'You're assuming they'd *want* to believe in something else. Religion as a word is both symbol and metaphor. They believe in a higher power, in a spiritual union.' Conor pointed to the equipment. 'This doesn't replace that. It can't!'

'Are you religious?' Sara asked.

'I'm not saying that.'

'So you're an atheist, then?' James pushed.

Conor exhaled a deep breath, wishing Ellie was there to back him up.

'People who adopt a faith don't *know* their religion, they believe in it. An atheist doesn't know that god isn't real, simply that there isn't proof to substantiate it.'

'That's the response of an atheist.' Sara said, smiling.

'Do I have to be one of the other?'

'Of course not,' the professor said, leaning away from his journal. 'People will choose to believe as they wish, and long may that continue.'

'Thank you,' Conor exhaled.

'Though in all things I would always recommend you form an opinion.'

'Why?'

'It defines you.'

The professor seldom offered his advice without purpose, his contribution often bringing closure to a dispute.

It wasn't their first disagreement, nor the last, Conor suspected. The *Hive* sessions were becoming more and more intense. When analysed, the affects the procedure would have seemed limitless.

'Think about it,' the professor had once said. 'If you could learn anything, be anyone without restriction, what would you be?'

'A stock broker,' Conor had responded instinctively.

'Why?' James asked. 'Because you associate that to money? Success? Comfort? Would that truly make you happy?'

'The money would.' Conor shrugged with honesty.

'Seems a waste considering all you could be,' Ellie said softly.

'A doctor?' James offered. 'A healer?'

'A life of service? Not for me,' Sara shook her head. 'An explorer. To see the world, to travel.'

'To what end?' the professor asked. 'What would you be searching for?' She lowered her head.

'What about you, Ellie?' James had asked.

She'd sat deep in thought before answering.

'A professor, maybe? Can any of us claim to know ourselves well enough?'

'Indeed,' the professor agreed. 'But in a world where this procedure is a reality, what is the worth of a profession such as mine?'

* * *

Conor was first to react when two gentle knocks came from the main door. Soft metallic taps that were still loud enough to echo off the walls. The door felt stiff and heavy as he opened it, revealing Ellie, wide-eyed and glowing.

She entered with an uncertainty, similar to the look Conor had brought with him on his first visit to the *Hive*. She glanced to her friends, noticing their readiness, their composure. They knew, they all knew, that the suspense was killing her.

Traditionally, when it was someone's turn to receive a *take*, they would arrive knowing what was on the menu, but tonight was different.

'It's a surprise,' the professor had answered, whispering playfully the previous night.

She sat down on one of the sofas, visibly nervous. The team gathered around her. Tonight was the big reveal, the fruits of their labour.

'We're at a point where we need to break new ground,' the professor explained. 'We need to broaden the scope of the project to include the adjustment of pre-existing memory. If we can understand the point in which the brain acknowledges a *take* as the primary thought it will lead to helping millions master addictive habits overnight, conquer phobias, perhaps in time help suppress abusive histories and psychological damage.'

'What do you have in mind?' Ellie asked.

The professor gestured to James before he took over.

'We want to try a subjective implant, a neuro-linguistic reprogramme. Therapists have been doing it for years with hypnotherapy and guided visualisations. If we pitch the *take* at the right level we should be able to dislodge deeply ingrained memories that lie at the root of an imbalance. Or, in your case, a phobia.'

'I've been working on a variation of *Galileo*.' Sara took a step forward. 'We believe that it will provide the right conditions in the hippocampus to adjust your thought patterns.'

Ellie felt her mouth dry up as the team went through the *take*. She felt a strange sensation in her stomach. It was no secret that she had long suffered from a fear of heights. She often needed a strong amount of will power just to file books away on the upper floor at Radcliffe Camera.

'We've collated nearly an hour's worth of code,' Conor said. 'We'll transmit birds-eye view images, video footage taken from the hull of flying planes, satellite imagery. If the professor's right your brain will digest it, accepting this as a form of memory. The more you experience something uncomfortable, the easier you find it. What's more, the effects should be almost instantaneous.'

'Synaptic redirection?' Ellie couldn't hide the doubt in her tone. It had been some time since she had felt concern or scepticism. Her belief in the procedure was almost absolute and her trust in the team resembled that of family. But they were talking about reprogramming her brain. This wasn't just changing memory patterns or redirecting pathways; they were talking about changing *her*.

Ellie's initial concerns were answered with a series of reassuring facts on cerebral redefinition: the process of changing someone's knowledge on a subject to address imperfections and misunderstandings.

She had taken to staring down at the floor by the time the team had dispersed. Glancing over her shoulder she could see James calibrating *Einstein*. Conor looked to be preparing the video camera whilst Sara worked on the new dosage of *Galileo*. It seemed clear that everyone had simply assumed she'd be fine with this.

She could feel her heart beating faster. Looking down she noticed her hands were visibly shaking. She felt warm, sweaty. Her neck was starting to feel tight, as though her jumper had suddenly shrunk.

The professor sat down beside her, placing a small glass of water on the coffee table and exhaling loudly as he got comfortable.

He briefly looked over to the team before speaking softly.

'You know you don't have to do this if you don't want to, Ellie. It's OK. There's no pressure.' He had kept his eyes with her throughout the explanation, noticing the subtleties of her concern.

'I'm OK,' Ellie said, trying to sound confident. 'But this is different from anything we've done before.'

The professor turned to his friends for strength before answering.

'I know,' he replied.

'You can't tell me it's safe, can you?'

'No.' Their relationship was always one of honesty. 'But I believe, Ellie. And I trust.' The professor folded his legs. 'But this isn't about faith. It's something else, isn't it? Something less biased.' He scratched his cheek in thought.

'Even with all we've achieved there will always be another step. To be able to know if we're on the right track, that's all we can ever hope.'

'And how do you know?' Ellie asked.

'I don't think you can.' He shrugged. 'Except perhaps to look back on the decisions you've made and ask yourself: 'Would I do it again?'. If the answer is yes, then if you're not already on the right track... It's close by.' He leaned back into the sofa. 'This is another leap of faith, Ellie, another moment of trial... Fascinating, isn't it?'

She closed her eyes, unable to respond.

'I'd watch over everything,' the professor said. 'I'd stay with you every step of the way. And believe me when I tell you that if I could take your place I would.'

'I know,' Ellie whispered. 'And if the worst should happen, you know what to do?'

Reluctantly the professor nodded.

'Promise me,' she said, her tone deadly serious.

'I promise,' the Professor replied, looking in to her eyes. Ellie had made it clear that she couldn't live in a vegetated state. If she awoke with brain damage the professor would do what was necessary.

She offered a smile and took in a deep breath.

'How will we test if it's worked?'

'Leave that to me,' Conor answered from across the *Hive*.

Ellie turned to find the team grouped together and watching over her. Conor, smiling with his hands in his pockets, leant against the operating table.

She could see the care in their eyes. The affection. It suddenly became clear. They had left her on the sofa not out of presumption or pressure, but to give her time. To give her the space she needed to prepare.

As the professor rose to his feet Ellie looked down and noticed that her hands were now steady. She reached over to take a sip of water, her throat feeling moist as she swallowed. Perched on the edge of her seat, she pressed her palms together.

'Alright,' she whispered. 'Alright, let's do this.'

* * *

Ellie was pale as she lay flat on the operating table, the professor standing over her as he went through the motions. Sara stood near Conor as he compiled the finalised code, often leaning in to take over and make adjustments.

'I've been meaning to ask you,' Conor spoke quietly. 'What made you think I was excessively mothered?'

'What?' Sara broke her gaze from the computer screen.

'When we first met, do you remember?'

'Sure.'

'What is it about me?'

Sara grinned, returning her focus to the monitor. Conor's insecurities continued to amuse her.

'The signs are all over you. The complexion of your skin, the time you'd spent doing your hair, the way you ironed and tucked in your shirt. When you learnt to do things for yourself you inherited the responsibility from someone who took great pride in your appearance. Besides, define 'excessive'; we've all been mothered.'

'Ready?' the professor asked.

'Ready,' Sara confirmed, typing in the final commands.

'September 4th, time is 11.35PM. Subject Swanson Elizabeth C, female, aged twenty-two. Members present are junior scientists James McCarthy, Sara Morgan and Conor Martin. My name is Professor William Daniels, project lead. This is procedure two four nine of the Betterment project.' The professor gave Ellie a gentle nod. The gesture was subtly returned to signify that she was ready.

'Administering the subject with fifteen millilitres of Estazolam,' he said, pushing the needle into the cannula in her arm and pressing down on the plunger. 'Ellie, you know what to do.'

'One, two, three, four, fiive, sixxxx…' Her head slightly tilted to the right as she drifted away.

'Administering twelve millilitres of *Galileo Beta*.' the professor said, pushing the second syringe into the cannula.

'Is it me or are doses increasing?' Conor whispered to Sara.

'It's necessary. The body fights routine, the brain adapts. Over time you need more to get the results.'

'When does that become unsafe?'

'We'll find out one day,' Sara replied. 'Hopefully when it's your turn.'

Conor smirked before turning his head to check that she was joking. Her face was difficult to read.

The professor gave James an assertive nod, and with a few keystrokes he typed in the commands to initiate the procedure.

'Here we go,' he said with a whisper, pressing down on the 'Enter' key.

Inside the keyboard, the key matrix on the circuit board sent an electrical current to pass through the binary signal into the CPUs processor. The program linked with *Einstein* retrieved the binary and ran the code through the head sensors.

Inside Ellie's brain, her hippocampus began channelling the foreign entity. Synaptic pathways formed in her cerebrum as the data pulsated through her cortex.

Conor stared at her vitals, monitoring the progress as the program delivered the *take*.

'Progress calculating...' James announced.

'I'll never get used to this,' Conor whispered. 'It's breathtaking.'

'Have you ever been to Devil's Pool?' Sara asked. 'It's at the top of the Victoria Falls in Zambia?'

Conor shook his head.

'There's a tiny rock basin at the very ridge of the falls, where the river is reduced to a soft current. A tiny pocket where you can literally sit at the peak of the waterfall and look over the edge without being pulled over. Believe me, breathtaking is what you make of it. This is something else.'

'Stay focused,' the professor said, his voice carrying a weight of fear that Sara hadn't heard for some time. 'Keep both eyes on her readings at all times.'

The professor looked down at Ellie lying helplessly on the table, her eyes twitching as the *take* transferred to her brain. His hands often rested on her arm or shoulder. True to his word he stayed by her side the whole time.

CHAPTER TWENTY THREE

CITY OF LIGHTS

Ellie stood close to Conor as they ascended the upper levels in the passenger lift. It was long past 2AM inside the Department of Biochemistry, an impressive, modern glass building, which housed some of Oxford's finest Biochemists, Developmental Biologists and varied extensive works in Biology research.

Moonlight shone through the glass roof, allowing a soft glow to sprinkle across the marble flooring. The inner ledges to each floor would steal the reflection, bouncing it through the floors off glass desks and monitor screens.

The evening security detail had stayed until midnight, but there was little need for overnight protection. The outer shell was secured through a series of key cards and rotating door codes. More than enough to deter any half-hearted burglary attempts.

It was Conor's idea. He made it happen. He had spotted the opportunity on a sunny afternoon whilst heading for the park, imagining the view from the roof. It was perfectly poised to offer everything on a clear night like tonight.

Things were changing in the team. Though the professor insisted that *takes* were never for personal gain, over the months Conor had found excuse after excuse to justify *takes* that would help improve him as a scientist. It surprised him how easily he could manipulate the professor to get what he wanted.

With infinite access to knowledge on a metaphorical tap, Conor now had the means to consider more than his own personal development. His ambition and desire for wealth hatched a new plan.

David P. Philip

He chose his first customer well, singling him out during a series of Digital Architecture workshops. He was mindful of the need to pitch at the right level. Too far behind and his assistance would be blatant and suspicious. Too comfortable or far ahead and there would be no opportunity to begin with.

Russell Watkins wasn't the worst in his class; far from it. But his feedback had consistently declined over the past couple of months. His body language was oozing the signs of pressure as the challenges overwhelmed him.

Conor could remember the look on his face, the shock and dismay when he offered to write his paper for a nominal fee. He immediately refused, swearing blindly that he'd find time and make it happen somehow. He even gave off a small speech on how he was insulted by the offer.

It didn't take long. Before the week gave out he was standing at Conor's door, holding an envelope and carrying the weak expression of defeat.

Conor wrote the paper over three afternoons with amazingly little effort. He was so focused. It was too easy.

With his work delivering the grades he promised, soon Conor found himself working on other assignments. His services became known among the hushed circles of the needy. He was making money from the rich and the slow.

Within three months he was making the first payment on a lease for a new Audi A3, buying designer clothes, enjoying meals in luxurious restaurants and the smell of expensive aftershave. He relished the taste of success. He would approach his prey carefully, researching their background and character. But, for Kevin Green he played things a little differently.

Studying for a Masters degree in Biomedical Sciences, Kevin was working as a temporary research analyst in one of the Biochemistry Labs.

From the outside he appeared to be comfortable; to the untrained eye he was knowledgeable. Conor did his research well. Kevin was struggling. Requesting extensions, meeting with his tutors out of class - fighting

148

against a decline that would see him on an inevitable course to failure. The odds were stacked against him.

Conor's approach had been subtle at first. A brush of the shoulder, a vague introduction. He observed Kevin for weeks, noting his drinking spots and where he read. Casually offering to buy him a pint. They struck up a curious friendship, drawn out over several nights. He worked his way in.

Before long Kevin was pouring his heart out. He was desperate to avoid a disgraceful exit from Oxford, from seeing the disappointment on his parent's faces. He was prepared to do almost anything. Conor chose his timing perfectly.

The fee was simple. He needed access to a card key and PIN number that would gain him and Ellie admittance to the Biochemistry Building for one night only.

Under relentless rainfall on a small disused lane within Botley Cemetery, Conor had presented his work.

'How can I be sure I won't get caught?' Kevin had asked, appearing nervous, looking around the cemetery to check if they were being watched.

'Nothing is for certain, but you need to trust me. The trick will be your own work following this up.'

Conor had appeared calm and, in a word, smooth. Somehow he was offering Kevin his complete focus whilst at the same time looking as if he was due elsewhere.

'OK,' Kevin had whispered, pulling out a small envelope and handing over what he had promised.

Standing close together in the glass elevator, Ellie's eyes stayed fixed to the display panel. She watched as the glowing floor numbers slowly incremented. With a ping they came to a stop on the seventh floor, the lift doors opening out to a set of stairs that led to the roof.

Conor guided Ellie up the stairs, her hands nervously clutching the rails as she ascended the steps. He waited until they were in front of the fire exit, before turning to her.

'Close your eyes,' he whispered playfully. 'No peeking.'

With her eyes sealed shut he opened the door to look out to a clear night sky. The view was everything he had hoped it would be. The fresh air was plentiful from this height.

He held Ellie's hand, slowly guiding her out on to the glass roof.

'Keep your eyes closed,' he said.

'I'm not looking,' she replied, her face cringing to exaggerate the point.

The stars were clear above them, the roof lighting giving an ambience as if they were surrounded by a hundred warm candles.

Conor took Ellie to the centre of the roof and gently let go of her hand. With her eyes still closed and her feet slightly turned in, he stole a moment to stare at her with affection. The feeling inside him had grown and it continued to grow. This was all for her, every second would be worth it.

'Can I look now?' she asked.

'Not yet,' Conor said, backing away, wanting her to be alone with a clear view. Everything needed to be perfect. 'OK, open your eyes.'

'I don't know if I want to,' she replied with a nervous giggle.

'Open your eyes!'

Ellie's eye lids slowly lifted. At first she held her breath, staring wide and mesmerised, her legs like jelly and her hands clammy and shaking. The view that greeted her was a city of lights, a picturesque display of life at night. She looked down to see only glass. She was standing on the skylight high above the ground floor. It was as if she were hovering.

She closed her eyes and waited for the fear to come; to overpower her thoughts and drive a sickening feeling into her stomach. Her body would tense up, paralysing her into panic.

But it never came. Instead she could think clearly, her shoulders dropped as her body relaxed, taking in deep, full breaths. She looked up to the stars and slowly lowered her gaze to the city.

'Beautiful,' she whispered.

'How do you feel?' Conor shouted from across the rooftop.

'I'm fine,' she cried out, laughing uncontrollably. She couldn't help it. 'I'm great!'

Her smile meant everything. From the moment he thought of doing this, he'd pictured the look on her face. The gleam in her eyes. Everything was as he had dreamed.

Conor found himself laughing along with her. He strolled over the glass to be close to her side.

'Sometimes I forget how lucky we are,' Ellie said with almost a whisper.

Conor smiled.

'You're a good person, Ellie... Nice things happen to nice people. You deserve this. You deserve everything.'

As he said it, she broke her gaze to look at him, suddenly realising the effort he'd put in to make this happen; humbled by the thought and attention. She couldn't pretend any longer; her barriers fell away when she was with him.

Before Ellie had time to be nervous she reached out to gently hold his hand, a simple gesture that told Conor everything he needed to know.

As he felt her hand lightly touch his, Conor kept his gaze forward, his heart racing, the smile on his face difficult to hide. Under the night sky they stood for what seemed like hours, holding hands and staring up at the stars.

* * *

Through his binoculars James watched in the shadows of the adjacent building. He observed intently as Ellie and Conor walked out on to the roof. He'd seen everything. Over-analysed every gesture. The pain in his chest made him sceptical and yet their silence and body language spoke volumes. He lowered the lens, revealing his watery eyes and the look of sadness on his face. In that moment and for the first time, James felt his heart break.

CHAPTER TWENTY FOUR

SARA LOUISE MORGAN

In the middle of her modest apartment, Sara curled her toes as she stood barefoot on the carpet floor. She was dressed in tight blue jean shorts and a low-cut grey vest.

With her curtains drawn and the lights off, the surrounding darkness was illuminated by the glowing screens of six wall-mounted televisions, each displaying their own channels: news feeds from three different networks; a documentary; a panel show; and a science fiction film.

A wall of noise and light; and yet the information flowed smoothly. Her eyes glanced from screen to screen. There was no feeling of chaos or white noise. It channelled to her as a steady current. A streaming river of data.

She first noticed the change in herself whilst working on the monitors back at the *Hive*. It was a fascinating side-effect to the development of her prefrontal lobe. Her peripheral vision was better than ever. She was a sponge, absorbing and digesting everything that could be taken in. Her subconscious was on overdrive.

At home she built on the concept slowly. She began by installing two televisions and running them side by side. It took a while to get used to. The blurring of colours, the mixed associations in sound. She pushed her boundaries, clearing the confusion from her mind before introducing a third screen.

Standing three to four metres back, she would try to keep up with the feeds. The financial markets scrolling to her left, the news to the centre, a repeating episode of HBO's The Newsroom to her right.

As she increased the number of screens she felt her brain fighting back, naturally reaching a threshold. She acknowledged the ache that would pulse in her head after around twenty-something minutes. But she practised with relentless tenacity, pushing the limits until they caved; eventually taking to another, her vision evolving over time. She now stood before six.

Should I tell the others? Sara still hadn't decided. At first the plan was to test her discovery before speaking to them, but she enjoyed the secrecy. With everything they had shared it was nice to have something for herself.

* * *

Raised on the south side of Stratford in East London, Sara Louise Morgan was the youngest of two sisters. Her mother was an assistant at a dental surgery, her father an account manager for a blue chip telecoms company. They lived off incomes that would cover the essentials in life but maintain an agonising orbit above the luxuries.

Though her middle class upbringing kept her grounded to social circles at a young age, it soon became clear that there was something special about Sara.

When tested, her uniquely high IQ put things into perspective, elevating her to the upper levels of state education and within reach of distinguished scholarships, granting an audience to the unique gifts she possessed. Her best gift was her curious ability to read peoples' reactions, along with her acute sense of observation.

During the latter stages of her schooling, Sara's focus drifted. She left behind the course in medicine her parents had hoped and saved for, and strayed off course towards an interest in athletics.

An appetite in sports built her a slender figure, matched only by a strength and motivation that had the capacity for rage when things didn't turn out her way.

Leaning towards her parents' wishes, Sara's first attempt at further education was to study Biomedicine at Kings College London in the Randall Division of Cell and Molecular Biophysics.

Her time there was to last four months before the first disagreement; a heated exchange between Sara and her tutoring professor on Structural Biology.

A month later, a visit from the section head ended in awkward silence when Sara openly questioned the College's approach to its research of Cell Motility, earning her the nickname 'The Unteachable'.

When a third incident followed soon after, it was suggested that Sara and the College part company.

Her move to Keble College in Oxford came at the ideal time, though her short fuse and hostile demeanour followed with it, igniting discomfort in lectures and disgruntling her tutors. History seemed set to repeat itself.

But then something happened. She met someone, a professor different from the others. A friend that would listen. Professor Daniels spoke to her as a young scientist, as an adult, allowing her to swear in front of him, to disagree and challenge. If anything he encouraged it.

The project was the first time she felt part of something, an ambition to channel her energy.

In hindsight the team would probably remember her as being the most cynical about their success, but she had enjoyed being wrong just this once.

These days she didn't spend a great deal of time looking back. Her broken family in London were an irritation she rarely checked in on.

* * *

With the glow of televisions reflecting in her eyes, Sara made fists with her toes on the soft carpet floor, the humming noise from her mobile ringtone gently rising above the sound of the channels, barely enough to be heard. Her concentration was slow to break, but on realising she muted the TVs with a master remote and took the call.

'Hey, Rolo,' she answered.

'I wish you wouldn't call me that.'

'I know.'

'We're on for tomorrow night.'

'OK.' Sara glanced to her watch.

'You're sure about this?'

'Of course I'm sure. And so are you.'

'I know, it's just... Shouldn't we tell the others?'

Sara sighed. 'We'll tell them when we're ready.'

CHAPTER TWENTY FIVE

EXQUISITE TASTE

Conor was greeted with a welcoming smile from the concierge as he walked through the main entrance, pushing aside the interior glass door and stepping into the main reception area.

'Welcome to the MacDonald Randolph, sir,' the man said. 'Have you made a reservation?'

'Table for two, under the name of Martin,' Conor replied, loosening his jacket from his shoulders and handing it to a servicing waitress. He was wearing a navy blue suit over a white shirt and a sky blue tie.

Scanning through the register, the concierge made a small mark against his records before glancing back to Conor with acceptance.

'This way please,' he said, gesturing to the restaurant floor.

Conor followed, keeping his chin high and eye line forward. He tried his best not to appear intimidated by the grandeur of the venue. All around him sat the wealth of Oxford; the cream of society - the unmistakeable sound of bellowing laughter and polished chuckling, the stylish business executives and their fake smiles, the popping of champagne corks and the light ting of toasting flutes.

To his left a pianist gave a soft rendition of the first movement from Mozart's Concerto Twenty One Andante. The main chandelier lights were dimmed, leaving candlelight and glowing table lamps to offer a perfect balance in tone.

The concierge walked with his hands held together behind his back, guiding Conor through the tables and flower arrangements, past the champagne buckets and the light, friendly gurgle of civilised conversation. They arrived finally at the table Conor had insisted on when he made his reservation. It was by the window, elevated slightly by a short step. A table with a view, it gave a sense of occasion.

The concierge gave a slight bow as Conor sat at the table.

'Have a pleasant evening, sir,' he said before returning to the reception desk. A tall and elegant waiter approached in his place, introducing himself as 'Marcus'.

'Are we expecting company this evening, sir?' he asked.

'She's on her way,' Conor sighed. Just once he'd like to pick her up, to take her out. He grew tired of meeting her in secret like a special agent.

It had been over three months since Ellie and Conor had started seeing each other. It was a relationship that had grown both cryptic and ambiguous over time. Neither were able to communicate their feelings well, and Ellie in particular often showed nerves that she'd struggle to control.

What they instantly agreed on was secrecy. No one was to know of their romance. The last thing either of them had wanted was for whatever this was to factor into the project. Sara was so perceptive and the professor missed little; they had to be careful.

'Will you be drinking wine?' the waiter asked, handing Conor the wine list.

'I hope so,' Conor replied. Missing the occasional glass was only natural. He grinned mischievously, wondering whether Ellie would agree to a sly one.

'Let's wait until the lady arrives, perhaps,' Conor said, digesting the prices under a breath.

'Of course, sir,' the waiter responded.

He waited patiently, attending to the finer details. The candle on the table was lit, the menu and solitary rose perfectly positioned.

The best view and chair reserved for her. He had arrived early on purpose to make sure everything was as he wanted.

Conor was picking at a bread roll from the centre basket when, from across the restaurant, he saw her.

Walking with beautiful uncertainty, a slightly tilted head, an innocence that was so endearing. He gazed at his date as she made her way, the concierge guiding her to the table. She was wearing a dark purple strapless dress, thin black high heels, a silver Tiffany necklace and matching earrings.

'Enjoy your meal, madam,' the concierge said, smiling before he left.

Conor stood up from the table, exhaling as he admired her up and down.

'You look stunning.'

'Thank you,' Ellie replied, giving a curtsy.

He walked round the table to give her an affectionate kiss on the cheek before pulling back her chair.

'Happy birthday,' he whispered.

After a short while Ellie was enjoying Conor's sweet, yet sometimes awkward, pillow talk and had conceded to a small glass of Sauvignon Blanc to accompany their food.

Conor did well, taking control of ordering Ellie's indulgent choice of a fillet of Limousin veal with braised shin, rainbow chard, Saint George mushrooms, shallot and sage jus, pronouncing the course with a passable familiarity. She was impressed.

Nearly two hours later and Conor was wiping the corner of his mouth with a serviette. He rested it on the table and looked down at his empty dessert plate.

Leaning forward he pressed down on his forehead with his left thumb and forefinger, feeling the familiar sting grow in his frontal lobe. He took slow and steady breaths.

'Headache?' Ellie asked.

'No more than usual,' he dismissed.

'They don't get any better, if you're wondering.'

'And that doesn't bother you?'

'If I let it I would fall behind. The project needs sacrifices.' Ellie shrugged her shoulders. 'A headache isn't really a sacrifice is it?'

'If that's all it is.'

'Are you all right?' she asked. 'You've been distant for the last few minutes.'

Conor's eyes wandered the room before returning to Ellie.

'I've just been thinking... Feeling... Like perhaps I'm a little out of my league.'

'Nice things happen to nice people,' Ellie said, smiling. Conor returned the gesture but it felt more condoling. 'What's bothering you?' she asked.

'I've been trying to figure it out.'

'What?'

'Why I was chosen.'

Ellie looked at him blankly, unable to give him what he wanted. Conor softened his voice.

'Look, Sara is well on her way to a Masters in Biomedicine and James has a degree in IT. You're an expert in Biology and Neuroscience and even with everything we know, none of us match the professor's experience in Neurology... and I'm... I...' Conor wasn't sure how to finish his sentence.

'You passed the test,' Ellie said, trying not to sound condescending.

'Maybe that's the problem,' Conor thought aloud. 'Maybe I shouldn't have.'

'Stop it,' Ellie dismissed.

'I don't feel like I belong here.'

'Don't be ridiculous.'

'Maybe the test wasn't hard enough.'

'Stop it!' Ellie was quick to realise that her voice had risen louder than intended. A couple on a nearby table had offered a curious glance before returning their attention to each other.

Ellie leaned in to speak quietly.

'You're still thinking in the old ways, Conor. Grades? Degrees? These are tools used to classify someone's knowledge of a skill. How is that relevant, knowing what we know?'

'So what am I? The simple idiot made interesting? Am I to be the shining example for the professor to parade before the Board when he plucks up the courage?'

'Don't talk about him that way,' Ellie snapped. 'He's sacrificed more than you know.'

David P. Philip

Conor gave a smirk before swallowing down the last of his wine. He glanced to his right, beyond the tables to the bar area.

At first sight he rejected it, a flash from the corner of his eye. He squinted, focusing for a better look but a table was clearing and the faces of strangers obscured his view.

'You don't feel it, do you?' Ellie asked, staring down at the table.

'Feel what?'

'The strength, the power, the privilege.' She looked up to meet his eyes.

'I feel something... I'm not sure it's what you feel.'

'But you do feel something... I can see it. You're changing, I've been watching as it happens.'

'Everyone changes,' Conor whispered.

'Yes, but when it's not for the better it matters. Don't lose yourself.'

'Look, stop wasting your time trying to figure me out, OK?! I've given up on that myself!'

Ellie recoiled at Conor's outburst, staring at him inquisitively as he sulked. He'd never spoken to her like that before. She didn't feel threatened by it; if anything she was intrigued, it was another interesting ingredient to his personality.

'Sorry,' Conor finally broke the silence. 'Words, that's all that was... Just words.'

'I hope so,' Ellie said softly.

He lowered his head, for a moment feeling ashamed and sorrowful, glancing away to return his gaze to the bar area. Leaning into his chair a look suddenly washed over him. He couldn't believe it.

The seconds were passing in slow motion, leading to the inevitable moment when they would be seen. Their elevated table had become a goldfish bowl. Vulnerable, exposed, there was nowhere to hide.

Samuel drank his whisky, resting up against the bar in a tuxedo. He didn't appear to notice them at first. But then it happened; the acknowledgement, the wave, a raised glass in toast.

'What?' Ellie asked.

A GAME FOR THE YOUNG

Conor's eyes danced across the surface of their table. *What were the odds?!* He tried to piece together the excuses in his head. There was no time. He looked up to see his friend closing in with a grin over his face.

'What is it?' Ellie asked.

'I know you, don't I?' Samuel jested to Conor. 'You look like an old friend I once knew.'

Conor looked up to acknowledge Samuel standing over them.

'Yes, yes. I've been busy,' he said, raising his hands with shameful apology.

'You've been invisible,' Samuel replied, his tone difficult to judge. 'I would have asked what you've been up to but now I see.' Samuel turned to greet Ellie. 'Samuel Milton,' he said, offering his hand.

'Ellie Swanson,' she replied, accepting it with a light shake.

Samuel pulled up a chair from an empty table next to them.

'Mind if I join you?'

Conor almost cringed.

'Of course not,' Ellie replied, picking up on Conor's discomfort with curiosity.

'Have we met?' Samuel squinted at Ellie. 'Your face seems familiar?'

'I don't think so,' she replied.

'Interesting, perhaps it was in a dream.' Samuel gave a charismatic smirk, suggesting his time at University had improved his charm with women.

'Who are you here with?' Conor looked over his shoulder.

'I'm meeting an intriguing beauty by the name of Chloe,' Samuel answered, glancing back to the bar. 'Or at least I thought I was! She must have got lost.'

He shrugged, placing his drink on the table. 'So... What's new? Tell me something interesting.'

'There's no such thing as the human regression theory. You made it up.'

'I make up a lot of things.'

'How's the degree coming?' Conor sighed, picking a bone from his teeth.

'I'm learning Algebraic Geometry.'

'What's that?' Ellie asked, playing it slow.

'I've absolutely no idea. What's more I fear I'll have no idea a month from now.'

'I'm sorry to hear that,' Conor offered.

'Oh don't be, in Oxford there are plenty of ways to keep a man preoccupied. Gambling, sports, women, riddles and codes. You of all people know that.'

Conor's reaction was instinctive, a telling look hidden behind a plastic smile.

'What does that mean?' Ellie asked, her tone calm and unassuming.

Samuel theatrically glanced to Conor

'It's not *still* a secret is it, old boy?' He spoke with a touch of sarcasm to his voice.

Conor's eyes rose from the table towards Ellie in apprehension. She wasn't reacting.

'He didn't tell you about that code? Well I suppose people are calling it a prank now, after all. I guess with hindsight you must feel a little embarrassed considering how it monopolised you.'

'I tried to forget,' Conor said. 'It's Ellie's birthday, by the way.'

'Happy birthday, Ellie,' Samuel offered.

'Thank you. So what happened with this code?' She looked straight ahead to Conor.

'It was nothing in the end.'

'Everything has meaning.' Ellie finished her drink.

'Well said,' Samuel agreed, noticing an atmosphere brewing. With both their glasses empty he rose to his feet. 'Let me get you guys a drink. What are you having?'

'I'll have an orange juice please,' Conor answered, his choice prompting a sigh in disappointment. Samuel turned to Ellie.

'A large gin and tonic,' she said. 'I feel rebellious.'

'A woman after my own heart,' Samuel said, grinning as he left the table. He strolled across the restaurant floor, gracefully waiving in and around the tables, over-familiar with his surroundings.

The smile on Ellie's face soon vanished, her body language turning cold and serious.

'You told someone?' she whispered.

'About the code, nothing more. I had no way of knowing...'

'Who else have you told?'

'No one, don't overreact. It's nothing.'

'What else does he know?' Ellie's voice nearly broke. Her piercing stare made it clear she was furious. This was no longer a date; it was an interrogation.

'Nothing.'

'Nothing? Absolutely nothing more? You're clear on that, yes?'

Conor sank, fearful as to how far this could go if he lied. He glanced to the happy couple standing up to leave by the table next to them, observing their affectionate giggles with jealousy.

'He knows why I checked into the Hospital. He knows I was poisoned.'

As he said it, Ellie stayed silent, overcome by disappointment. Trust meant everything to her. This was a betrayal of the worst kind.

'Funny, he didn't mention that. Did he? Why is that, I wonder?' Her tone was cynical.

'I don't know. Look, he doesn't know anything.'

'He knows plenty. More than you realise or are prepared to accept. I can't believe you hid this from me.' Ellie breathed in deep for composure, under the table her hands were clawing at her chair. Conor's sorrowful eyes tried to meet hers.

'Are you going to tell the others?' he asked.

Ellie didn't answer. She couldn't. Reaching into her bag for her purse, she stood up to place a twenty pound note by the candle. A token gesture.

'Are you going to tell the others?' Conor repeated, his face showing the signs of desperation. Tucking in her chair, she gave him nothing before turning to leave.

Conor watched as she made her way towards Samuel. Holding a tray of drinks, he appeared confused as she approached him. They exchanged a few words, before she took her drink from his tray, downing it in one swift motion and cringing as she swallowed.

Conor made out her mouthing the words 'Lovely to have met you Samuel,' before she walked in to the reception area to collect her coat, disappearing from view. He slumped his head into his hands.

'Well, dear boy,' Samuel said, approaching the table to sit in Ellie's chair. 'Fancy telling me where the fuck you've been?'

CHAPTER TWENTY SIX

A SMARTER OPPONENT

'Rook to bishop four.' Conor spoke his move quietly, nudging his piece into position and thumping his hand down on the Jantar Chess Watch to his left. His face was calm and motionless, his palms flat on the table. Chess at this level was as much about composure and self-control as it was tactics and skill.

James stared at him intensely from across the coffee table, searching for something to go on, subtly probing for weaknesses. The clock above them bore down on 2AM.

Across the *Hive*, Sara lay asleep on the operating table. A *take* on Neuraxial Anesthesia neared ninety-five percent. The progress bar slowly drew to completion.

The professor stood over her, arms folded, offering an occasional glance to the duel of wits in the corner. Introducing a casual night of chess had made things interesting.

Some believed it to be a relaxing night off - a comforting gift sandwiched between their studies. But Conor and James saw things differently. To them this was a test, an opportunity for the professor to establish a natural hierarchy of intellect within the team. He wouldn't confirm either way.

Over the passing minutes Ellie observed the readings fed from *Einstein* until finally nodding in acceptance.

'Transfer complete,' she said, turning to face the professor.

He made his way around the table to pick up the syringe he'd prepared.

'Administering stimulant,' he said, gesturing in a slow and clear motion, speaking loud enough for the video camera to pick up his voice. He pushed the syringe into the cannula on Sara's hand and pressed down on the plunger.

It was too soon to declare success but the team had recently switched from slowly reviving a subject with Ritalin to the more rapid arousal in Modafinil. The results were pretty convincing.

Moments later and Sara was blinking her eyes repeatedly, taking slow and steady breaths.

The professor briskly took her through the checks before she leaned forward, holding her forehead and offering a quiet groan.

'Headache?' Ellie asked. The symptom had become routine.

Sara nodded her head, approving the standard prescription of Hydrocodone to be placed in her hand.

From across the room James responded with a snigger.

'Too obvious. Bishop to Queen six.' Conor sat back into the sofa, glancing over to the operating table before standing up.

'Where are you going?' James asked, opening a packet of pills to take with a glass of water.

'Just move my pieces for a second, will you?' Conor made his way towards the professor.

'What's your move?'

'Bishop to king three.' He didn't look back. 'It's my turn on the next *take* right?' Conor's tone made it practically a statement.

'Correct,' the professor responded, apprehension in his voice. He opened the medicine cabinet and took out some pain killers. He'd been suffering from a migraine himself for most of the night.

'I was hoping to learn about Econometrics.'

'Why?'

'It would help with our research. Quantitative analysis, data relationships.'

The professor exhaled as he closed the cabinet. 'No.'

'No?' Conor winced.

'No,' the professor turned to face him. 'You don't want to learn quantitative analysis. You want to learn about

Econometric models, a methodology that equips you with the skills to work the stock exchange... or some other financial market. Either way, the answer's no.'

Conor tried to appear insulted, his expression as defensive as he could make it. He soon dropped his shoulders. The professor was right on point.

'Aren't we past this?'

'We've been through the rules,' the professor said. 'If we use this procedure for personal gain then what are we doing here? It undermines everything.'

'Queen to knight five,' James shouted from the corner.

'We've been receiving data packets for months,' Conor argued. 'I can list all of the elements of the neuron doctrine off by heart. I could take you through the pros and cons of each of the eight different neuroimaging techniques available today. If you like, I could recite, in date order, the key events that led to the discovery of Cognitive Psychology and draw a picture depicting the stages of growth in a biological neural network with the use of...'

'Queen to knight five!'

'Knight to king six... Check!' Conor responded instinctively.

James stared at the pieces on the table.

'Son of a bitch,' he whispered.

'I know how to prove algorithms that would stump most senior scholars,' Conor continued. 'I don't care what social circles you swim in, you can't tell me this knowledge isn't valuable.'

The professor raised his hands.

'OK, I appreciate what you're saying, but if we start simply learning what we want, is that a research project? What message are we sending to our peers? When the time comes, one of the first questions they'll want to address is how this is controlled.'

'Controlled?!' Conor appeared angered by the suggestion.

'Queen to bishop four.'

'Licence,' the professor explained. 'The decision on who can use this and when? In the wrong hands this procedure is dangerous. The means to build explosive weaponry, mortal combat at someone's fingertips. Years are spent building this knowledge in controlled environments. This technology has the potential to open up subjects that are difficult to learn for good reason.'

'If someone is intent on causing harm they'll find a way with or without this,' Conor disagreed.

'Queen to bishop four!'

'That doesn't imply immunity,' Ellie spoke. 'If this was used to achieve deadly force that would practically make us accomplices.'

Conor turned to face her. It was the first time she'd spoken to him for two days.

'So this can only be used by nice people wanting to learn nice things?!' He bit his tongue in frustration. 'Why is everyone focusing on the negatives? This should be a celebration! Now is the time to demonstrate that you can learn what you want with this procedure. You can change your life overnight.'

'Are you forfeiting?' James shouted.

'Rook to bishop three, check mate!' Conor snapped.

James shook in his chair.

'Fuuuuck you!' he screamed, staring at the board.

The professor sighed, looking away in thought.

'Just let me think about it, OK, Richard?'

Conor frowned.

'Who's Richard?' After all this time, the least the professor could do was get his name right.

His response jolted the professor. He glanced to the floor, rubbing the left side of his forehead with an open palm.

'Sorry, Conor,' he said, grimacing. 'Look, we're all tired and it's starting to show. Let's take a couple of days off, enjoy some sleep. I'll have a think about what you've said. I promise.'

The professor could feel himself slipping. Caffeine tablets could only do so much.

Almost daily the rules were being tested. He'd set them in stone from the beginning to prevent this from happening and yet there it was all the same, slowly unfolding before his eyes. Perhaps it was human nature to dwell in disappointment at what you can, rather than ponder in hope at what you could.

The team around him were becoming sharper, more receptive; alert and questioning. The clock was ticking, counting down to that inevitable day when they would mutiny. Needing time to think was an excuse; a stalling tactic that was both obvious and weak. No one was impressed.

CHAPTER TWENTY SEVEN

JAMES THOMAS MCCARTHY

James turned up his coat collar as he opened the door out into the cold. Cautiously he looked in both directions. Unlike the others, the use of the fire exit on the east wing of the warehouse wasn't optional. The door led to an eerie ground level car park. He was exposed every time. The last to leave before the professor.

His journey home was always uncomfortable. A man in a wheelchair on the streets at 3AM simply stood out. If he caught someone's eye it was difficult to dismiss. The reasoning that bit harder to justify, or at least that's how he used to feel.

What he came to realise was a depressing truth. People generally go out of their way to ignore each other. Eye-lines often low, hands in pockets.

For as long as his head was down and he appeared disinterested with his surroundings, he wasn't acknowledged, approached or remembered.

In any case the initial mystery and excitement had worn off. No one was watching. No one cared.

James made his way along the pavement near Jowett Walk, his hands cold against the steel as he turned the wheels.

Born in Edinburgh, James was raised able-bodied; agile, even. He spent his childhood attending private schools and enjoying privileges that were accustomed to a family born into money.

By nine he was an accomplished swimmer, showing little fear on the diving board and an above-average skier, frequently relishing trips to the Alps to help master the art of the black slopes.

A GAME FOR THE YOUNG

But five weeks after his eleventh birthday everything had changed. Whilst on a morning ride in the hills of Drimsynie in Argyll, his horse suddenly startled and broke into a canter on uneven ground. James lost his right foot stirrup and held on with all his strength, but when his horse began to gallop she lost her footing.

His father watched in horror as they fell, rolling helplessly down a jagged embankment and landing on the rocks with a series of deafening cracks.

James remembered little of that day. He was told how his horse, a beautiful chestnut Clydesdale called Red Night, broke two of her legs and was covered with deep and aching cuts. They had no choice but to put her down.

James was found ten feet away, flat on his back, staring up at the clouds. Traumatised, in silence and unable to move. He was covered in cuts and bruises. His rib cage was cracked and broken, his left arm fractured and twisted. But the worst was yet to come.

At the base of his back he had picked up extensive spinal injuries. The doctors did what they could, attempting procedure after procedure, but it was too late. He had become semi-paraplegic and was unable to control the motor functions in the lower half of his body. His mother wept as they delivered the news, delicately taking them through the reasons why he was destined to remain in a wheelchair for the rest of his life.

His rehabilitation took years. James became fearful of sudden movements, of change, the dark, anything that discomforted him or made him feel vulnerable.

He was privately tutored through secondary school, living a secluded and lonely childhood. It wasn't until he was fifteen that he finally turned a corner and began to venture outdoors. His communication skills improved with his confidence.

Over a decade on from the accident and James was now twenty two, carrying a self belief and determination that was inspiring. Many marvelled at his achievement of an honorary degree in Computing and IT, finishing second in his class at Nuffield.

There was a time when things had come so quickly to him, he could see so clearly. The *takes* amplified his intellect and sharpened his mind. But those days had drifted from him. He couldn't even say when it happened. Perhaps two months ago, maybe three, but gradually he felt a shift. His brain slowly straying from centre, his focus failing despite his efforts.

James hadn't slept properly for months. The longest scientific study of a person going without sleep was eleven days and he'd come close to it on several occasions.

Eventually he found using Estazolam helped him sleep. But what did that mean? Was he now dependant on drugs to support the procedure? Was this an inevitable conclusion waiting for the others? Every night he'd look for signs within the team but they seemed so sharp.

James had seen them get the headaches, receiving the usual dose of Hydrocodone or Oxycodone to deal with it, but James had to be honest with himself; he was now addicted to pain killers.

He had to raise this. He had to explain what he was going through. It was agonising.

What would happen if they knew? Would he be cut from the team? Would his secret end the project altogether? There were days when his head was on fire, but with every *take* he learnt more. Perhaps he was addicted to more than pain killers.

If only that were everything. Nights with Ellie were unbearable. His heart ached in misery and became only more exasperated by the knowledge that she was oblivious to his pain. *Conor!* It all started to go wrong when he came on the scene.

James turned his mind back to the chess match, reciting the positioning of the pieces, trying to play out the game in some other way. He couldn't understand it. Conor had never beaten him at anything until recently. Never. It was now a regular event. The frustration enraged him.

As the lift opened out on to the second floor of Holywell buildings, he began wheeling himself down the corridor. His mobile rang in his pocket.

'It's late,' he answered with a whisper, approaching the door to his home.

'We need to talk,' Sara said, her voice sounding agitated.

'I know.'

'You promised to help me.'

'And I will,' he assured her, reaching into his jacket pocket for his keys.

'Then when?'

'Soon.'

'Make it sooner, Rolo,' she hung up.

CHAPTER TWENTY EIGHT

PROOF YOU'VE LIVED

Scuffing his feet along the river bank, Conor stumbled to a slow walk, profusely sweating and coughing until his throat was sore. He leant forward to grip just above his knees, spitting saliva onto the footpath. His breath was wheezy.

It had been more than six months since his last run. For the life of him he couldn't remember why. Finding fitness was always a steeper climb than maintaining.

The crisp morning air had woken him as he made his way out of the car park of Tennyson. His legs felt the cold. His feet were spongy and soft.

But he wasn't far into Gloucester Green before his first pause. Panting with frustration and glancing to his watch, his body felt tired before he had even got started. The sting in his chest reminded him of when he needed an inhaler.

A long morning passed in slow motion, leaving Conor's pride battered, his swollen feet and calves raw.

The warmth of his shower came as a soothing relief. Resting his head against the tiles he slowly lowered until he fell with a thud to slump on the shower room floor. His eyes closed and head slouched.

Six months.

Saying it now he gave it the respect it deserved. His mind was sharp but his body was a blunt disgrace. The procedure was supposed to make time, free him to do as he pleased. But to a man his age, free time would often mean downtime. He'd become lazy, slow.

Struggling to his feet, he fumbled his way to the sink basin, wiping the condensation from the mirror to peer at his reflection. Gritting his teeth, he threw water over his face.

He lowered his head, staring in disbelief at the sight of blood trickling down his chin and dripping into the sink. A solitary line of red was flowing from his nose.

'Shit!' he grabbed some toilet tissue and tilted up his head to stop the bleeding. 'Shit, shit!'

The blood in his nose was slow to clot. An hour later and Conor was still shaken. Had he pushed himself too far? What was wrong with him? *No, no. I'm fine. I'm great... I have to be.*

* * *

'What are *you* doing here?' James asked, staring up at Ellie, who was standing in the doorway of the *Hive*. He wheeled himself past her before glancing to his watch. It was 10.35PM. He was sure he'd be the first to arrive. He needed to be the first.

As he looked back to Ellie, James caught a brief look of uncertainty on her face. There was a discomfort in the room.

Ellie glanced to the professor, standing by the operating table, acknowledging an approving nod before she spoke.

'We've been working on digital signatory.'

'What's that?' James frowned.

'Marking a *take*,' Ellie simplified. 'A digital marker to home in on the resting place of an implanted memory, like a map co-ordinate to the neurons.'

'You two love birds needed to be alone for that?' James smiled, humoured by their private club.

Ellie and the professor gave each other another telling glance, notably proud with their achievement.

'There's more,' the professor explained. 'By mapping a *take* with digital signatory, we've found a way of redirecting the synaptic pathways with remotion.'

James eyes widened.

'Redirecting synaptic pathways? Like what we did with Ellie's fear of heights?'

'This is the next step.'

'Removing the *take*?' James voice stammered.

175

'We're talking about isolating the memory,' the professor corrected. 'Allowing it to dissolve into grey matter.'

'You're serious?!'

Ellie could see James's face grimace.

'It's still theoretical.'

'Don't do that,' the professor said, turning to her.

'Do what?'

'Dilute our achievement. This will work and you know it. Be proud.'

'Erasing memory?!' James spoke a little louder to bring back their attention.

'I know,' the professor smiled, misreading the tone. 'We should be in a position to try it within the next few days. Perhaps with some support we could...'

'Haven't we done enough?' James interrupted, his voice breaking as he said it.

The Professor took a step back to compose himself.

'We have to learn each step before racing to the next,' James pleaded. 'The risks are too extreme. I'm uncomfortable with this.'

He could see the confusion in their eyes. His reaction was clearly disappointing them. *What did they expect?* He would never have agreed to this. The professor had chosen his accomplice well, exploiting Ellie's gratitude and desire to please.

'I had hoped you'd have a little more faith, James?' The professor held back his disheartenment.

'I'm sorry,' James whispered. 'But this is too far. I think you both know that.'

'What makes you say that?' Ellie asked, taking a seat.

'The secrecy. The fact that you've done this off-plan. This was never part of the project.'

The professor's face was difficult to read. Had it finally happened? The moment James knew would eventually come. Had they finally reached a breaking point in their unity? A difference in opinion that divided them conclusively, bringing an end to everything?

They had always presumed the grandeur of their achievement would reduce the consequence of their betrayal when everything was pitched to the Board. James was beginning to understand how naive that was.

Listening to them proudly announce their accomplishment had put him in the shoes of the senior professors. For a moment he had stepped out of the exclusivity of the project and was feeling as he imagined they would. Furious, angered by the deceit.

James squinted a look of concern to the professor. He needed to speak to him alone.

'You're just bitter, Rolo,' Ellie whispered.

James turned to face her, struggling to control the ferocity burning in his veins. She'd never called him that before. As he went to speak a thud came from the door, breaking the awkward silence in the room. It was almost sympathetic in its timing.

At first no one moved to answer, each mindful of the suspicious glances, the cold atmosphere in the *Hive* awaiting the new arrival.

Ellie finally sighed, slowly rising from her chair to open the door. Sara was quick to push her way in.

'What took you so long?' she asked, noticeably annoyed.

'Did you know about this?' James asked.

'Know about what?' Sara rubbed her hands together to warm herself.

'They're working on a way to remove a *take*.' James gestured to the professor.

'Oh, yeah, how's it going?' she asked, turning to the others.

'Very well,' the Professor responded, the sound of achievement returning to his voice. 'We're just preparing the algorithms to...'

'You *knew* about this?' James grimaced.

'Sure, didn't you?'

'It was practically Sara's idea,' the professor said, his palms gestured open. 'You've each been given your own assignments.'

James had never felt more alienated.

'Why is this such a surprise?' Ellie challenged. 'What kind of hypocrite does the things we've done and then starts talking about risk?'

'Why would you ever need to erase a memory?' James pointed to his right temple. 'If something isn't needed your cerebrum has a perfectly efficient way of disposing of it.'

'Does it?' the professor winced. 'When considering that knowledge changes us, our perceptions, our perspectives. Is it so hard to imagine that someone would need to remove unwanted memory?'

James could feel himself outnumbered, the others encircling him with their opinions, their biased views. He lowered his eye line to the floor.

'Is there anything else? Is there anything more I need to know?'

He glanced up to the professor in hope, willing him to shake his head or smile, but he gave up nothing.

'I think we need to agree a point where this stops. A point where we've proven enough. Maybe it's time to speak to the Board?'

As James said it everyone jumped.

'We're at a pivotal stage,' the professor said.

'It's always pivotal. There'll always be another procedure!' James tried to reason with them. 'We can't keep going on this way, blindly moving from one objective to the next.'

His words cut the professor deep, his composure recoiling in concession.

Before he had a chance to speak, two knocks came from the door.

Ellie gave a smile in response, quickly rising to her feet to answer it.

* * *

Conor picked up the pace as he ascended the inner stairs of Tennyson, keen to leave the eerie corridors behind him. The creaking steps always seemed louder at night.

A GAME FOR THE YOUNG

The reception hall had been quiet when he arrived home a few minutes after midnight. The whole floor offered a strange feeling of desertion.

The dispute in the *Hive* was still ringing in his ears. The team's anger lingered with his thoughts. Not that an argument was anything to be surprised by. After all, walking in on a disagreement was common, but this was unlike anything he'd seen.

The group were fiercely divided, furious with one another. The implications of a regression procedure could have been interesting, but for James it was a notion that sewed doubt into everything.

Before long the atmosphere had turned toxic, the team arguing amongst themselves, exchanging verbal blows and bitter stares, the sound of frustrated huffs settling.

The trust in the room was shattered. They finally dispersed early into the night to cool their tongues.

Coming off the stairs, Conor kept his head low as he made for his room. He was thinking hard on his feet, often oblivious to his surroundings. It took a sudden crashing noise from down the hall to startle him back into focus - the distinct sound of snapping wood and smashing glass.

He slowed, waiting to see whether any of the doors along the hall would open. *It sounded like it was coming from his room.* He stared at his door at the end of the corridor. Inching closer, he tried to make out from a distance whether it had been forced.

As he drew nearer the noise steered him away to the opposite side of the corridor, to Samuel's door, resting slightly ajar. Gently he pushed it open.

First the smell hit him. An odour of sweat, cigarette smoke and the remnants of drunken beer cans. The room before him was a mess. The bed mangled and up-turned, the TV was face down in the corner, the desk broken into four or five pieces with shards of wood and glass spread across the floor.

Sat barefoot pressed against the back wall, in ripped jeans and a red T-shirt, he found Samuel. He was unshaven, with an open bottle of Jack Daniels whisky by his side. His expression was cold and vacant.

Samuel squinted, his blurred eyesight making out Conor in the doorway.

'Oh, Conor. Welcome,' he mumbled. 'Be careful where you tread, there's smashed glass on the floor somewhere over there.' He pointed to the corner whilst picking up his cigarettes and lighter.

Lighting a cigarette, he discarded the packet somewhere to his right.

Conor was speechless. It took him a moment to find the words.

'What the hell are you doing?!'

'Corresponding,' Samuel replied, flicking the ash from his cigarette on to the carpet with a faint smile.

'With what?'

He pointed with his hand shaped like a gun to the base of the bed. Among the wood splinters and bottle fragments lay a screwed up piece of paper.

Conor bent down to pick it up, shaking the pieces of glass free. Quickly he opened it, noting the official emblem of the University in the letter heading.

'Dear Mr Samuel Milton Esquire,' he read aloud. 'It is with regret that we must inform you, having reviewed your latest assignment and in light of suspicious...' Conor lowered his voice as he read on, Samuel watching as the words registered on his face.

'Expelled with immediate effect,' Samuel announced, the drunken slur evident in his voice. He raised his whisky bottle in salute.

'Cheating?' Conor's face scowled in disbelief. 'This isn't right! There are steps they need to follow. You can appeal against this!'

'Oh, Conor you innocent soul. Everyone cheats. Everyone lies.'

'Not everyone.'

'Then perhaps the best of Oxford will be left behind.'

Conor stepped towards him, the crunching rustle of debris under his feet.

'Still, it's worth trying to...'

'My dear boy, why would I bother? I have everything I need.'

As he said it Conor saw the acceptance in Samuel's eyes. There was no fight in him. He lowered the letter to his side and leaned up against the back wall, sliding down it to sit beside his friend. He took the whisky from Samuel to have a drink of his own.

'Proof you've lived?' Conor offered, lifting the bottle to his lips. Samuel nodded. 'Then why?'

Conor gestured to the chaos.

'A parting gift.'

Conor raised his knees to his chest.

'What will you do now?' He passed back the bottle.

Samuel sniggered before breaking into a series of coughs to clear his throat.

'I'm sure my father already has something lined up.'

'You told him?'

'No, but my parents' expectations of me are so low that I have to work very hard just to disappoint them.'

'And he can get you a job? Just like that?' Conor clicked his fingers.

'How do you think I got here in the first place?' Samuel laughed. 'Dear boy, where I'm from it's all phone calls and favours.'

How the other half live. Conor looked down to the crumpled letter in his hand.

'Then maybe you should get your father to call the University, straighten this whole thing out? This is a matter for Pembroke anyway, it doesn't make sense.'

'Oh, it makes perfect sense,' Samuel said, taking a drink from the bottle and swallowing it down with a slight cringe. 'They're making an example of me and rightly so, spoilt little rich kids can't have it all their way.'

Conor placed the letter on the floor. Samuel watched as the emotion drained from his face.

'Look, try to imagine that the world doesn't revolve around Oxford. I know it's hard,' he jested.

Conor paused before choosing his words.

'You know, there was a time when maybe that would have been difficult, but no. Not now.'

Samuel smiled.

'Yes, I can see it. You've changed. Whatever it is, I hope it's made you a better man.'

'I'm going to miss you, you bloody idiot.'

'You've got your hands full.'

'Not for much longer.'

'You looked like a nice couple?'

'All things end.'

Samuel chuckled lightly as he took another turn on the whisky bottle.

'I need to ask you something.' Conor leaned forward. 'It's important.'

Samuel tilted his head as he stubbed his cigarette out on the carpet.

'That code...' Conor took a breath. 'Did you break it for me?'

He wasn't even sure he wanted to know the answer, but this was it. His only chance to learn the truth. He turned his head to find Samuel offering an odd smile.

'What makes you think I could? Or more interestingly, what makes you think you couldn't?'

'Please, no riddles. I need to know.'

Samuel could see he was serious.

'I knew about your code long before you told me. You really must lock your door, old boy.' He leaned back against the wall and sighed, shaking his head. 'No, I didn't break your code. Christ, I wouldn't know where to start. But it sounds like you're not convinced you did, either. Will you still not tell me what you've been doing?'

Conor looked away before taking the whisky bottle from Samuel's hand for another drink.

'I'm sorry, I can't,' Conor replied, cringing as he felt the whisky pass down his throat. 'But it's important. It's changing my life.' He offered the bottle back.

'I hope you know what you're doing. Just get what you want from this place and then get the hell out. I don't need to know any more.'

Conor came within a whisper of telling Samuel everything. He owed him that much. But as he went to speak, the words didn't come. The moment merely came and went.

Together they made empty promises. Modest talk of meeting up later in life. Trading stories and reminiscing on some of the funniest nights they'd shared. Conor sat with him for nearly an hour.

But when Conor turned to leave and offered a final glance back to his friend, he couldn't help acknowledge a bitter truth. They'd never see each other again.

CHAPTER TWENTY NINE

GOVERNED BY RULES

Conor's fist slammed against the steel door of the *Hive*, leaving his hand aching. He stood poised, his eyes piercing the door, waiting, daring it to open. His blood pumping from the pace he'd marched through the maze. The pieces had clicked into place.

Ellie barely had the chance to bring the door ajar before he burst through it.

'You son of a bitch!' he yelled.

'I beg your pardon?' the professor calmly replied, standing by the reading table.

Conor raised a finger in warning.

'Don't do it. Don't even try to pretend you weren't part of this.'

'Part of what?'

'Samuel Milton. You had him expelled.' Conor's voice growled as he said it. 'Tell me why?'

The professor remained placid and composed, lowering the lid of his laptop to give Conor his full attention.

'He was cheating.'

'Don't treat me like an idiot. You had him expelled to stay in control. To keep *this* safe.' Conor gestured to the *Hive,* glancing to Ellie just in time to see her look away. He scanned the room and noticed Sara by the coffee table. James hadn't arrived yet.

'And you want an apology?' the professor asked, seemingly confused by Conor's distress.

'I want you to undo what you've done.'

'Don't we all.' his response carried a sting in its tail.

'Why get him expelled?'

'You expelled him, Conor,' the professor scowled. 'You and your mouth. Even if your friend didn't know, he had cause. You gave him just enough to be curious and that was a danger we could not risk.'

'We?!' Conor turned to the others, but no one would give him eye contact. 'He may have been good for this,' Conor said, gesturing to the operating table.

'That's not your decision to make.'

'Oh, I see.'

'Oh, you do, do you?' the professor patronised.

'You've got everyone convinced that we're a team. A unit. But it's all for nothing if it's not under your conditions.'

'You're damn right!' the professor snapped, his outburst surprising even Ellie. 'Forgive me for being selfish, but *I* am the project lead. It will be *my* career that will be over when they find out the risks we've taken down here. I am the one who has remortgaged his house twice to pay for all this equipment and I am the one who's watching over you as you sleep. So yes! This project *will* be governed by my rules!'

'You talk like none of us have made sacrifices.'

'Oh, you've taken risks, sure, but you've measured them against the rewards. My fate is certain, what you've done isn't illegal.'

'Isn't illegal?! What about Begbroke? You think that little stunt was legal?'

Sara looked up.

'That was a test in a controlled environment.'

'Controlled?! I was chased by security guards!'

'Overweight and in their fifties. Anyway, we killed the security cameras.'

'What about our late night MRIs at the Hospital?' Conor challenged. 'Is it right that I know the roofing schematics to that building off by heart?'

'Calm down, we're all friends here.'

'Can that be my decision?'

'Everyone knows exactly what they've done and exactly what they're prepared to do,' the professor dismissed.

'Really?' Conor cringed, refusing to swallow the professor's response. He took a breath to think. His head was clouded with rage.

'You call this the Betterment Project. Why? Because we've found the path?! Because we're the savers of humanity?! How are you not ashamed of such arrogance?'

'The name was my idea,' Ellie whispered, pointing to the poem that hung on the wall. 'It seemed to say everything we feel.'

Conor noticed that the professor's focus had drifted, his eyes now pacing across the floor in thought. Leaning closer he spoke softly as if he were counselling.

'Why do you continue to hold back publishing this research? You can't honestly believe with everything that's been achieved that it would be rejected again. Why are you stalling the growth of our team? Be honest with everyone. Be honest with yourself. You're holding us back because right now *you* have control. That's all this is.' Conor could feel his words registering. 'Let it go,' he whispered.

'WHO THE HELL DO YOU THINK YOU ARE?!' the professor shouted furiously, his voice was an explosion. Conor recoiled in silence. 'Do you think that when this gets out, I'll be standing before a Board of senior professors? That it'll be posted on the University intranet? Announced in a newsletter?' He shook his head.

'You have no idea. Conor, we will stand before governments, before the world's finest... And they will demand we justify our claims conclusively. You forget this procedure is bigger than us - it changes everything!'

Conor could see the professor's eyes watering, his chin shaking as he spoke.

'How do you want us to be remembered? As visionaries? As scientists? Or a team of amateurs stumbling upon something we couldn't possibly understand? A bunch of chancers, rushing recklessly from one procedure to the next?'

The professor lightly punched the reading table.

'You think I don't want this published? You think I don't want what we've achieved acknowledged?' He looked away before returning with a piercing gaze. 'We have stood on the shoulders of giants, looked into our future one step ahead of the rest. I will not hold us back, but I am not about to rush in forsaking this project to quench your pathetic thirst for fame. And you ask if I am ashamed?! How dare you to think the worst of us.' He turned his head away.

'Get out!' he growled.

Muted in shock, Conor glanced to his friends for support. But it was clear where they stood. Alone he felt his feet drag as he turned for the door, strolling to a stop by the exit.

'How far will we go?' he said, with almost a whimper. 'How far is too far? What would we do to keep this safe?' He looked to the team. 'Would we lie? Cheat? Steal? Would we kill to keep it ours? We need to know... We need to know before it's too late.'

He left the room, leaving the professor staring at the wall, contemplating the words they'd spoken in anger. It was difficult to gauge whether he was disappointed with Conor or himself.

Sara broke the silence. Reaching into the top drawer of the professor's desk she pulled out an envelope and placed it on the table.

'I take it you still want these?' she asked, holding up printed images of Conor leaving Begbroke Science Park holding a leather bag.

The professor sighed before reluctantly nodding.

'Keep them for now.'

* * *

Conor's anger had dulled to a petty sulk by the time he came off the stairs to the third floor of Tennyson. He felt a growing ache slowly rise across his temple as he scuffed his feet on the carpet along the corridor.

Stood outside his bedroom, he turned to notice Samuel's door ajar and pushed it open to find the room gutted of life.

He was gone. The mess on the floor had been tidied, the broken furniture removed. His wardrobe doors were wide open and emptied of designer clothes.

His musty odour still hung in the air. The smell of cigarettes, sweat and expensive aftershave slowly blew away through an open window. By morning it would be as if he had never been there.

Conor walked into the centre of the room and stood in the darkness, the outdoor street lighting coming in from the windows to offer just enough light to see.

'You know, he's not a bad person,' Ellie said from the doorway, her head resting against the frame. She must have followed him home. 'You know that, right?'

Conor didn't turn to greet her; he knew her voice.

'The professor?' He shrugged. 'I don't know him. I don't really know any of you.'

'You know me,' she whispered, walking into the room to stand next to him, offering her hand. He was slow to accept it but when he did, he held her tight.

'I'm sorry,' she said. 'You believe me, don't you?'

'Words, just words.'

'Mine count.'

Conor thought about turning his head to look her in the eyes but he couldn't.

'Do you remember your dreams?' he asked. 'I've stopped remembering mine. Perhaps I don't dream any more. But I suppose that doesn't bother you, does it?'

'Don't give up on us,' she pleaded.

'This isn't about us. This was never about us,' he whispered. 'I..' he stopped himself.

'What is it?'

'I can't trust you, can I? Not when it comes to the project. Not the professor, not the others.' His head turned towards her. 'You're capable of almost anything.'

'I want you to trust me.'

'Then tell me what you wouldn't do? Tell me how much our secret is worth.'

Ellie stared at him, her face searching for the words to keep him. She missed him so much. Lowering her head, in that moment Ellie knew she had no response. Nothing that she could comfort him with or stand by.

Her eyes watered as she accepted what was inevitable. Gently, she let go of his hand.

CHAPTER THIRTY

AN INTERESTING CHOICE OF WORDS

Dr Arthur Zimmerman had been a fully qualified psychiatrist for gone thirty years, graduating with honours from Oxford's prestigious Keble College back in the days when students were gentlemen and study was the product of paper, ink and a library card.

Strolling around his office with notable pride and holding a dusting cloth, he polished the surfaces of his bookcase, the drawers on his antique pine desk, always excessive in his attention to detail.

His day had begun as any other, the morning appointment spent negotiating the inevitable divorce between a distant couple struggling under the delusion of their marriage. A tedious series of backward conversations, encouraged along by the odd probing question. It was all in the timing.

By midday he was sat back in his crisp leather chair, spraying his table plant with cool fresh water, half-way through the chicken sandwiches his wife had made him. He followed it with the one solitary cigarette he'd allow himself every day.

But finally he had come to it. An intriguing appointment that made its way into his schedule only two days earlier. A referral from an old friend at the University.

The doctor repeatedly peered to his watch in anticipation, the minutes baring closer to 2PM. He perused through the online Guardian. He was reading a business article when the phone rang, breaking the calm ambience in the room.

Closing the browser window, he answered the call on loud speaker.

'Susan?'

'Mr Daniels is here for your two o'clock, Dr Zimmerman,' a lady's voice responded.

'Send him in,' he replied eagerly, rising from his chair and repositioning his pad and pen.

Looking up to the door, he watched as it opened to a man he'd never seen before.

'Professor Daniels?' he asked.

'Good afternoon, Dr Zimmerman,' the professor replied, stepping forward and offering his hand. Zimmerman walked round his desk to shake it gladly.

'Take a seat,' the doctor said, gesturing to the leather sofa positioned just off-centre in the middle of the room. He took up his usual seat on the opposing chair.

'So, Professor Hendry pointed you my way, did he?'

The professor rested into the sofa, responding with a friendly nod.

'How is Mike?'

'Getting married,' the professor replied.

'Again?'

'Fourth time lucky.'

'Yes, well, I should know...' Zimmerman stopped himself there. 'Would you like a drink? I can get you a pot of tea?'

'No, thank you,' the professor replied, looking around the office. 'Do you mind if I smoke?'

'If it makes you comfortable,' Zimmerman retrieved an ashtray from his desk drawer and placed it on the small glass table between them. Neither felt the need to fill the silence as William lit his cigarette. Zimmerman opened a small window to let the smoke escape.

The professor took in a long exaggerated drag, followed almost instantly by a series of coughs and splutters.

'Do you often smoke?' Zimmerman frowned.

'No, not really,' the professor confessed, looking down at the cigarette. 'Not since the Gulf. I started up again about a month ago, filthy habit,' he flicked some ash into the ashtray.

'So, William - can I call you William?'

'Of course.'

'I hope you don't mind me saying but when we spoke on the phone you seemed a little guarded.' He chose his words carefully.

'Yes, well the last psychiatrist I spoke to was appointed by the Forces. Our conversations didn't flow, shall we say.'

'I see, well let's see how we get on. This is a place where we can discuss in confidence what you like; free of embarrassment, guilt or self doubt. I am here to listen.'

'And judge?' the professor swiped.

Zimmerman kept a straight face.

'Think of me as a guide. I will ask important questions to steer us, offer an opinion perhaps, but we're only here to discuss what you want to talk about.'

The professor rose from the sofa, leaving his cigarette burning in the ashtray, and began pacing around the office, staring at the paintings on the wall and soaking up the literature on the shelves. Dr Zimmerman watched with interest.

'How do we get started?'

'Why don't you tell me what you're thinking?'

The professor stood for a while, frozen, before finally turning to speak, his palms placed together.

'Look, I don't want you to think that I'm wasting your time or being frivolous with your company. It's just that I need to talk to someone, someone that will listen. I don't know if we'll have many sessions, if any after today.'

'Could you talk with anyone else if not me?'

'My life has been very... Specific, for the past...' William tripped up on his own words. 'However many years it's been now. I've been very focused.'

'And distant?'

'My friends, family, they're a distraction.'

'Why is that?' Zimmerman asked, making notes in short hand.

'They wouldn't understand.'

'But you hope I will?'

The professor folded his arms as he leant against one of the bookcases. Dr Zimmerman continued to write on a small notepad, never straying his eye contact from the professor for more than a few seconds.

David P. Philip

'What would you like to talk about?'

The professor pushed away from the bookcase, pacing back and forth.

'I'm... I'm involved in something, an experiment if you will. It's something that will change a lot of people's lives. In time maybe even everyone.'

'In what way?'

'It's complicated. No, sorry... I don't mean to be patronising,' William apologised. 'It's just that there's only so much I'm prepared to say. I trust you understand?'

'What are you able to tell me?'

The professor wished he'd thought this through better; scratching his head, he retreated into silence.

'Is it a cure?' Dr Zimmerman asked.

'Oh yes,' he smiled. 'Very much so.'

'And you wish others understood and were thankful?'

'What makes you say that?'

'A theory. Human nature.'

The professor shook his head, reaching into his pocket to pull out some pain killers.

'Teaching is a thankless profession,' he said, tapping two pills into his hand.

'Are you OK?'

'Fine; well, I've been suffering from migraines.'

'Interesting.'

'Painful,' the professor sighed, pinching the bridge of his nose.

'Do you crave... Rest? Peace?'

'I'll get all I need when the job's done.'

'Do you crave... Acknowledgement?'

'Must I crave something?' William asked, appearing defensive.

Dr Zimmerman paused his line of questioning.

'Perhaps not. I'm simply trying to understand the reason you wish to talk with me.'

He allowed a moment to settle the tension.

'Is what you are doing dangerous?' Zimmerman asked.

'There's risk with the project, yes, but great reward.' He pointed at the doctor, holding his gaze for several seconds to amplify the point.

'How so?'

'It will help a lot of people change their lives for the better.'

Zimmerman smiled.

'Wouldn't this be easier if you simply told me? I am bound by the laws of confidentiality if it helps.' He gestured to the room, hoping he wouldn't have to draw attention to the numerous certificates on the wall.

The professor tapped his right foot on the floor, appearing anxious and unsettled before finally shaking his head.

'Let's look at this another way.' Zimmerman changed his approach.

'Why would someone not appreciate what you're working on?'

'Fear.' The professor's reply was instinctive. 'Change.'

'Fear of change?'

'Perhaps... That's the risk we've taken.'

'*We've* taken?'

'Soon, I'm going to have to take the next step, I'm out of time, I can feel it. But I've put this off for so long, I'm not sure how to take it. I'm at a crossroads. You're a therapist, you've heard all the metaphors?'

'Are you afraid?' Zimmerman asked.

'Not for me.'

'So you feel responsible for others in your... Project?'

'Their lives will never be the same.'

'They're not ready?'

The professor frowned, unable to answer, settling for a shrug.

'Don't worry,' Zimmerman assured. 'I expect to ask more questions than I get answers.'

The professor glanced to the doctor's pad, noting a few of the scribbles with curiosity.

'What have you got?'

'It might be better to wait - until the session is over, perhaps.'

'Humour me,' he pushed.

Zimmerman sighed as he held up the pad.

' "William indicates signs of fatigue and stress. Symptoms extenuated by migraines, the renewal of smoking habit and an irritable demeanour. Dismissive towards friendships and family, demonstrating trust issues with insecurities potentially routed by childhood trauma. Gives reference to a project which may or may not be metaphorical, but appears to be the source to representations of anxiety and unresolved tension." '

'Interesting,' the professor rolled his eyes.

'There's more, I just haven't written it down,' Zimmerman explained. 'By not sitting or accepting a drink you've made it clear that you don't want to associate this session with comfort. You've avoided three or four questions by either responding with opposing questions or ignoring them entirely, all of which has been done, subliminally or intentionally, with a view to staying in control. You're accustomed to managing the environment around you. I appreciate that letting go can be difficult.'

'Mike was right about you,' the professor said, heading back to the sofa to sit down.

'I'll presume that to be a compliment?'

'It was.'

'Thank you... But we both know this doesn't scratch the surface.' Zimmerman briefly looked at his notes.

'From what I've seen and what you've said and not said, we'd need ten sessions or more to go through all of this. So I'm left wondering how I can help you, William? Or whether you really want my help?'

The professor leant forward to pick up the cigarette he had left burning in the ashtray and took an exaggerated drag before stubbing it out.

'I came here wanting to know if how I'm feeling is the only way I could feel? I know that in the long run what I've done will make lives better.'

'And yet you don't know if what you're doing is the right thing?' Zimmerman offered.

'Exactly. It's a paradox... And it's consuming.'

'Given the choice, with hindsight, would you have done anything differently?'

'Yes, I believe so,' the professor answered almost instantly.

'That's good to hear.'

'It is?'

'Yes, by acknowledging that there are better alternatives you're showing that your mind is open. It would be more concerning for you to think that the things in your life are the only way they could be. Although it does suggest that you could be dwelling on the past.'

The professor broke his eye contact to look away to the window.

'Is there anything about the past that could be relevant?' Zimmerman pushed carefully.

'There are things that I would do differently, but nothing that I'm ashamed of.'

'Ashamed?! That's an interesting choice of words.'

'Perhaps a poor choice,' the professor replied softly.

Dr Zimmerman made some more notes before raising his head.

'Let's try some simple word associations. Say the first word that comes into your head.'

The professor rose to his feet and began pacing, eventually turning to explain.

'I think better on my feet.'

Zimmerman smiled in response.

'Home?'

'Oxford.'

'Work?'

'Teach.'

'Sleep?'

'Memory,' the professor sighed.

'Future?'

'Hope.'

'Past?'

'Dar...' the response was instinctive.

'Dark?' Dr Zimmerman queried.

The professor shook off the question.

'Look, it's not metaphorical. The project's real.'

'But you can't tell me anything about it?'

'That's right.'

Dr Zimmerman made some more notes on his pad.

'Perhaps you're right.' The professor put his hands in his pockets. 'Maybe this should be a weekly thing for a while. Why don't we pick this up in a few days? I'll check my diary and we can set something up?' The professor picked up his packet of cigarettes from the table and began backing away to the door.

'William, if you leave now we both know I'm never going to see you again.'

'I promise I'll think about it.'

'Before you leave may I offer you some advice?'

The professor turned with curiosity, sparing one last minute to give the doctor his due. Zimmerman tried to make his words count.

'The end of anything is often bittersweet. Sometimes you need help to make it over the finish line. Now in your case that might not be me, but it does need to be someone. Keep your friends close, William, you appear very much alone.'

The professor nodded, for a moment appearing to ponder the doctor's advice. Poised with indecision, he offered a respectful salute before turning for the door.

CHAPTER THIRTY ONE

THE END OF SOMETHING PURE

Sara killed the lights as she slowed her car along Robert Robinson Avenue, the brick road softly rippling beneath the tyres, the surroundings darkening into shadow.

Just ahead and to her left she made out the Magdalen Centre; the Innovation Hub to Oxford's Science Park. The Centre had a heritage spanning over half a century; the prestige of scientific excellence, acknowledged by seven Nobel Prize winners and a history of acclaimed achievements.

Gliding down a short ramp, she drove into the multi-storey car park to her right, pulling into a secluded space and bringing her Honda to a stop. She glanced over her left shoulder, peering to make out the revolving door entrance. The bleeping lights of motion sensors and security cameras glinted through the windows, offering a glimpse to the surveillance inside.

Sara turned back to the campus blueprints she'd downloaded onto her tablet. Up close, the task was more daunting than she had expected.

'You wanted this, remember?' James taunted, sat on the passenger seat beside her. 'You pushed for this.'

'I know.'

'Good, then do this right. You can't cut the power until you've patched the loop, the guards will be alerted when you kill the sensor.'

'Got it,' Sara dismissed.

'Do it properly this time. You're getting sloppy.' James appeared agitated. Opening his laptop, he brought up the structural schematics of the Magdalen Centre.

Sara held her tongue as she got out of the car.

'I like you, Rolo, I don't care what they say.'

'What do you mean? What do they say?' James winced as she slammed the door shut. His voice muted against the window.

She took a few steps away from the car, pressing half her face against the inner stone wall, allowing the other half to appear from an opening. She stared up at the building before her as if it were an adversary.

James was right. The first few retrievals had been smooth, well thought through and executed with calm swiftness. No traces left behind. It was almost easy. Blind accuracy. But recent attempts had been less graceful. Close calls that gave an initial rush but carried the bitter aftertaste of an amateur whose luck was wearing thin.

Crouched low she made her way to the east side of the building, weaving in and out of the tree line, carefully avoiding the pockets of space where she would be seen. She moved briskly on the balls of her feet. The purr of traffic from the A4074 gently grumbled in the distance.

From outside the building appeared clean and polished, a stylish exterior. The windows were tinted and mysterious. From the online pictures she knew the layout inside would be open. Light walls and silver rails. The occasional painting would give some colour and culture. The ground floor was tiled with dull grey and crimson squares, the staircase carpeted with light brown striped fabric. There would be large plants in each corner, common features accustomed with plain office space and perfect hiding spots as she progressed through the floors.

Sara knelt down in the shadow of the final tree, taking the bag from her shoulder and unzipping a compartment. She pulled out an ear piece.

'Rolo?' she whispered, plugging it into her left ear.

'You're not funny, you know that, right?'

'Later,' she said, taking one last look around before covering her face with a black balaclava. Reaching further into her bag she pulled out a pair of night vision goggles and placed them on her head.

Inching closer to the rear entrance, she pressed her hand to her ear.

'Going in.'

* * *

Conor sat slouched at the bar, downing a shot of tequila and cringing. The drink was turning on him, slurring his words and blurring his vision. He gave each passing stranger a drunken glance.

He picked up his pint of Guinness and pressed the cool glass surface against his forehead. *Don't close your eyes.* His head span even faster in darkness.

Conor leaned forward to try and control his breathing, holding back the impulse to spit the drunken saliva that had built up on the side of his mouth. He looked back at his reflection in the mirror from across the bar, mindful of a presence to his left.

He turned his head to find the professor watching over him.

'How did you find me?' Conor asked, looking away.

'Stands to reason,' the professor said, looking around before sitting down. 'Considering all we've been doing and your rebellious mood, I assumed you'd be looking to kill a few brain cells.'

Conor stumbled as he tried to stand.

'Conor, wait.' The professor held up his hands. 'Please, I just want to talk.'

Mumbling, Conor slumped back onto his stall.

'You sure you want to be seen with me?' he teased. 'Out drinking with a student? They might guess our little secret. Do you hear them whispering?' he gestured to the punters, using his hand as if it were a puppet. 'Pss, pss, pst... Do you hear them?'

'Are you finished?'

Conor held up his drink.

'You offering?'

'That's not what I meant. Anyway, you've had enough.'

'You're damn right I have.' Conor drank down the last of his drink. 'Are you here to lecture me, professor?'

'I'm here to apologise... Look, you were right and I was wrong,' the Professor explained. 'Wrong about a lot of things. I've been staring over the ledge, preparing to jump, for so long now. I got used to the view. This can't be our secret for much longer, I understand that now. But when the time comes we're going to need each other.'

'Have you ever heard of the human regression theory?' Conor asked, slurring his words as he spoke. The professor shook his head.

'It's got something to do with our species peaking,' Conor said. 'For me that was about three hours ago. But I've got to be honest, the way down is just as much fun.'

'Come back to us, Conor. Let's finish what we started.'

'I didn't start anything.'

'But you're part of this team now. You've earned that... When the time comes, I want us all standing together.'

Conor lowered his head.

'You can't tell me you don't miss it,' the professor pushed.

'Maybe that's the problem... Let me ask you something, what's the difference between *this*,' he held up his pint glass, 'and what we've been doing? Cause to tell you the truth I can't tell between them anymore. Both make me happy. Both make me sad.'

'One of them will kill you.'

'And which one is that?'

The professor looked away, his demeanour changing to acknowledge that perhaps this was a mistake.

'You don't need me,' Conor sighed.

'She needs you. For what it's worth.'

Conor looked up as if he were about to speak, but changed his mind.

The professor got up to leave.

'Look, you're not a quitter, Conor. It's not in your nature. Come home. You know where to find us.' He tapped him lightly on the shoulder and began walking away.

'Are we close?' Conor asked.

The professor turned.

'You wouldn't believe me if I told you.'

* * *

200

A GAME FOR THE YOUNG

Outside the Magdalen Centre, the temperature was slowly dropping as the night air cooled. The wind had picked up, blowing through the trees whilst the distant grumble of nearby traffic muted to almost silence.

Sara rattled the windows as she burst through the fire escape onto the balcony, her eyes petrified, her composure frantic. She ran to the ledge, looking down two levels to the concrete slab floor beneath. *It was too far.*

'Stay where you are!' the security guard shouted, panting in pursuit.

Instantly Sara took in her surroundings, thinking fast and gauging her options. The guard appeared from the fire exit, carrying a podgy frame and breathing heavily. Quickly he looked right to see the intruder ascending the ladder to the roof.

'Keep moving!' James spoke into her ear.

'Shit, shit!' Sara growled. 'You said...'

'Never mind what I said. Keep moving!'

She made it to the roof, nearly tripping on the last step and gasping for air. It was difficult to breathe, her face trapped in the balaclava, the cloth sticking to her skin as the sweat poured from her forehead. The bag felt heavy on her back.

'The roof cameras!' she said, looking across to see the surveillance boxes on the East Wing.

'Don't worry about it, I've killed them.'

The roofing was sloped and unsteady; she had to be careful. From the corner of Sara's vision a blur passed. Distant but growing. She turned to see him, the figure of a chubby security guard clambering onto the roof. His physique offered her a moment of confidence. She could lose him.

'Fifty metres to your left, there's a drain pipe. Move!' James shouted, reviewing the building schematics and monitoring the radio frequencies.

Feeling more in control, she leapt across the roofing at pace, holding tightly on to the tile fixtures, stabilising herself when needed. The roof was damp and slippery in parts.

'Come here you little shit!' the guard shouted.

Behind her she could hear his huffing, the exhaustion of a chesty wince. The tiny spotlight of his torch hectically bounced across the roof surface. Sara crouched down, closing in on the ledge near the drain pipe. *Almost there.*

With a sudden crack she heard a shivering cry of panic. The sound of crunching tiles and timber, a half second of silence and then a sickening thud.

Sara slowed, her face shaken by a new fear. Her legs almost buckled.

'Oh no... Please no,' she whimpered.

'What's going on?' James froze.

She couldn't move, it took all her strength to drag her feet. But slowly she retraced her steps, physically shaking, her eyes watering. Breathing erratically, she came closer to the ledge. There was an opening, ruptured and broken.

Leaning forward, she peered over the edge. A vision of horror and tragedy reflected back at her.

Faraway below on the stone slabs of the pavement lay the security guard. His left leg was clearly broken. His neck was twisted and distorted. A small oozing puddle of deep red was building by his head.

'What's happening?' James whispered.

'He fell,' Sara spoke in shock, her voice breaking as she said it. She crouched down on to her knees. 'I think his neck's broken.'

The words echoed in James's ears. His eyes closed.

'Come on. We've got to go.'

'I think he's dead,' she whimpered.

'Sara, we've...' James croaked at his mistake. *No names on an opening frequency.* 'There's no time, we've got to go!' he shouted.

Sara's eyes filled with tears, and her pale hands became numb.

'He's dead,' she cried, her nose running. 'What have I done?'

'We can't do anything for him. Come on, one step at a time. Move, you have to move.'

She watched helplessly, letting the seconds pass, her eyes clouding over. The man's haunting face was now vivid in her memory. The image buried deep in her mind.

He would be there forever more, waiting for her when she slept. A white stranger staring with an empty gaze, forever unknowing. Asking why. Desperately reaching. Sara would never be able to explain, to defend or justify, but would her words mean anything? Slowly she pulled back from the ledge.

CHAPTER THIRTY TWO

THE ART OF NEGOTIATION

Anthony Portman gave an uncertain look to his polished black Bexleys as the footpath beneath his feet changed in terrain. The smooth tarmac switched to ruffled stone, the feeling of chipped pebble and dry mud under his feet. Dust kicked up as strolled into Witney Lake Country Park. Just off the A40 dual carriageway, the sound of passing traffic faded as he walked further down the pathway.

He kept his eye line low, mindful of the unwanted leftovers from nearby dog walkers. He ignored the tranquil view of the lake to his left, the sun setting faraway to his right. The tide had brought the smaller pebbles up the shore line, brushing moss against the dying shrubbery yearning for spring.

Portman's dark navy Hugo Boss pinstripe suit and slick city boy comb over amplified just how out of place he felt. The plush offices of E.C Stanley were a distant memory.

Less than fifteen minutes earlier, he had passed through the glass doors, enjoying a sly moment to flirt with the blonde secretary before strolling with pride towards his new Porsche 911 Carrera, recently shipped in on tailored order from Germany. Only two weeks old and still gleaming. The strong smell of fresh leather and polish greeted him as he opened the driver's side door.

Established in the early 1920s, E.C Stanley Ltd was a powerhouse in the Pharmaceutical Industry. A growing enterprise with a reach that spanned all continents, their accounts were some of the most strategic and influential among the emerging markets in Europe and Asia.

Life was good, which was to say that business was good. In 2011 global spending on prescription drugs topped £590 billion, with E.C Stanley quietly earning its percentage. The commission he was taking was criminal considering his work rate. Profits were up 6% on the last quarter and the share price was holding at a healthy 27.6 - sitting pretty, ready for Portman to collect his annual stock entitlements at the turn of the financial year.

Gingerly he approached the wooden bench overlooking the lake, peering over his shoulder to see if he was being watched. He enjoyed the mystery as if it were a satisfying indulgence.

It had been several days since Portman received his first encoded message. Shrouded in secrecy, a cryptic communication, he found it all quite amusing. Though his contact was skating on thin ice, he had done just enough to warrant interest. *An opportunity worth anything you could fear losing.*

Standing by the bench, he gave a moment to check that it was clean before sitting cautiously on the edge of the seat. He glanced to his Rolex, sighing loudly. He wasn't prepared to wait; he'd give it five minutes maximum.

Across the lake, a pair of dark binoculars lowered in response. The contact dialled out on his phone.

Portman soon felt his inner pocket vibrating and reached in to retrieve his mobile.

'Go,' he answered.

'There's a phone taped underneath the bench you're sitting on. I'll call it in ten seconds.' The caller hung up.

Portman raised his eyebrows, clearly unimpressed as he stood up to search for the phone. Spotting it quickly, he pulled it free from under his seat, it rang almost instantly.

'Yes?' he answered.

'Thank you for coming.'

'Thank you?' He looked down at the phone before returning it to his ear.

'Forgive me, young man, but I'm really not interested in these theatrics. It was you who made contact, through unconventional channels I might add.' He sat down on the bench. 'To this point you've done just enough to interest me. But I should warn you my patience is bone thin. Now, what is this about?'

The caller paused. Anthony's tone was harsh and ungrateful.

'I'm offering the specifications of a unique procedure. Property rights and access to three years-worth of research material.'

Portman leaned back into the bench.

'The brief?'

'Neurological enhancement.'

'Neurological? You're going to have to give me more than that,' he chuckled, bordering on patronising.

'Not today.'

'How many players?'

'Five.'

He didn't seem enthused.

'Status?'

'Advanced stages of testing. By all accounts... conclusive.'

'And you're aware how many research projects we've got running out of this city?'

'This is unlike anything you've seen.'

'You'd be surprised what I've seen.' Portman looked again at his watch. 'Is it sanctioned?'

'Not exactly.'

The response made him frown.

'Privately sponsored?'

'No.'

'You're sure about that?'

'Positive.'

'Interesting,' Portman crossed his legs, his bottom lip protruding. 'I take it you own the patent?'

'There is no patent.'

'It's pending?'

'No.'

'Then you have nothing?!' Portman's face cringed. 'You're looking to float the findings of an unsanctioned, illegitimate project, without backing or patent?' He rubbed his forehead, fighting off the urge to end the call. 'Do you have group consent to be speaking with me?'

'Not yet.'

'Why would I want to get involved with this?' he sighed.

'It will be the single greatest discovery of your career. It would make you.'

'What makes you think I'm not already made?' Portman adjusted his purple silk tie.

'It will make you more.'

'And you're prepared to sell out your friends?'

'This isn't about that.'

'Then what is it about?'

'I'm worried for them... Their health. This needs to turn legit before it's too late.'

'You're performing human trials?'

'Correct.'

Portman shook his head. *Christ, these guys are amateurs.* He took a second to think, glancing out to the lake.

'You do realise this isn't how it's done? If I move on this I'm going to need everything up front. I won't risk embarrassing myself.'

'Fine.'

'And you will have everything ready when I give the word?'

'I will.'

'Very well. We'll arrange a face-to-face to discuss your proposal. If you pass, I'll organise an opportunity to pitch to the Board. That is, if it's as good as you say it is. If you're green lit, we'll file for corporate patency. But you understand that I'm not going to hand hold you through the legalities?'

'I understand.'

'If it is approved, and only if, we'll discuss your percentage.'

'I want assurances.' The caller's tone raised slightly.

'Assurances of what?'

'The other players. My friends. I need to know they'll be taken care of.'

Portman smiled.

'I think you should worry about your friends for the time being, don't you?'

James gritted his teeth as he ended the call. He despised corporate folk like Portman. His arrogant self importance floated across the lake like a bad odour. His suave suit and city boy swagger.

He only wished he could approach one of the smaller pharmaceuticals. The ones that deserved the chance. But it was no good, this was a global discovery. He needed the vast reach of a giant like E.C Stanley to do it right.

Things were moving fast, the project was breaking at the seams. Sara's haunting words still echoed in his ears: *I think he's dead.*

Placing the phone in his pocket, he thought clearly about his next move.

CHAPTER THIRTY THREE

A FICTITIOUS LIFE

This wasn't betrayal, that much James was certain. This was not betrayal.

After finishing a chapter from one of his more pretentious self-help books, James returned the hardback to its resting place on the shelf. He hadn't read any of these books in years. Not since the earlier days of his recovery had he immersed himself in such well-constructed metaphors; times had changed. To him the words now read patronising rather than helpful.

But with every passing day his confidence grew and for the first time, in as long as James could remember, *he* was taking control.

Three days had passed preparing for his moment in the spotlight; his speech was all but chiselled into memory.

Though the science spoke for itself, he finally understood the stress the professor must have been feeling. There was so much to cover and justify: the approach; the key components, *Einstein, Galileo, Hawking*; their reasoning to maintain secrecy and undertake human trials in such an unsanctioned fashion.

The composure of his explanation was imperative. This wasn't stumbled upon or the reward of circumstance. He had to convey the sacrifice and devotion his friends had shown. The pressure bore down on him like a curse.

The fact that E.C Stanley were interested paid compliment to the project's success. The team had simply enjoyed the benefits for too long; it was their only sin.

Popping a container of Vicodin, James tapped three pills into his palm and reached out for a helpful sip of coffee.

Indonesian Luwak came at a price, though he made no apology on being a coffee snob. The professor had long since surrendered the debate on its taste versus his beloved French roast Cappuccino.

Glancing to his phone, James's thoughts turned to the call he had promised himself to make. A conversation that needed to happen and yet it made the hairs on his arms stand up on end.

Hovering his hand over the receiver, he recoiled briefly, pausing for a second to think. The words he would use still eluded him. He took a final sip of his coffee and picked up the phone, his hands shaking as he listened apprehensively to the dial tone ring out.

'Hello,' a woman's voice answered, speaking with a strong Scottish accent.

James took a breath.

'Hi Mum.'

'James? Jimmy, is that you?' His mother's cold telephone voice quickly turned warm and caring.

'It's me.'

'Where have you been, hun? Did you get my messages? It's been so long. Your father was convinced you'd gone travelling.'

Emotion crept across his face. The sound of home almost brought him to tears.

'Yeah, I know. I'm sorry. I've... I've been away.' *Was he lying?* 'But I'm back now... How are things at home?'

'Everyone's fine, darling, don't worry about us. Tell me about you. Are you good?'

James managed a smile. 'People are nice here.'

'Are you coming home?' Her tone rose with excitement.

'That's not really possible at the moment.'

'What do you mean?'

James held the handset away from his face before nodding with commitment.

'Mum, I've met someone... I guess you could say I'm in love.'

'Oh Jimmy, that's wonderful! Tell me about her. What's her name?'

James choked.

'Ellie.' His eyes swelled with water. 'Her name's Ellie and she's perfect, Mum. You'll like her.' A tear rolled down his cheek.

'And how did you two meet?'

He closed his eyes.

'We're both part of something special down here. It's sort of a team.'

'Can we meet her?'

'Soon, I hope. There's something I need to do first.' He wiped his nose. 'It's important, Mum. You'll be proud of me.'

'We've always been proud of you, Jimmy.'

'I know,' he whispered. 'I miss you guys.'

'We miss you more, sweetheart. Are you OK? Do you need any money?'

'Not for much longer,' he smiled. 'Oh, wow, I can't wait to tell you.'

'Tell me what?'

'It's a surprise, Mum. It's a surprise for everyone.' He could feel his self-discipline starting to buckle.

'Look, I've got to go. But I just wanted to let you know that I think I'm almost done here. I'm coming home soon. I promise'.

'I can't wait. Your father will be thrilled. '

'Say hi to Dad for me.'

'I will. We love you Jimmy, we're so proud. You tell that new lady of yours to take care of my boy.'

He lowered his head.

'I love you too, Mum.'

After ending the call, James sat and contemplated the fictitious life he had just portrayed. He was conflicted by guilt and a confused sense of reason. After all he hadn't lied. Granted, he hadn't exactly told her the truth, either. But it was the call he wanted to make, the conversation he'd always hoped they'd have. With hindsight it was quite therapeutic.

His moment of reflection passed quickly. Startled by the two loud knocks that came from his front door, he dried his eyes and closed down the lid to his laptop.

'Be there in a second. '

CHAPTER THIRTY FOUR

IN DARKNESS

Ellie anxiously hovered her hand over the door before knocking for a third time.

'James? James, it's Ellie.' She glanced from left to right. 'Are you there? We're worried about you.'

Her tone was gentle, her face bearing the signs of concern as she pressed her ear against the door.

'I'm alone.'

She owed him that much, just in case certain words needed to be said.

Backing away, she stood pensive in the hallway, resting against the opposing wall on the second floor of Holywell Buildings.

James's disappearance had left Ellie in a bemused state of shock. More than a week had passed since he was last seen. She couldn't be sure how many days, as they all blurred together as one. She imagined the fallout, acknowledging that perhaps their research may have finally gone too far. But time had made way for new questions.

Where was he hiding? Should they call the police? Where would that lead? James rarely spoke with his parents back in Edinburgh and he didn't have a job or anywhere he was due to attend regularly. There was no explanation or warning and, like the others, he had submerged himself in the research for so long now; all of his other friendships had dissolved.

His absence could last weeks before it was noticed. It was a painful reminder on how lonely they had all become.

'I'm going now, James,' Ellie said with a whimper. 'I'm here if you need me.'

She backed away slowly, hoping that he would rush to the door to open it in the last moment. Turning to leave, she sensed another dear friend slip away from her.

Descending the stairs, Ellie reached into her jacket pocket to pull out her mobile phone before opening the main door onto the street. She dialled out.

'Any luck?' the professor answered.

'No, I don't think he's there.'

'You're sure?'

'As I can be,' Ellie replied. 'I'm worried.'

'I'm sure he's fine.'

'We don't know that. Did you get hold of Sara?'

'There's something I need to show you,' the professor said. 'Be here for ten o'clock?'

'OK.' She hung up and spun round in the street. Keeping still, Ellie looked up to James's window, desperately holding on to the hope that his face would appear. *Please.*

* * *

Ellie tried to be positive.

Knocking at the *Hive* entrance, she imagined Sara or Conor answering. Welcoming her with a smile, a comforting hug.

She masked her disappointment well as the professor's face appeared in the doorway.

'Did you talk to Conor?' she asked, walking in to find him alone.

'I did,' the professor replied, closing the door and backing away to his desk.

'And?'

'We'll see... Perhaps you should reach out to him?'

Ellie threw her jacket over one of the chairs.

'I wouldn't know where to start,' she sighed.

'He'll be back. They'll all come back.'

'What makes you so sure?'

'Intuition. Failure is positive once you learn from it.'

Ellie lightly stroked the equipment. 'Everything's falling apart. First Conor, now James. We kept arguing over the changes this would have on the rest of the world. Maybe we should have been focusing on what it was doing to us?'

'I'm inclined to agree. That's what I wanted to talk to you about.'

'What do you mean?'

The professor typed a few words on his laptop before bringing up a file on to one of the larger monitor screens.

'This is a data entry on Receptor Molecules.' He highlighted the file on the viewer. 'It contains key equations on chemical signalling and cellular direction that formed part of the level four beta everyone received two months ago.' He zoomed in on the file. 'It went a long way to helping us establish the conditions to dissolve your acrophobia.'

'So what's the problem?' Ellie asked.

'I don't know where it came from.'

Giving a moment's pause, he glanced to Ellie, stumbling upon her look of bemusement.

'Every piece of data we've utilised has been taken from the University network or open source. Our progression was subsequently limited but at all times fair and legal. This file goes way beyond what we should have had access to. The explanations and complexities have been researched to an almost definitive conclusion.'

'So where did it come from?'

'I think it's been stolen.' He minimised the file to bring up a series of websites. 'I've been doing some checking and there's a project running at the Biochemistry Research Centre covering this subject at an advanced level. This file came from there, I'm sure of it. Someone planted it on our network. What's more I've found at least five other files from our transfer history which originated from an unknown source.'

The professor arched and clicked his neck.

'Which means someone in the group has been stealing research. And in doing so you have all gained knowledge in areas way beyond what we should have been able to use.' He shook his head. 'To the benefit of the research, I'm sure, but whoever has done this has placed us in a moral dilemma which jeopardises everything.'

'Where's Sara?'

'I spoke to her briefly. She's laying low for a while.' The professor reached into his desk drawer.

'Laying low? Why?'

'She didn't say, but I have a pretty good theory.'

Retrieving a copy of the Oxfordshire Guardian, he folded out the paper to an article revealing the headline 'Security Guard Dies In Tragic Accident.'

Ellie squinted as she made out the print. She took the paper from him, pacing as she read the article.

'What's this got to do with Sara?' she asked, raising her head from the paper.

'Sara... and, I think, James... I believe they've been...'

With a sudden spark and sharp snap the room went black. Ellie shrieked in shock and dropped the paper as the Hive disappeared from around her.

There were no windows. No glowing pockets or glimmering signs of light. She couldn't see her hand in front of her face.

'Professor?'

'I'm here,' he replied calmly. 'The power must have blown. Just stand still for a second. I've got a torch somewhere.'

Ellie stood firmly to the spot, listening to the sound of the professor rummaging through his desk, stationery being pushed aside and drawers opening and closing.

Stretching out with her hands, she reached for something to lean up against. Her breathing became noticeably loud.

In the deepest black, she heard it. The unmistakable creak of grinding metal. A sound she knew well. The sudden feeling of an icy soft breeze brushed against her cheeks; her legs quivered, her heart thumped heavy in her chest.

It took everything to fight off the urge to huddle into a ball on the floor. The main door was quietly opening.

'Professor,' she whispered, turning in blind panic. He didn't respond. She made out the gentle click as the door sealed shut. 'Professor,' she spoke louder.

'I know, I know,' he responded, still rummaging. 'It's somewhere in here, I'm sure it is.'

'I think someone just used the door,' Ellie whispered.

The noise from the professor's direction stopped.

'What did you say?'

She struggled to repeat it 'I think someone is in the room with us.'

The words carried a chilling stillness, the atmosphere turning cold.

'Hello?' the professor shouted, his voice echoing off the walls with haunting repetition.

'Listen,' Ellie whispered, her hands shaking.

Near the door, perhaps a couple of metres from the wall, somewhere to her left, she could hear something. The airy whistle of someone's breath. Just above the ground, maybe crouched.

The professor's tone became harsh, almost threatening.

'Conor? Is that you? This isn't funny!'

'Professor?' Ellie whimpered, the sound of fear growing in her voice.

'Ellie, slowly walk towards my voice.'

With awkward steps, she moved towards the sound of the professor, cluttering his desk with a renewed sense of urgency and frustration.

She couldn't tell where the breathing was coming from any more, the noise the professor was making allowed the intruder to be invisible to sight and sound. She had all but lost her bearings.

With a rush of fear she ran in his direction.

'Professor!' Her arms stretched out, her steps fumbling on the uneven floor. Suddenly she felt herself smothered, pressed against the warmth of a chest.

'I'm here, Ellie,' the professor said quietly, comforting her.

With a click, a light appeared in his hand, illuminating the floor beneath them. Quickly he lifted it to enlighten a small portion of the room.

The torch was poor, flickering as the cheap battery life faded. It barely covered a few metres in front of them. The black gave out to a pitiful glow, lighting up pockets of space to show the *Hive* in an eerie state of dormancy.

'Is someone there?' the professor shouted.

Ellie huddled close. 'I'm scared.'

The professor held her hand, squeezing it tight.

'It's OK, it's OK.' He held up the light, pointing it towards the door.

'Slowly now,' the professor whispered, inching them closer.

As their feet scuffed the floor, the professor quaked, turning around to point the light behind them.

'Who's there?' he yelled.

With blinding brightness the lights returned, filling the room with texture and detail. The beams overhead buzzed with electricity. Their eyes slowly adjusted, blinking as they scanned the room. They were alone.

CHAPTER THIRTY FIVE

HIDDEN IN PLAIN SIGHT

Ellie nervously glanced over her left shoulder. Her pace stuttered with insecurity as she climbed the small set of steps leading up to the Department of Engineering Science. She walked through the main double doors, taking the time to close them quietly behind her before turning to make her way down a long, open corridor. The ground floor looked different from the last time she saw it. The darkened route through the hallways cloudy and muffled by memory. It had been a while.

Reaching the white door to one of the laboratories, she took one last look around before softly turning the handle. Pushing the door slowly, the look of anticipation in her eyes turned to relief at the sight of the professor stood waiting by the main desk.

The laboratory was lit up by glowing desk lights, their rays glinting in the reflection of test tubes and glass wall cabinets. The window blinds were closed. The welcoming sterile smell greeted her like an old friend. Quickly she stepped inside, closing the door behind her.

'Did you contact the others?' she asked.

'I'm here,' Sara replied, stepping out of a shadow. Her hair was greasy and covering half her face. Her skin was pale and blotchy. She appeared overcome by grief and shame, hunched as she stared aimlessly at the floor. Her confidence had been broken.

Ellie was quick to comfort her, offering a long and affectionate hug.

'I'm so sorry,' she whispered. 'It's going to be OK.'

'What are we doing here?' Conor asked from the doorway, his face unshaven and his hair appearing shaggy and unkempt. He stepped inside and shut the door behind him.

'Conor, thank you for coming,' the professor said, smiling and gesturing to the chairs laid out in a semi circle around the main desk.

'What's going on? Why are we here?' he asked, taking off his jacket and noticing Sara and Ellie's embrace in the corner. The mood was sombre as the team gathered. Their body language spoke volumes, removing any need for small talk.

'We've come full circle,' the professor explained. 'It was almost a year ago to the day, in this very room, that we decided to take the next step, a leap of faith... I have no regrets.'

Sara and Ellie held hands as they sat down, Conor chose to stand for a minute before joining them.

'As with all things, when you lose control you return to the beginning... And the sad truth is we've lost control.'

'Where's James?' Conor frowned, looking around the lab.

'We don't know,' Ellie told him. 'We've not seen him for nearly a week now.'

'Who was last to see him?'

'I was,' Sara cleared her throat.

'And?'

Sara turned her head, her eyes blood shot and watery.

'I don't know where he is,' she said. Her tone was final.

'We've checked the Hospitals,' the professor assured. 'No one has been checked in under his name or matching his description.'

'This doesn't make sense,' Ellie whispered, holding her head in her hands.

'It makes some...' Sara glanced to the professor, picking up on his hesitance. 'James wanted out, you knew this.'

The professor cringed.

'He never said that to me directly.'

'What?!' Ellie sat up in her seat.

'The procedure was too much for him.' Sara sighed. 'He wasn't well, the sleep deprivation, the headaches... He wanted to stop. James was sick.'

'Why didn't he tell me?'

'You were busy.' Sara glanced to Conor.

'That's not fair.'

'I know.' Sara wasn't looking to blame anyone.

Ellie thought back to the moments she had shared with James, pondering on the times they had spoken. She slowly realised how often she had spent the time talking about Conor. A shameful sting hit the back of her throat. *How could she not have known?* Her eyes began to fill with water.

'Am I the only one prepared to say this?' Conor tread carefully.

'What?' Ellie whimpered.

'Is it possible that he's gone off on his own? Set up another *Hive* elsewhere?'

'How could you think that?'

'Is it so hard?' Conor turned to the professor. 'You said yourself that some of our Microbiology literature went missing only a few weeks ago?'

'That's true,' he acknowledged. 'But the equipment is all accounted for. It would be too expensive for James to start up alone. He'd need backing.'

'Is that possible? Well if he's not sick or branching off, he's lying low. Science of deduction. He'll come back when he needs a fix.'

'A fix?' The professor squinted, intrigued by the choice of words.

'When he starts to miss it,' Conor rephrased. 'When he begins to forget. The *takes* fade over time, right?'

'All memory degrades over time.'

'But what happens if you want to bring it back? Receive the same *take* again, I mean?'

'In theory the brain would categorise everything the same, reinforcing the memory as the *take* implanted.'

'Like reloading software on a computer.'

'Like a drug.' Ellie sank into her chair, glancing down to the needle marks on her arms. James had once described the burst as euphoric. Under scrutiny she began to imagine how it could be perceived. The thought made her uncomfortable.

'There's more,' the professor said. 'But, before I say any more, does anyone have anything they want to tell me?' The professor looked to his team, watching them one by one shake their heads in puzzlement.

He recited the events of the previous night, the black out, the noises in the dark.

'Couldn't you have been imagining things?' Conor dismissed.

'I checked the fuse box. Everything was fine, the power had been tripped.' The professor seemed certain.

'But it's a stone floor? If someone was there you would have heard their footsteps!'

'Would we?'

As he said it, Ellie's face dropped. *James?* 'How long have you known?'

'It's merely a theory.'

'Guilty until proven innocent?' Sara looked disappointedly at all of them.

'If it's true, he will have his reasons,' the professor said, sighing. 'We're all entitled to go our own way.'

Ellie had heard enough. 'We have to stop.'

'What are you talking about?' Conor snapped.

'You agree with me, right Professor?' Ellie looked to him in hope. 'You've been looking for a way out just as I have? You can't honestly say your heart is still in it?'

The professor appeared deep in thought.

'If something is achievable with time then it is inevitable. History has taught us that.' He spoke as if he were trying to convince himself. 'If we were to stop here, it ensures nothing. Others will follow in our footsteps knowingly or not.'

'Then we carry on.' Conor fell back into his chair, relieved to reach a conclusion.

'No, our part in this is played. We've taken it as far as we can. I ignored the signals, but it's the lies you want to believe that are always the easiest to tell.'

'What?' Conor rose to his feet.

'It's time,' the professor said, raising his hands.

'Shouldn't this be a vote?!'

'It doesn't need to be,' Sara sighed. 'I'm done.'

'So we're quitting?' he argued.

'We're taking the next step.' The professor checked his watch. 'It'll take me a while to gather the senior professors, maybe a couple of weeks. What happens then, I can't be sure.'

'Will you need help?' Ellie offered.

The professor shook his head. 'I'll face them alone. When it's done, they'll come for you. Try to get word to James if you can.'

Conor was restless.

'Can we talk about this?'

'We are talking about this,' Ellie replied.

'What will happen to you?' Sara asked the professor, her eyes closely watching with intrigue.

The question stirred a mixture of emotions. He looked back without response. The team always knew the risks he'd taken.

'This is bullshit!' Conor shouted, putting on his jacket.

'Let the dust settle, Conor.' Ellie tried to calm him. 'Let's see where we are.'

'I'll tell you where we are... fucked!' Conor kicked away his chair in disgust. His disappointment turned into a tantrum he couldn't control. 'Bullshit, fucking bullshit!'

Bursting out of the lab, Conor left the door reeling as he stormed down the corridor. Punching and kicking segments of wall along the way.

'I'm here if you want me,' Ellie offered, tightly squeezing Sara's hand as she rose from her chair.

'I'm OK,' Sara replied. 'I might go home. See my family. I can barely picture their faces it's been so long.'

They hugged a long and affectionate goodbye, both knowing that the next time they met the weight of the world would rest on their shoulders.

Sara turned to shake the professor's hand, lightly nodding her head. A look of understanding was shared between them. She looked around the room, smiling, taking mental notes, until reluctantly she left, closing the door behind her.

For Ellie, thoughts of home began to drift in to memory. Thoughts of a life she had long forgotten. She tried to remember the nights out she had enjoyed with Marie and Sally during the early days, the times she had spent reading in Bury Knowle Park, the morning walks along the Oxford canal bank.

She put on her jacket, the sadness of the end showing on her face.

'I'm going to miss our nights together, Professor,' she said softly.

He smiled. 'Ellie, you of all people should know. You could have always called me William.'

'I know, Professor,' Ellie replied, but she wouldn't. Through everything they had achieved he had been there. Their leader. The one they could always depend on. He'd earned that title.

For the last precious moments they hugged, Ellie doing her best to control her tears.

'Good luck.'

CHAPTER THIRTY SIX

PLEASE, BE WRONG

The Academic Records Office was charged with the keeping of Oxford's illustrious graduate history, a legacy of pupils encompassing Prime Ministers, Nobel Prize winners, Archbishops of Canterbury and Olympic athlete medal winners.

Sandwiched among them were the unrealised talents. The auspicious resumes of the hopeful undergraduates, housed within the infamous 'Examination Schools' centre, designed and built by the visionary architect Thomas Jackson.

The distinguished building stood apart from its surroundings. From Merton Street, the grand entrance was fronted with tall black-railed gates, offering a view to its tranquil courtyard resting beneath the clock tower. The words 'Dominus Illuminatio Mea' chiselled in stone beneath the columns represented the motto of the University of Oxford, a passage taken from the opening words of Psalm 27, meaning *The Lord is my Light*.

Gone were the darker days of the World Wars, where the halls were used as a Military Hospital. The large function rooms now served as conference centres for corporate business events and exhibitions.

At night, the staff and security dispersed, leaving the empty corridors and eerie hallways to resonate a ghostly silence, forsaking the bustling activity that would be common during the day.

Across the first floor on the east wing, a soft echo bounced against the walls as the intruder's footsteps tip-toed over the marble flooring. Access via a concealed side entrance had cut her a way past the main lobby, the cameras left behind to focus on the communal areas, giving her the freedom to wander.

The Oxford record chambers were laid out across a vast number of spacious rooms. A library of documents slowly modernised among PC terminals. The walls were decorated with elegant oil paintings and fine wooden furniture polished to shine. There were dark oak bookcases standing firm next to chiming antique Grandfather clocks. All this was in keeping with the building's famed history.

The side door clicked with acceptance as the lock pick sliced its way through the keyhole. It opened with only the slightest margin to allow for the intruder to slide in before quietly closing it shut. Tiptoeing across the floor she positioned herself at a terminal, suddenly enlightened as the monitor awoke from dormancy. From where she sat she could access the University's student files for the past twenty-five years.

The balaclava covered Sara's face well. Her dark, tight-fitting shirt helping her to feel agile and swift. She logged on.

The light sound of tapping from the keyboard pin-pointed her position in the room like a buzzing cricket in an empty corn field. Her leather gloves ensured that no finger prints would be left behind.

The terminal began searching, displaying a rotating hour glass to indicate its progress. Sara looked over her shoulder, glancing around the room with impatience, her eyes wide and gazing.

The search completed, bringing back a name. *The* name.

As the record appeared on the computer screen, Sara studied the history notes.

She read through a number of files before raising the balaclava above her face to breathe easier. Her expression was cold and calculating. Scanning through the final record she nodded her head with acceptance. It was time to make her move.

CHAPTER THIRTY SEVEN

ATONEMENT

Stumbling out of Tennyson's car park, Conor gave little thought to where he would go or what he'd do when he got there. With his head low, he walked aimlessly through the streets. His hands nestled in his pockets to stay warm. The greasy dinner he'd finished off two hours earlier was sitting uncomfortably just below his chest. His eyes were heavy with exhaustion and yet rebelliously staying open.

He could hear the sound of distant traffic and a dog barking from a direction he couldn't pin-point. The night's breeze was dropping to near freezing.

His broken body clock would ensure he lay awake long into the night.

And so he walked, blindly turning the corners, breathing in the cool air until he realised where his feet were taking him.

Earlier that night Conor had stood alone, naked in the shower; cold water running over his prickled skin, his body clean of sweat and odour. His eyes closed as he tried to calm the storm in his head.

He just needed one more *take* before they took it from him. *Just one more.* Why couldn't he find the words to justify this?

The depressing truth pained him. He didn't return to the team to be with them. He didn't miss their company. He needed what they could give him. He needed the *takes!* Something had changed inside of him, something biological or neurological. But whatever it was, it owned him.

Wiping the fog from his bathroom mirror, he'd stared back at a stranger. Trying to think back to the *takes* he'd been given, already slipping away. His brain was struggling to hold on to the wealth of information pouring from his memory.

Without purpose it was all for nothing. His brain ruthlessly discarded without obligation or bias. With a towel wrapped round his growing mid-section he'd slumped at the end of his bed, consoling himself to one absolute fact. The research *had* to continue. He just needed one more...

What had he become?

Turning on to St Clements Street, Conor held out his mobile, staring longingly at her photo before dialling. He didn't know what he'd say; his instincts would have to take over.

The call was answered with silence.

'Ellie, Ellie are you there?' he whispered, the light whistle of her breath told him what he needed to know.

In her room, Ellie sat cross-legged on her bed, regretting how quickly she had answered the call. Staring at the framed picture of the team on her bedside table, she focused on Conor. She imagined him turning to drink to fill his evening, craving more than just her company.

'Probably easier this way,' he sighed.

For a moment Ellie went to speak but she couldn't.

'This is hard for me,' he stammered. 'I've become so confident. So arrogant... I'm used to the right words being there when I need them...' He cringed. 'You know you were right. You were right about me... I've changed. I'm not the man I was... I can barely remember him. Can you remember who you were Ellie? Before all this?'

Standing outside her home, he looked up, hoping to see her face in the window. But the blind was lowered. Inside she had picked up the photograph to hold it close.

'And now we're expected to present our discovery.' Conor shrugged. 'To proudly announce our achievement... Should I rehearse something? I... I don't know what I'll say.' He walked into her building, through the outer doors and into the hallway.

'Ellie, talk to me, please. I need to hear your voice,' he pleaded.

Gripping the picture tight she gathered her courage, before returning the frame to her bedside. He needed to know the truth.

'You're outside aren't you?' she whispered, looking to her door.

'If you ask me to leave I'll go.'

Rising from her bed, she stopped herself before reaching for the door handle.

'Conor, I need to tell you something,' she spoke through the door. 'And it needs to be like this. If I open the door, I'm not sure I'll be able to get it right.'

Conor waited for her, resting against the wall opposite her room.

She clutched the back of her neck with her left hand, unsure how to start.

'You see, I figured when the time came, you'd thank me. I never imagined...' Ellie shook her head. 'In the beginning, the candidates weren't all chosen by the professor... Sara came up with a few. James added some more... I chose just one.'

She rested her forehead against the door.

'When the professor agreed to send you the code, I allowed myself to hope. I watched. I waited.'

Ellie grimaced at the memories of Conor drifting past her along the riverbank. The nights she had seen him from across the bar. How she had stared adoringly at him in Bury Knowle Park. *'There's something about him.'* Even then Ellie couldn't describe the way she felt. She'd never been in love before.

'I couldn't let you go,' she whimpered. 'You were right not to trust me Conor. I lied to you. I finished your code to keep you close... I wanted you, I wanted *us*... And I still do.'

As she said it she realised what she was doing. What it could mean for them. Her confession was supposed to offer atonement and yet she was nervous.

'I understand if this means you hate me,' she said, her chin quivering. 'But, the thing is, I'd do it again. I'd do it a hundred times if it brought us together. Nothing's made me feel more happy.'

She paused in hope of a response. Anything to break the silence, her right ear pressed against the door before she pulled away.

'Look, I don't deal with confrontation well. If you want to leave... Then just go, please, Conor. Please just go.' Tears had begun to form in her eyes. She could do anything but what she wanted. Take it back. Fold back the truth and hide it away in her pocket. She rested her head in her hands.

'I love you, Ellie,' Conor whispered.

His words wrapped around her like a soft blanket. She opened the door to find him there. Her hands were shaking. Standing face to face, she let the weight she had carried slip away.

Conor leant forward, his eye line lowering to meet her lips. His arms welcoming her to the warmth of his chest. They kissed as if for the first time. Her hands cuddled around the base of his back to pull him close.

The sudden noise of Ellie's phone broke the moment, an annoying ringing sound rising over her left shoulder, spoiling the mood, a collective sigh came from both of them.

'Just wait one second,' she said seductively, hoping she could dismiss the caller quickly.

Picking up her phone, she looked down at the number to see it was the *Hive*.

'Professor?' she answered.

'No it's me. Ellie, it's Sara, I've found something. You have to see this. It's...'

Ellie glanced back to her phone. The line had gone dead.

'Sara?'

CHAPTER THIRTY EIGHT

THE INVESTIGATION OF SARA MORGAN

Across the City, sub-basement level to the University's storage faculty, Sara approached the doorway to the *Hive*. A heavy duty tool bag was slung over her right shoulder. A torch tucked under her left arm.

The hunch she carried niggled at her like a cut that wouldn't heal. This wasn't about being right. Sara was desperate to be proven wrong.

Clutching the tools she'd need to break in, she paused to contemplate what she was about to do. If she did this there was no turning back.

Shining her light on the lock, she dropped the tool bag on the floor before pulling out her crowbar. Sara took a deep breath.

The door put up a good fight as it ground open, leaving a panting Sara stood in the doorway peering into an empty void. Lifeless and black. She hit the lights and watched as the room she once knew came alive around her.

Inside, the *Hive* spoke of a time that had been and gone. The equipment was covered with plastic sheeting. The operating table was blanketed with a transparent mesh as if it were a crime scene. The surfaces looked sterile and the light stone flooring felt icy.

Sara glanced to the sofas by the coffee table, reminiscing on moments she thought she'd cherish. With awkward steps she approached the professor's desk, placing the tool bag on the floor and taking the time to put on her leather gloves before sitting down.

His seat was firm and weathered, the wheels squeaky and stiff. She leaned forward to search his desk.

The top drawer was almost bare, but for blown up photos of Conor and the odd piece of stationery. Swiftly moving on to the second, she came across a copy of the Oxfordshire Guardian.

Her heart sank at the sight of the family picture they had used for the article: '*Security Guard Dies In Tragic Accident'*. Nathan Jones. That was his name. A name she would never forget. Nathan had left behind a grieving widow and a three year old daughter named Bethany.

'I'm so sorry,' Sara whimpered, softly placing the Guardian to one side.

She pulled hard at the bottom drawer, but the wooden handle held firm. It was sealed by lock and key.

With a snapping crunch the drawer gave out to Sara's crowbar. Its contents rattled as she pulled it open. Placing the iron bar to one side, she looked down with intrigue.

Reaching in she retrieved a pair of night vision goggles, an mp3 player and a collection of the literature she thought was missing.

She sat upright, her thoughts turning to the Professor's laptop resting on the desk in front of her.

Breaking through his login security was easier than she expected. He proved trusting or at least presumptuous. Sara drew a breath as the loading page faded with acceptance, each keystroke making her situation more real than the last.

For the first time feeling as though she had crossed a line, she began studying through his private files. Scanning through MRI pictures with interest, his browser history and the array of procedural documentation that had amounted over time.

Her searching gaze slowed with curiosity at the sight of an unmarked program, littered with frequent access logs and archive transactions. It was running as a background service, recording and cataloguing the output from a remote feed. With a shrug Sara ran the program.

As the screen loaded, the monitor split in to four evenly sized square panels, each generating their own video feed. *Oh my god.*

Gradually the panels loaded, some taking longer than others, but straight away she knew what they were. She was watching silent video feeds, *live*. Each panel was streaming camera footage from their homes.

In the top left panel she could see Ellie, sat cross legged on her bed. The secret camera placed just above her window, obscured by the roller blind.

Sara glanced to the top right panel to see her home. Her private space. *You bastard*. A sickening feeling grew in her throat. The camera was hidden in the living room, top left, overlooking her television screens. It must have been sandwiched between some of the books on her shelf.

To the bottom left was Conor's studio room at Tennyson House. Positioned above the door frame to the right. A twisted angle, he'd have no idea it was there.

The final panel was black. *James's flat?*

They were all under surveillance, secretly being scrutinised. Like mice in a cage. *'I am the one who's watching over you as you sleep'*. The son of a bitch had meant it literally.

He knew everything. He'd watched as Sara stood before her numerous television screens, recording the results. No doubt making notes in his journal. *'Does anyone have anything they want to tell me?'*

She tried to gather herself. Her thoughts turned to the fourth panel. To the empty feed that should have shown James, unknowingly going about his business.

She thought back to the last night she saw him, studying the archives and finding the final feed that had come through, five days after that fateful night.

Loading the file, the feed showed James sat in his room, reading and typing on his laptop, oblivious that he was being filmed, making calls on his phone whilst drinking cups of coffee. Sara forwarded the video, speeding through him drinking and disappearing to the toilet, returning, downing some pills, talking on the phone, turning to answer the door... Sara slowed the feed to play the video, watching closely as a man entered his living room, his face blurred by poor quality. His back to the camera.

She knew that walk, the coat, the mannerisms. She watched as they exchanged words, trying to lip read, the conversation building for several minutes. Sara recognised the hand gestures and the subtleties of a dispute growing more and more heated. She leaned in. It was the professor, she was sure of it.

He stood up, gesturing to the window and pacing around the room. Controlling the tone, as if he were giving a lecture. James shaking his head in disagreement. Speaking calmly now. Circling.

What are they talking about? Is he quitting? Sara could see the look on James's face. He seemed sad.

And then, in a moment of horrific betrayal the professor lunged at him. Covering James's face with a polythene bag and pulling it down to circle around his neck.

Sara gasped for air, pulse racing as her stomach churned.

She watched as her friend struggled for breath, as the polythene bag pressed skin-tight to his face. Desperately reaching. Suffocating. Slowly weakening. His arms becoming loose, his shoulders dropping. Sara's hands started to shake. James had now sunk into his wheelchair.

Gathering the strength within her, she forced herself to lean closer, to watch as James's head rolled back lifeless and still. The professor was breathing steadily, his composure returning.

In a glance that chilled Sara's blood, he stood up to look at the camera. As if he knew she'd be watching, his cold eyes peering back at her.

She paused the feed, the picture frozen on the professor's face, glaring through the lens.

Instinctively grabbing the phone on his desk, she dialled quickly, punching the buttons with impatience. The line rang for several rings before Ellie picked up.

'Professor?'

'No, it's me,' Sara replied, staring at Ellie and Conor on the video feed. 'Ellie, it's Sara, I've found something. You have to see this. It's the professor, Ellie. Nothing is what it seems. Nothing. You have to... Ellie?' The line had gone dead. 'Ellie!'

Sara looked down to the phone, tapping the receiver repeatedly in search of a dial tone.

'Good evening, Sara,' a voice spoke from the doorway.

Sara's mouth turned dry. His words stung like an ice pick. The door must have triggered a silent alarm.

Slowly she turned, keeping her eye line low in a bid to compose herself. She kept her breathing steady. She raised her head to see his face.

'Do you mind telling me what you're doing?' the professor asked, looking at the door and gesturing to her sat at his desk.

Sara glared back at him, her eyes white with fear, barely able to recognise the man she once knew. Glancing to the monitor, her focus drifted to the tool bag positioned on the floor between them, to the crowbar by her side.

'I tried to ignore it at first,' she said. 'But you were right, the lies you want to believe are the easiest to tell.'

The professor frowned with intrigue, his head slightly tilting to one side as he took a step forward beyond the doorway.

'But the idea grew like a cancer. I just couldn't let it go,' Sara whispered. 'Why Professor? Why? I thought you trusted us? I thought you believed in us? We were in this together. Weren't we?'

He gave her nothing. His left foot inched with another step.

'We were prepared to do anything for this. For you... Even steal.' Sara lowered her head. *'We'll do whatever it takes.'*

'I know,' the professor replied calmly.

'Of course you knew. Ignorance doesn't suit you.' Her eyes had turned red. 'I suppose you're wondering what gave you away?' She raised her head to look at him.

'No,' the professor whispered, shaking his head. 'I always knew you'd find him.'

Sara reached over to clutch the handle of the crowbar, picking it up to rest it across her lap.

'I watched you use the mirage of stress to manipulate us. Always in control. Every move analysed, everything a test. Our reluctant leader. What was it you said to Conor? *'This project will be governed by my rules.'*

The professor squinted, for a brief second offering a glint of emotion.

'What did James say to you, Professor?' Sara asked, gesturing to the monitor. 'Did he tell you about the data we'd stolen? Did he tell you about the accident?' She whimpered as her voice broke. 'Was he sick? Did he want to quit?'

The professor glanced to the tool bag.

'You positioned your pieces well, Professor.' Sara rose to her feet. 'But it's a lot harder to play master when your puppets have cut the strings.' She held the crowbar up with both hands. 'Now get out of my way!'

He barely blinked. His right hand resting in his pocket. His composure solid. He turned to the door, appearing to contemplate leaving. His shoulders dropped with a sigh. An acceptance. *How did it come to this?*

'Nothing's fair,' he whispered, slowly reaching out to push the door closed.

In the corridors, the sound of cargo lifts and buzzing air conditioning vents diluted the noise to beyond recognition. From only a few metres away the shouts were reduced to mumbles. The mumbles reduced to a distant scream, the slightest cry. A whisper in the air, a deadly stillness as the hush fell, finally softening into fateful silence.

CHAPTER THIRTY NINE

THE LOSS OF INNOCENCE

Conor pulled hard at the cargo lift shutter, the grill grinding and snapping as it opened out onto the basement floor. Ellie quickly walked on ahead, swiftly making her way through the maze, guided by memory and a sense of home. The phone call was still fresh in her ears. *'Ellie, it's Sara, I've found something. You have to see this...'* The line had gone dead. The sudden silence was haunting her.

She knew the number of the *Hive* when she saw it, but she'd never heard Sara sound so frightened. Conor was quick to agree when she told him where they were going.

As they approached the *Hive* Ellie's pace wavered. The door was ajar. The glow from the lights beamed around the ridges of the door frame. The distant purr of electricity whistled.

Ellie lightly pushed the door allowing the room to reveal itself. The plastic sheeting and cleanliness took her off guard. Conor peered over her shoulder.

There was no sign of Sara. The room was empty. Abandoned. An odd feeling lingered in the air.

'Sara!' Ellie called out, standing at the edge of the room. She crept through the doorway, scanning the corners. The library, the coffee table and the sofas.

Conor stood by the door, noticing the dents and scratches by the lock. It had been forced.

'Ellie, we should go.'

She couldn't help herself. Entranced, Ellie drew towards the professor's desk like a moth to flame. The video feeds on the monitor pulled her closer. Her eyes focused on the detail.

'Conor!' she cried out, her voice shaking him.

He left the entry way to join her, approaching the desk and squinting with disbelief at the discovery. Neither of them moved but to look at each other.

From behind, the door made a fearful crunch as it slammed shut.

Spinning around they found the professor, his right palm resting flat against the steel. He was visibly sweating, looking shaken and disorientated.

They didn't notice it at first, the professor's left hand was obscured behind his leg. Conor almost missed it entirely. But as their attention focused the horror sharpened into view. In his left hand, lowering to his side, the professor held a black Walther P99 pistol. A sight so out of place, so alien.

For seconds they stood. The professor motionless, despairing, unwillingly deciding on his next move. How could he let this happen? How did it get so out of control?

A silence held for as long as it could before Conor found the courage to speak.

'What is this? Professor? Where's Sara?'

Offering a look of uncertainty he stared back at them.

'Professor!' Conor pushed.

Scratching his chin, he stood by the door, his eyes almost closed.

'Why don't you both take a seat,' he said, gesturing to the reading table.

Ellie took a single step towards him.

'Professor? What's going on?' she asked softly. 'Talk to me.'

Gently her steps drew closer.

'Professor, where is she?' She reached for his shoulder to comfort him. Conor followed with a reserved step forward.

'Don't!' The professor suddenly jolted, raising the gun in reflex to point it at them. They backed away, their hands raised. He looked stressed and hesitant. Out of options. He was cornered.

'Believe me, friends. They say that to kill someone is the hardest thing a man can do.' He shook his head. 'It's a lie. The hard part is living with yourself afterwards. But even that is made easy when you know you had no choice.' His hand wasn't shaking any more. This wasn't his fault. He'd make them understand. Slowly he lowered the gun. 'Now sit down!'

As he said it Ellie tried not to buckle. It was written all over his face. *Is she gone? Oh god, this isn't happening.*

Tearful and lost, she broke away to gaze at the floor, to go within herself. Conor gently placed his hands on her shoulders, holding her tight and offering words of assurance he couldn't promise.

Slowly they backed away towards the table, glancing back to the Professor. Conor's eyes were piercing with rage.

Remaining still, the professor waited until they were at a safe distance before turning to secure the door with a bolt lock from inside.

Lowering into their seats, they stared back at the man they had once admired, reluctantly making his way towards them. Conor held Ellie's hand tight.

'Why Professor, why?' he asked. 'We were a team.'

'Please sit opposite each other,' the professor said, gesturing Conor to move with a wave of his pistol.

With a look of disgust, Conor rose from where he was sitting to move round the table, offering Ellie a comforting squeeze of her hand.

'We were *something*, Conor' the professor said, sitting at the head of the table. 'I don't think you can call it a team.'

'Then what were we?' Ellie whispered.

'Fortunate,' he replied.

'Fortunate?'

'That's right. I gave you a chance to experience something extraordinary.'

'Gave? We invented this together.' Ellie spoke without any pride in the achievement.

'Did we? In all honesty, what is it that makes you think I couldn't have done all this by myself?' He gestured to the operating table, looking to them with a patronising stare. 'You'd be surprised how easily someone can be manipulated. The right guidance, some helpful books left out in the open. A comment here or there, the opportune moment. Perhaps it's uncomfortable to know that a person can be directed so willingly with suggestion. After all, wasn't the research material all my idea? The techniques? The approach? You think Sara came up with *Gallieo* by herself? You think James could have come up with *Einstein* alone?' He shook his head, lightly tutting.

'You've stood on the shoulders of years of research, on the minds and intellects of the finest in modern day science. You think without direction you'd be sat here knowing all that you know?'

Ellie and Conor fought with every word. Their worlds were crumbling.

'So why do you think I needed you?' the professor asked, appearing to humour them.

'Bullshit!' Conor barked. 'We're not going to let you take all the credit.'

The professor sighed.

'You do not understand.' He wondered how best to explain.

Ellie took a sharp intake of breath.

'We didn't invent this?!'

'Warm,' the professor taunted.

'We weren't the first?'

The professor smiled, pointing to Ellie before tapping the table in appreciation.

'You know you were always the brightest.' He leaned back into his chair. 'It was inevitable really, borrowed time. Sara had an uncompromising gift.'

'What did she find?' Conor scowled.

'Ellie?' The professor offered her the chance, but she had no response. 'I'm surprised that none of you picked up on it sooner, really. Christ, half the books in our library are initialled with his name. It was my first mistake.'

'Richard Myers?' Ellie's eyes widened.

The professor gave an acknowledging nod.

'Richard enrolled in Oxford six years ago. Pembroke. A brilliant student, top of his class. You would have liked him.'

Ellie looked away in disgust.

240

'We made the discovery together. Working tirelessly. Breaking the rules of conventional science. The results were, as you know... Breathtaking. But there wasn't the focus or control we had this time. He learnt what he wanted, when he wanted. It's impossible to know exactly when it happened.'

'What happened?'

'Memory dysfunction, reality impairment, over time... Cerebral swelling, memory loss, the early symptoms of neurological disorder. I tried to pull the plug before it was too late.'

'Tried?' Ellie didn't look convinced.

'Richard refused to stop willingly. He'd become addicted. I wanted to close the lab, to secure the research, speak to the Board.'

'Then why didn't you?' Conor growled, pushing back the professor's reaches for sympathy.

Ellie already knew; she could see it on his face.

'He died.'

The professor lowered his gaze for a moment before composing himself, shaking off any sign of pain or regret. 'He suffered a cerebral seizure. Soon after, the doctors induced him into a coma to save his brain activity. They couldn't determine the cause. How could they?' He lightly shrugged. 'Richard died eight days later.'

'You didn't tell them?' Ellie felt sick. 'You son of a bitch!'

'You have no idea how difficult it was for me,' the professor explained. 'Watching from the corridors as he slowly slipped away. His family by his side. The doctors trying treatment after treatment.'

Conor could feel the professor manipulating them.

'Sara found out, didn't she? She knew, so you killed her.'

'Oh, grow up! Nothing is that simple. I told her everything I'm telling you now. I gave her the chance to see reason.'

Ellie felt nauseous, suddenly mindful of the pieces the professor had offered. *'We're all entitled to go our own way', 'The lies you want to believe are always the easiest to tell', 'Failure is positive once you learn from it.'*

David P. Philip

This wasn't about invention or the good of mankind. The professor had positioned them like pieces on a chess board.

'Why?' Ellie turned to him. 'Why reinvent it?'

'Why do you think?' he replied, looking disappointed by the question. 'There is no greater commitment than a sense of ownership, Ellie. You of all people know this.'

'But why do it again, after Richard? I don't understand?'

The professor composed his response.

'I've said it many times. *'This is bigger than us.'* What did you think I meant by that? We talked as though we were visionaries, as though our discovery would bring *change to the world.'* The professor gestured with his hands as he imagined the words hovering in mid-air.

'Well... The truth is, this procedure isn't for everyone. Less than thirty percent, in fact. The conditions are so specific it's maddening... When I realised this my research became one of natural selection.'

'Natural selection?'

The professor looked to Conor.

'Let me ask you something, why do you think you were chosen? Honestly, tell me why? Let me guess... Because you thought I saw something special in you? Something unique?' He smirked. 'Isn't it amazing how self gratifying we are? How easily we can accept that if someone was to look at us closely we'd be considered exceptional. What did you think I was looking for? What was it exactly that made you think you were worthy?'

'I know why I was chosen,' Conor whispered, glancing to Ellie.

The professor grimaced.

'And you think Ellie swayed my decision? Christ, you kids are incredible! Consider the specifics of this procedure. Consider that both Richard and James suffered multiple forms of brain dysfunction.'

'James?!' Ellie cried.

'He was indicating symptoms of temporal lobe impairment, narcolepsy, terminal apraxia. Weeks, perhaps days from excruciating pain.' The professor's response felt

242

rehearsed. 'Don't question how you'd treat a friend slipping away in your arms. You have no idea what I've been through.'

'Where is he?' Conor shouted.

The professor held a long breath before speaking.

'I'm not a murderer, but I've made my choices. If this procedure is presented as a discovery suited to only a small percentage, the key factors being a series of unrealised gut instincts...' He took a breath. 'Our sacrifice will be for nothing.'

Ellie cringed, thinking back to the way they had begged the professor for help.

'You didn't present anything to the Board, did you?'

The professor offered no response.

'Then what was your plan?' Ellie scowled. 'To deal with us one at a time? Make us think that James had betrayed us?'

'Oh, he betrayed us. Believe me,' the professor swiped. 'And though you may be the brightest, Ellie, you need to work on reading a room. It was clear to me after last night that Sara wasn't going to let things go. From that moment I knew tonight was inevitable. So I did what was necessary.'

He gestured to the plastic sheeting, the polished surfaces. He'd scrubbed everything. Wiped away their fingerprints and disposed of the evidence.

'I told you,' the professor said, pointing at Ellie. 'I pleaded with you, *'Let it go',* do you remember me saying that?'

She shook her head.

'Of course not,' he sighed. 'You weren't listening. You didn't want to hear it.'

Conor felt the rage swelling in his arms. This wasn't their fault. *'You wouldn't believe me if I told you'.*

'Lab rats,' he whispered, realising the truth.

'I beg your pardon?'

'You used us like lab rats. Observing how we changed, how we responded to the procedures. You watched as we suffered.'

'Suffered? Are you trying to be funny?'

243

'The headaches, the sleep deprivation, the memory loss. You made your little notes before passing us the drugs to ignore it.'

'Which was your decision.'

'We're not going to let you get away with this,' Conor warned. 'All the procedures were recorded. Others will know what you've done.'

'Young man, those recordings are long gone,' the professor dismissed.

Ellie felt cold.

'Covering your tracks?'

'Laying new ones.'

'How could you?' There was nothing of the man she once knew.

The professor's face contorted to become threatening.

'No one's innocent, Ellie. You know this better than most.'

Conor raised his head, the professor turning to him to gauge his reaction.

'Why did you collapse outside Radcliffe Camera, Conor?' He smiled. 'Did you take the time to think on it?'

'I tried not to.'

'How ironic that on the eve of learning something so profound, you would take comfort in trying not to think.' He scratched his cheek. 'I read your medical report, did you really think that mould spores could put a man your size in Hospital for two days? What do you think, Ellie?'

'Shut up.' She knew what was coming.

'What are you talking about?' Conor shouted.

'I was surprised you thought it did?' the professor pondered aloud. 'I suppose it doesn't matter now. The truth is always more sinister. Would it sicken you to know that Ellie poisoned the book? Watched as you opened it? Looked on as you gasped for air and collapsed on the grass?' he turned to Ellie. 'And then, while you lay there helpless, she walked over, stole the novel from your bag and injected you with twenty millilitres of Vecuronium. She even called out for help, rang for an ambulance, all very convincing.'

'Shut up.'

'It gave us just the time we needed. A risky dosage, but worth it, wouldn't you agree?'

'Shut up!' Ellie exploded.

Conor's eyes drifted from the table to meet hers. Did he know her at all?

The professor basked in their looks to each other.

'No one can claim to be innocent, Conor, not even naive. As I've told you before *'Everyone knows exactly what they've done and exactly what they're prepared to do.'* You think I don't know about your little enterprise? Making money on the side finishing other students' coursework?' The professor gestured to Ellie. 'You've batted out of your league within this group in more ways than one.'

He knew everything. The words stuck in Conor's throat.

'I told you,' the professor said to Ellie, with almost a whimper. 'I warned you. *'You don't know what you're asking'.* What did you say? Do you remember? *'All we're asking is that you believe in us, Professor.'* Well, I did. It was the risk we took together and here we are. Now only one question remains.'

The professor rose from the table to walk over to the medicine cabinet. The gun by his side.

'It'll be alright,' Conor said, holding out his hand to Ellie. Her gaze focused on the table. She'd gone within herself.

The professor returned, holding a small glass container of pills and a bottle of water. Gently he placed them on the table.

'What's this?' Conor frowned.

'The game for the young is over,' he said. 'So a new game begins.'

CHAPTER FORTY

THE FINAL CHOICE

As the container touched the table surface it brought with it darkness, a sense of fate that stood the hairs on the back of Ellie's arms on end. She felt dizzy. The pills blurred with the tears streaming down her face. The man she never knew sat at the head of the table, looking at her without emotion, without warmth or remorse.

'What is this?' Conor repeated, grimacing.

The professor picked up the glass, rotating it with his left hand.

'I have given everything to this project, it's time you both risked the same.'

Ellie wiped her eyes clear.

'I won't,' she whimpered.

'You won't what?' Conor cried.

The professor lightly nodded to Ellie, acknowledging how perceptive she was.

'It's been called Russian Roulette before now.' He lightly tapped the lid of the container, for the first time lifting the gun so it was held sideways on the table.

'By now you must realise that we cannot leave this place. Not all knowing what we know. Not all three of us.'

Conor felt a shiver crawl down his spine. Glancing to Ellie, he saw her face was white with fear. She was ten seconds ahead of him.

'There are three pills,' the professor explained. 'Two pills are a small dose of Ketoprofen, a harmless painkiller your body will digest without difficulty. Needless to say the third pill is not so apathetic...'

Ellie closed her eyes. *Wake up, please wake up.*

'You will not be able to tell the difference. Not with the naked eye... Within three minutes you'll know. The first sign will be your fingertips turning numb. Your eyesight will begin to fade. You'll start to feel tired, faint... By this time you should have made your peace. Within the fourth minute you'll be all but paralysed, ready to die. I'm not saying your death will be painless, but it's as good as we can do considering the circumstances.'

The professor held the glass up to the light, staring at each of the unassuming tablets, wondering himself which one carried the death sentence. He opened the lid and tipped the three pills on to the table.

'Any questions?'

He was met with silence. An empty gaze of fear and disbelief. Ellie's face now appeared drained. She swallowed hard before speaking.

'What of the two remaining?'

'If it's me, then of course you are free to leave and do as you please. If it's one of you... The other will be freed from the memory of this place.'

Conor cringed.

'That's not ready. It hasn't been tested. Besides you can't erase someone's memory without digital signat...' He stopped himself, suddenly aware of how stupid he looked. The professor had played them like puppets.

'Not unless the *takes* had already been sent with signatures,' Ellie finished. The professor once again tapped the table in respect. 'And even then...'

'And even then it doesn't address the memories acquired outside of the *Hive*, I know,' the professor nodded. 'I'm not saying that you won't lose a few years from your childhood. It isn't an exact science. But you'll be alive. Alive and free.'

'But how have you tracked the memories of the *Hive*?' Conor asked, fearful of the answer. 'The team? The location?' As he said it he suddenly remembered. His first *take* had included information on the procedure, the *Hive*, everything.

The professor saw the recognition on his face.

'I mapped your brains from the very beginning.'

'That's what really happened, isn't it?' Ellie growled. 'Five years ago? You tried to wipe Richard's memory. That's why he had a seizure.'

The professor squinted before pinching the bridge of his nose.

'I'm going to miss you, Ellie.'

'What makes you think it'll be any different this time?'

'A leap of faith,' the professor offered. 'That sounds familiar, doesn't it?'

'Why?' Conor cried. 'Why kill Richard, James, Sara... Only to risk everything now? It doesn't make sense?'

The professor bowed his head.

'At last, you're asking the right questions, Conor.' He looked around the room in reflection. 'I suppose the truth is... Everyone needs reassurance. I have taken lives - I'm in no denial over this - but the time has come to let fate step in. I need to know that I'm on the right path... Or at least, that it's close by.'

'If you're unsure then stop this,' Ellie pleaded. 'There's still time.'

'No, there is no other way.'

'There is always another way!'

'No! If it's meant to be then both of you will walk free. I can only perform the procedure on one of you. Two patients, students of similar ages, both with sudden amnesia. They'd perform all kinds of tests to determine what was wrong with you. If they compared your MRIs, your brain activity. No, it's not an option!'

'Who will you have to test the procedure after we're gone?' Conor asked, staring down at the pills.

'What makes you think I need anyone?'

'My god. You son of bitch,' Conor sneered.

Ellie flinched in her seat. 'You can receive *takes*?'

'Not often,' the professor replied. He didn't appear satisfied by their pain. 'I tend to suffer from migraines for several days afterwards. Old dog, new tricks.' He pointed to his temple.

'You're risking terminal brain damage.'

'This is my choice. It's a chance I'm prepared to take. Now, enough talk. I've protected you long enough.'

'You never protected me!' Ellie winced, insulted by the suggestion.

'Never protected? Are you serious?' The professor glared. 'I hope you're joking. Who do you think helped you stay on track during the first two years? Grading you above average despite the poor excuses you passed off for coursework? Did you honestly think you were balancing the research with your studies? I protected you for as long as I could.'

The professor raised the gun, pointing it at Conor.

'Enough!' he shouted. 'Choose. Do it now.'

Conor, now shaking, peered intensely at his options on the table. He always thought near-death experiences would prompt thoughts of family, home, a rushed flashback of his life. But his mind was blank, blinded in fear.

Ellie couldn't watch.

In a lightly stuttered motion he reached out to choose one of the pills, picking the one furthest to his right and staring at the professor as he held the pill close to his mouth. 'Go to hell,' he hissed before placing the pill on his tongue. Taking the bottled water he swallowed it down. The professor watched him closely.

Ellie went limp, dead inside. This was a dream, a nightmare. She barely reacted as the professor relentlessly turned the gun towards her.

'No speeches, no quotes. Just choose. Now.' He pulled back the trigger.

She closed her eyes. The taste in the air had turned stale. Her skin prickled and paled. Her thoughts turned manic and yet empty. Raising her eyelids she took in a quivering breath before glancing to her left.

Her vision was blurred and confused, but there they were, the faces of James and Sara sat next to her. Her friends, her family. They didn't say anything, they didn't move, but they were with her. She allowed herself the faintest smile, allowed herself to hope. *Watch over me. Give me strength.* With a blink they were gone. An empty space. She was alone.

Ellie reached out to take one of the capsules from the table. It didn't matter which one, nothing mattered any more. Conor watched as she placed the pill in her mouth, taking a turn on the water bottle before swallowing.

The professor's composure and strength faded as he looked to the remaining pill. Grunting to gather himself, he took the final capsule and opened his mouth, swallowing loudly with a gulp. He drank a third of the bottled water to prove it was gone.

To Conor it was like observing a magician before he tricked the crowd. *Three minutes.*

They sat studying each other from across the table, exchanging glances with one another. Conor listened to the sound of his heart.

'What were their last words Professor?' Ellie asked, her face dry of feeling. 'Did they cry? Did they feel pain? Do you remember the last look in their eyes?'

The professor glared at her.

'You think it was easy for me, don't you? Do you dream, Ellie? I can't remember the last time I did... We have all made sacrifices.' He sighed. 'Life makes its own choices for us.'

'The things we tell ourselves.'

His face screwed up in anger.

'Little girl, do not try to understand me. This is my life's work. I have devoted myself entirely. I have given everything.'

'Including your soul?'

'Oh, please,' the professor dismissed with a sneer.

'Who are you?' she asked, shaking her head.

He closed his eyes.

'Necessary...'

With a whisper Conor silenced them.

'It's me,' he mumbled, his face faint and eyes bloodshot.

'No!' Ellie screamed, reaching out across the table for his hand.

Conor slumped in his chair, drifting to his right and coughing as he fell to his knees.

'I don't want to die. Please, there must be another way. Please...'

His hands were numb. The energy was draining from his body, turning him cold. His eyesight blurred as he lay down flat onto the stone floor.

Ellie rushed around the table to hold him, crouching on her knees to be close, tears pouring from her face.

'I'm so sorry,' she whispered. 'I'm so sorry.'

He stared back, reaching, praying. His throat seized shut, his arms turned to a lifeless limp. He was so tired, so bare.

'It was real, I promise,' Ellie cried helplessly. 'It was real... I loved you.'

Conor began to lightly shake, convulse, his lungs fighting for their final breath. Ellie stroked his cheek as she watched over him, closing her eyes in the hope that she could hold onto this moment, delay the inevitable.

She opened her eyes to stare down at the man she loved. Conor lay still, staring back with dead motionless eyes. No breath, no pulse. He was gone.

* * *

The professor rose from the table, his face sorrowful and pained.

'It's OK to feel it, Ellie,' he said, turning for the medicine cabinet.

Ellie closed Conor's eyelids with her fingertips before lightly kissing his forehead. Resting his head on the stone floor as softly as she could, her heart in pieces, she looked up at her enemy, her eyes full of malice and rage.

'It's OK to feel it,' the professor repeated. 'Relief. No one wants to die. Some things just turn out the way they are meant to.'

'FUCK YOU!' Ellie erupted, rising to her feet. '*YOU* made this happen, don't try to convince me or yourself of anything different!'

The professor recoiled, almost shaken by Ellie's outburst.

'I didn't want this!' he cried. 'You think I wanted this? Ellie, not once did I imagine this would happen. You think I don't wish I never discovered this? That I don't curse that god forsaken day?!'

As he spoke Ellie's eye line lowered to the table, noticing with sudden clarity the professor's mistake. A look of hope appeared on her face. The gun rested freely on the table.

By the time the professor realised, it was too late. Ellie snatched at the gun, reminding him just how young and agile she was. Holding the pistol firmly in her hands, she aimed it at his chest. She had never held a gun before; it was heavier than she expected.

The professor gave her little reaction. He seemed broken.

'When there's blood on your hands it doesn't wash off, Ellie.' He walked towards her without fear.

'Don't!' Ellie shouted.

He glanced down at Conor lying dead on the floor.

'And we came so close... Maybe I'll have more luck with the next team.'

As he said it Ellie's face changed, the rage that had built beyond control now dulled to a sad acceptance, an overpowering grief. She couldn't let this happen, she wouldn't let this happen. With her last ounce of strength she firmed her right arm, using her left to steady her aim. Her nerves had steadied. The fear had left her. She was without option or doubt. With lifeless eyes, she squeezed the trigger.

The pistol offered a metallic click as the empty chamber gave her nothing. She glanced down to the gun, pulling the trigger again to hear the same idle click returned. It was empty. The gun was empty. Her chin quivered in shock as she looked up at the professor, his face telling her what she knew.

With a sudden lunge forward the professor covered her mouth with a cloth soaked in chloroform.

'Shhhh. It's OK,' he whispered, holding the back of her head.

Ellie tried to scream, to fight him off. Her body was turning light as the fumes filled her lungs, stealing her strength. He was too strong.

A GAME FOR THE YOUNG

The professor closed his eyes, tears rolling down his cheeks. He held her tight until she was gone.

CHAPTER FORTY ONE

STEP OUT OF THE DARK

A blurring white light brought Ellie out of her sleep. Her body felt light and fresh. Warm and well rested, she grew heavier. Her head was drowsy and confused. Her eyes squinted as she slowly opened them. The view was unfamiliar, characterless and plain. Light walls and cheap furniture. A thin white door to her right was open to the passing strangers in the aisles.

Ellie groaned, unable to move her head more than a few inches before it throbbed with pain.

'How are you feeling today?' the nurse asked, standing at the foot of the bed. 'Feeling up to talking?'

Ellie tried to sit up, breathing deep to regulate the pain. She noticed that, to her left, there stood a parade of 'Get Well Soon' cards on her windowsill.

'We've informed your mother of your recent progress,' the nurse said, going through her notes. 'She'll be coming up to see you at the weekend. That's nice, isn't it?'

Ellie raised her eyebrows.

'What day is it?' Her throat was sore.

'It's Wednesday, my love,' the nurse responded, updating her records before hanging the clipboard at the base of the bed. 'Can you remember what we spoke about yesterday?'

Ellie closed her eyes.

'Vaguely.'

'Good, your short term memory is getting better.' The nurse seemed pleased. 'Would you like me to take you through everything again?'

'Please.'

The nurse sat near the end of the bed.

'You're at the John Radcliffe Hospital, my love. You were brought to us eight weeks ago. Your condition was considered unstable at the time so the doctors induced you into a coma to keep you safe.' She spoke tenderly.

'Let me get you something to eat. Are you hungry?' she asked.

'What's wrong with me?'

The nurse's face dropped at the question, for a moment looking unsure as to how she should answer.

'You've been diagnosed with, what the doctors believe to be, an acute case of Transient Epileptic Amnesia. You need to be patient. Your memory should return in time.'

'But I don't understand,' Ellie winced. 'I can remember most things, my family, my home, my life more or less. It's just the pieces, the detail. I've got holes here and there. I can remember the beginning of some days but not the end.'

'Partial memory loss, I know,' the nurse said, moving up the side of the bed. 'But the doctors believe your memory will return. Look at the improvement we've seen in just the past week!'

Ellie gave a faint smile. *Must be patient.* The first few minutes when she awoke were always disorientating.

The nurse rose from the bed.

'Would you like some tea?'

'Yes, please.'

She gave Ellie's shoulder an affectionate squeeze before leaving the room.

Ellie rested her head on the pillows. The days were growing longer. There was nothing to help pass the time but gaze aimlessly at the television. Her senses were returning to normal at their own confusing pace. And yet something still felt wrong; something distant and elusive.

Outside her window the sun now shone full and golden, an inviting light resting over the warmth of spring. She longed for freedom.

The nurse returned holding a small cup and saucer, a sachet of white sugar with a teaspoon on the side.

'Are you up for visitors?' she asked, placing the cup down on the side table.

'Who is it?'

'He didn't say. Elderly chap,' said the nurse. 'I can go ask if you'd like?'

'No, it's fine.' Ellie sat up, patting down her bed.

'I'll go get him,' the nurse said, turning for the door.

Ellie ran her hands through her hair, mindful as to how greasy it might look. She had little choice but to tuck it behind her ears.

A light tap on the door echoed across her room. Ellie responded with a turn to see the face of a man she didn't recognise. He was dressed in a black suit and blue shirt.

'Miss Swanson?' he asked.

'Yes?'

'I'm sorry to bother you, my name is Detective John Eagleman of the Oxford Police Department. May I come in?'

Ellie tried not to flinch.

'Of course,' she said, puzzled by the introduction. She hit the remote control to turn off the television.

'Thank you. May I have a seat?' he asked, pointing to the chair beside her bed.

'Please,' Ellie replied, gesturing to her right.

'Thank you.' He pulled up the chair before making himself comfortable, taking his time and giving out a slight groan as he took the load off his knees. He placed a large A4 envelope by the side table.

Appearing in his late fifties, the detective came across as well educated and calmly composed. His rich English gentleman accent and impeccable manners gave the distinction of experience and authority. He crossed his legs, placing his palms together and linking his fingers before speaking.

'How are you feeling?'

'Fine, I guess,' she replied. She didn't know enough herself to answer truthfully.

'Glad to hear it. And your memory?'

'On the mend... Apparently.' Ellie rolled her eyes with a nervous giggle.

The detective smiled in response, holding his eye contact with Ellie a few seconds too long.

'I'm sorry, is there a problem?' she asked, before it felt awkward.

'Forgive me, no,' he replied. 'I'm just wondering how much you know and how much you are yet to remember.' He tilted his head.

'Allow me to explain. I've been assigned to a series of unexplained disappearances within the University. The students in question appear to have lived a life in recluse leading up to their disappearance, but when cross-checking their whereabouts and social activities one name has consistently come up.'

The detective studied her reaction before continuing.

'Do you know a student by the name of James McCarthy?'

'No. I don't think so.' Ellie broke eye contact with the detective to think, staring ahead to the wall in front of her.

'No, should I?'

'How about Sara Morgan?'

Ellie tried to concentrate, thinking hard and sighing before shaking her head.

'What about Conor? Conor Martin?'

Again she offered no response. The detective scratched his chin.

'Interesting,' he said, opening his jacket pocket to pull out a notepad and pen.

He flicked through his notes.

'You don't remember having dinner with Conor, January 17th at the MacDonald Randolph Hotel?'

Ellie leaned forward, nervously gripping the back of her neck with her left hand, for the first time feeling anxious.

'No?' She couldn't remember anything. 'No,' she repeated suddenly feeling vulnerable, as if her body wasn't her own. 'Conor Martin, you say?'

The detective went through his notes.

'Conor Joseph Martin, white male, twenty two years of age, born in Leicester. He was taking a degree in Computer Science at St John's College. Staying in a studio room at Tennyson House. I'm updating his mother on an almost daily basis.'

Ellie was still lost.

'And I knew him?'

'Perhaps if I showed you some pictures it might help?' he said, opening the envelope by his side and producing a collection of blown up photographs.

'This is Conor,' he said, holding up one of the photos. 'Does he look familiar?'

Ellie glanced at the picture. He was attractive. Seemed her type and yet she couldn't remember him. She shook her head.

The detective moved onto the next photograph.

'How about this lady here? This is Sara.' Ellie looked closely. She had never seen her before.

'This is James McCarthy,' he said, moving on to another picture. 'Anything?'

'I'm sorry,' Ellie offered.

'Don't be.' The detective smiled, showing another photograph. 'How about this gentleman?'

'Yes!' Ellie shouted, relieved by the recognition and pointing at the photo. 'Yes, this is Professor Daniels. He's one of my Biology teachers at St Anne's.'

'Indeed,' the detective agreed.

'Is he missing too?'

'No, not exactly.' The detective placed the pictures back in the envelope.

'We found a letter in Conor's bedroom. It doesn't make a great deal of sense, but what it does suggest is that whatever happened to him may not have been an accident. He mentions the professor by name. Can you think why that might be?'

Ellie winced, shaking her head.

'No, sorry. Why don't you ask him?'

'I wish I could.' The detective sighed, leaning back. 'He was brought into the Intensive Care Unit a week ago after collapsing in the Botanic Gardens. He suffered from a near-fatal brain seizure. The doctors don't hold out much hope that he'll speak again.'

Ellie drew a short breath.

'Jesus,' she whispered. 'I can't believe it. He was such a nice man.'

'Yes, so everyone keeps saying.' The detective made some notes.

'I'd like to leave these photos with you if you don't mind? Perhaps you could take a moment to look at them every once in a while. It may help resurface some of those lost memories, help me get to the bottom of what's happened. Is that OK?'

Ellie nodded in agreement, keen to be helpful.

'Sure.'

'Here's my card.' The detective handed her a small white card with his details. 'If you remember anything else, anything at all, please give me a call.'

'I will,' Ellie assured him.

Detective Eagleman rose from his seat.

'Well, I'm going to leave you alone to rest. Get your strength back. We'll speak again at some point, I'm sure.'

'Thank you.'

Ellie watched as he moved the chair back to where he found it and headed for the door.

'You think they're connected?' she asked, the detective turning to look back at her. 'The professor's seizure? My memory loss? The other students?'

He smiled in response.

'Oh, I'm a detective, Elizabeth. Everything has meaning.' He offered a thankful nod before turning to leave.

Smiling as she watched the door close, Ellie's gaze drifted, pondering the photos he'd left behind. Never before had she felt so lonely, isolated from the mind she thought she knew.

The dull ache from her forebrain was groaning, as if it were a caged animal trying to break free. Whatever drugs they were giving her, she needed more of them.

Her life in Oxford suddenly felt like a forgotten dream. Her cherished memories were an afterthought. She yearned for the detail to piece it all together. Ellie turned to the photos once again, giving a subtle glance to the door to make sure she wasn't being watched.

'Conor,' she whispered, holding up his picture. Something the detective had said resonated with her, though she couldn't place it.

CHAPTER FORTY TWO

ALL YOU DREAMED?

The sun's warm gaze shone through the windows of the waiting area, teasing it's hostages with the promise of a beautiful day. A day like the one he remembered, the day that had been taken from him. The professor now lay helpless on a cheap thin mattress, paralysed by his brain. His memory a broken glass. His thoughts, the water that now drained away. Forever lost.

The Intensive Care Unit had long since stabilised him, allowing the professor to painfully tread water. He longed for the medicine to fail, for the machines to let him go; for the nurses to let him die in peace.

'There you go, William, all clean,' the elderly nurse said, tucking the bed sheets under his mattress. Such embarrassment, such indignity, he would cry if his body could remember how. He closed his eyes hoping to open them and find himself back in the Botanic Gardens, gazing upon the birds nesting in an old English yew tree. Beautiful.

He looked up to the ceiling, the dull-white canvas doing nothing to stimulate him. The nurses gathered round him to lift his paralysed body back into bed, covering him up as if he were a baby.

'Who fancies a cuppa?' one of the nurses asked, rewarded with a string of accepting replies of 'oh, that would be nice.'

Ellie stood in the doorway, watching over him with her head resting against the doorframe. The nurses walked passed her as if she were furniture.

'Can I help you?' the final nurse asked.

Ellie suddenly focused.

'Sorry, I... He's my Biology teacher,' she said, gesturing to the professor. 'I knew him.'

'Well, you can still know him,' the nurse replied, looking somewhat offended by the comment.

'Of course, sorry. I just... I don't know what to say.'

'Well, let's start with your name and see if he's up for visitors.'

'Ellie, Ellie Swanson.'

'Wait here for me will you?' The nurse walked over to the professor.

'William, William? It's Nurse Rose. There's a young lady here to see you.'

Ellie could hear her speaking softly to him, her tone affectionate and mothering.

After a short while she returned.

'He's not very responsive today, but you can try by all means. We have a system. One blink for 'yes', two blinks for 'no'. Try to keep it simple for him.' The nurse pointed to the chair resting by his bedside.

'I'll be down the corridor if he needs me,' she said, turning to leave.

Ellie took a breath for courage. Pushing away she stepped into the room, taking in the sterile smell of disinfectant, a hint of bleach, and the unmistakable fume of stale body odour.

She walked slowly around the bed, gingerly with each step until she saw his face. Frail and helpless. She sat down on the chair next to him, meeting his eyes for the first time. There was no reaction.

'How do you feel, Professor?' she asked, looking him up and down. 'Was it worth it?' Her composure hid the rage boiling inside of her.

'Was this all you dreamed?' Ellie motioned to his bed, studying his face before she caught it. His eyes dilated, his breathing pattern subtly changing. *There you are.*

Ellie leaned forward.

'That's right, Professor. I remember everything. I'm so sorry, does that disappoint you?' She lightly tapped her head. 'It was Conor. Wasn't it? He kept me safe. Kept the memories deep. I can close my eyes and picture his face.

You couldn't take that away from me, not for long. And to remember him is to remember everything.'

She looked around his room, his prison cell.

'I bet you wish you'd been there? When everything returned, the burst of emotion, the feeling. I cried. The anger, the love, the sadness.'

She rose from the chair to walk around his bed, the professor's eyes now watching intently, desperately trying to keep up with her. She paused to look at his notes at the end of the bed, turning the pages with interest.

'It says here that your parietal lobe and cerebellum are damaged, extensive inflammation. Swelling of the entorhinal cortex and hippocampus yet to be diagnosed. Although, your MRI shows that your frontal lobe is hanging on.' She looked up from the clipboard.

'So you *can* remember? You can understand what I'm saying. But you can't structure a response?'

She put the notes back and returned to his bedside, leaning over to antagonise him further.

'How frustrating for you. How lonely.' She smiled, savouring the moment. The professor was now physically straining, screaming inside, his breathing fluctuating. A glint of agony in his eyes.

'I noticed you left the *take* on my Biology degree alone. What was that, Professor? A parting gift? A peace offering?' She looked at him pitifully. 'One last desperate attempt to maintain control? Was that to be your hold over me if I remembered?' She sneered. 'For what it's worth, it would never have worked.'

Ellie stood up again and walked around his bed, moving to the doorway to peer down the corridor. She looked left and right before closing the door.

'I wish I could describe it to you,' she said, walking back over to his bedside. 'I can feel the *takes* fading. The knowledge dissolving. The older memories of my life returning. It's like waking from a bad dream. I'm a drug addict going cold turkey. I feel free.'

She sat by his side.

'It will happen to you too, you know. All that knowledge. Everything you made out to be your own. All that power will dissolve, leaving you with nothing.'

Ellie stared at his heart rate monitor, watching the ripples, for a moment remembering the seismometer at the lab and hearing James's elated voice. *'Ellie, I think we've done it. I think we've found Hawking.'*

'I suppose you're wondering what I'll do now?' she asked. 'Alert the authorities? Tell the world?' She brought herself closer to the machine regulating his oxygen. Her eyes were full of hatred and contempt.

'Tell me, Professor, blink once for yes and twice for no. Do you regret what you've done?' Ellie brought her hand up and poised her finger over the off switch to the regulator.

The professor's breathing grew fast and erratic, his eyes begging, seemingly willing her to do it. Defiantly he blinked twice.

Ellie lightly nodded her head.

'Given the chance would you do it all again?' The professor didn't hesitate before blinking once. She offered the briefest of smiles, lowering her gaze to the floor.

'I thought so,' she whispered, her eyes raised to meet the professor. Slowly she took her hand away.

'No,' Ellie shook her head. 'This is exactly as you should be. I didn't come here to put you out of your misery. I came here to tell you that I'm going to destroy our research. I won't give you the satisfaction of being remembered. It dies with you. Alone.'

Ellie reached inside her bag and pulled out the framed group photo from her apartment. She looked at the picture of the team before placing it on his bedside table, positioning it so that he could see their faces. The professor closed his eyes, unable to turn his head away.

'I keep trying to understand what we did wrong,' she said, staring at the photo. 'Whether it could have turned out any differently.' She paused to breathe through her nose.

'But I'm starting to realise. This was never about a cure. This was greed. Vanity at its most awful. We should be ashamed, Professor. Don't you see? Your memory is your identity. It's you. What you choose to learn, the time you invest, that's what defines you. That's what makes you who you are. I forgot how pure it was just to be me.'

Ellie dared to look at him one last time before standing up to slowly back away. His chin wobbled in desperation. The steady monotone of his heart rate showed signs of struggle.

'I guess we're not ready... But is that a bad thing?' She paused to ponder the question. 'Goodbye, William.'

Feeling satisfied, Ellie opened the door to walk out of the room. She didn't look back.

The professor lay empty and hollow. A single tear slowly rolled down his cheek.

With confident strides she walked down the corridor at pace, passing the hostage waiting area to her left. The crying children, the elderly man reading a newspaper, a bickering couple sat opposite each other.

Her thoughts were clear. A smile grew across her face. Her heels clicked with rhythm over the Hospital floor. She could feel Conor with her, remember his touch, his smell. Remember her friends and the moments they had shared.

She could hear Conor's voice whispering, reciting the poem that had once defined her.

> *What of a selfless life lived, if not for hope?*
> *To strive, to build and be remembered,*
> *In tides of fate, for the betterment of all.*
> *With eyes closed and hearts open.*
> *Our deeds shall not be forsaken.*

In the waiting room Detective Eagleman slowly lowered his newspaper. Glancing back to the professor's room with curious interest, he offered a grin that spoke of a hunch paying off. Folding his newspaper, he rose from his seat and tucked the paper under his right arm.

Keeping his distance with intrigue, he followed Ellie down the corridor.

Walking out of the Hospital doors, Ellie stepped into the light. The sun was warm and glowed in a way she'd never seen before. Her new life was ready to begin.

THE END

AUTHOR PROFILE

David P. Philip lives on the South Coast of England, with his wife and daughter.

Fascinated by stories that explore the brain, and challenge human behaviour; David's first novel A Game for the Young tells the story of a team of Oxford students who invent something that is set to change the course of history.

Exploring obsession, addiction and abuse of power, A Game for the Young toys with the idea of knowledge being a drug.

This novel is the end result of over three years of writing, proof reading, and editing. Including the months of research David did in the field of cognitive neuroscience.

Set in the present day, and dripping with realism; the tone of this story is gothic, and will keeping you hanging on every page.

David P. Philip is currently working on his next project, and hopes A Game for the Young will be his first of many novels.

Rowanvale
Books

PUBLISHER INFORMATION

Rowanvale Books provides publishing, writing and marketing services to independent authors, writers and poets all over the globe. We deliver a personal, honest and efficient service that allows authors to see their work published in a way that suits them. By making publishing services available in a cost effective and ethical way, Rowanvale Books hopes to ensure that the local, national and international community benefits from a steady stream of good quality literature.

For more information about us, our authors or our publications, please just get in touch.

www.rowanvalebooks.com
info@rowanvalebooks.com